PEDESTRIAN WOLVES

PEDESTRIAN WOLVES

JAMES L. GRANT

PRIME BOOKS

PEDESTRIAN WOLVES
Copyright © 2004 by J. Grant

All rights reserved. No part of this publication may be reproduced or transmitted in any form or by any means, electronic or mechanical, including photocopy, recording, or any information storage and retrieval system now known or invented, without permission in writing from the publisher, except by a reviewer who wishes to quote brief passages in connection with a review written for inclusion in a magazine, newspaper, broadcast, etc.

Published in the United States by **Prime Books**
an imprint of **Wildside Press**
www.primebooks.net

ISBN: 1-894815-14-9

For Melissa Hynes, without whom this book would not exist.

PROLOGUE

"Welcome to New Orleans!"

My roommate spoke these words with the passion and bravado of a Shakespearean actor opening the stage for a great drama. Marcus always talked like that. I would not be surprised to discover, for instance, that he spoke in that manner while wiping his ass. I was lying in the backseat illegally, with the seatbelt on but completely prone. His wife giggled as I raised my head to look at the downtown sprawl, and my mind registered that *we had arrived*. It was time to get a little crazy. If anything I'd heard was correct, then I would be carousing and wreaking havoc soon enough in such an abundance that arrest and prosecution would be very real threats. Fuck work, fuck responsibilities, and fuck any kind of behavior that the peons of corporate America would consider "sane." My vacation was *on*.

From the back of the car, I watched the touch of the dying sun splash across the skyline of New Orleans, tongues of fire gilding the structures in flickering hues of gold, red, and purple. The superdome resembled a giant demonic tortoise overlooking the pits of hell in the distance. A cemetery the size of a small city whisked past my window, crammed full of ancient headstones the color of a dead man's teeth.

My grin felt like it was going to split my face in half.

CHAPTER ONE

I could never be referred to as a man of wealth by any stretch of the imagination. Even the most hard-bitten liar would have a difficult time using the word *tasteful* to describe me. Regardless; Please allow me to introduce myself (as the song goes.) My name is David Livingstone, and I probably wouldn't like you very much. Nothing personal, I just don't like most people. Sure, I get along with others just fine in public, and can be tactful when it behooves me to do so, but usually I like to speak my mind without pussyfooting around the emotions of the morons I meet. We'll just get that one out of the way—*I'm an asshole*. There.

Caroming through my late twenties, I have been described by many as "stocky," a leftover from a weight lifting spree in the year 2000. My skin looks moderately white, with a half-Japanese heritage lending an almost imperceptible cast to my brown eyes, and naturally black hair when grown out. For years, however, I've taken to shaving my head bald—a no-stress, no-worry hairstyle. I can simply run a razor over my scalp every three days, and then I don't have to worry about what it looks like. At 5'10" my body doesn't appear exactly imposing, but when clad in a leather jacket and boots, people usually leave me the fuck alone on the street. This is how I like it.

On September 13th of 2002, I stoically limped into work with five minutes to spare before my shift started, and leaned against the wall of my cube. I was a network technician for a fairly large cellular phone company, and my desk was in its usual state of disarray. Collapsing into the chair, I sat for a second, and then rubbed gently on the tender spot where my left thigh met my abdomen. It still hurt like hell.

"Motherfucker," I mumbled, and turned on the power to my computer.

"Such language!" The exclamation came from behind me, and I turned in my chair to focus on the source of the voice. A little too quickly, as it turned out, and this time both of my hands pressed to the side of my stomach. Smiling in the entryway was a chubby man in his forties, obviously pleased that he'd caught me unaware. "Mother*fucker*," I hissed at him. Realization came slowly to his lazy features, and he slapped his forehead comically.

"Aw, hell," he said in his usual Texas drawl. "I totally forgot about that. You okay?"

"Yeah. I can work, but it still twinges at me," I grumbled. "What's up, Murray?"

"Oh, not a lot," he said. "You were gone these last two days with your, ah . . ."

"Groin injury," I said, swiveling the chair back around to log into my computer.

"Yeah, that. How'd you get that anyway?"

"Went out dancing," I said, waiting for the programs to finish loading. "I went on a date with this chick on Wednesday."

"Oh, yeah?" He leaned his ellipsoid frame against the wall of my cubicle, making the entire contraption creak. I let him endanger the structure any way that he liked, without saying a word. After all, chummy or not, Murray was my manager. "How'd that work out, then?"

"Hell," I said, slumping forward to rest my forehead on my palms. "I'm just getting old. It was great, and we got along really well, but at the end of the night I felt this weird stitch in my gut. I dropped her off, and long story short, I woke up Thursday with this horrible pain stabbing me in the stomach."

"Jesus. What was it?"

"Just a pulled groin muscle, but I tell you what, Murray: The next time you see an NFL player on TV getting pulled off the field on a stretcher and the announcer is talking about a groin pull, know that the overpaid goon on the screen ain't faking it. That shit *hurts*."

"Well, good to see ya back," he said amicably, and I could tell that he was thinking about clapping me on the shoulder like he usually does.

"I'm good," I said carefully, "As long as nobody jostles me."

"Wouldn't dream of it," he replied, and took his weight off of the cubicle panel. "But I do have news that might shake you up some."

"What's up?"

"You," he said while leveling a rounded finger at me, "have been working too much." He chuckled, and the fluorescent office lights reflected off of his bald head in a manner that reminded me of a disco ball.

"What?"

"We tallied it up, and you have some vacation days left."

"I do?" Clicking the mouse, I popped open the screen of my schedule, looking at the little yellow frame in the screen that showed how much Paid Leave I had accrued. "Wow. I do. 33.4 hours . . . that's four days . . . "

"Yes sir, and if you want any time off for the rest of the year, you need to request it today. HR wants all requests turned in by two pm." He turned to go, and waved a hand at me. "Later."

"See you, Murray," I mumbled, still staring at the screen. Four whole days off left? Cool.

Of course, I had no idea what in the holy fried hell I would do with that kind of time off. Christmas had never been a big deal for me—call it a bias left in my mind after growing up poor in Los Angeles, but I didn't normally use any time off around the end of the year, preferring instead to work through the holidays and make some extra dough.

At about 1:38 pm, an idea came to me, and I decided to use it.

"Outrageously cool!" Marcus slapped me a high-five, his other hand holding a slice of the pizza halfway to his mouth.

"Yeah," I said, helping myself to the food. "Now, if I just knew what to do with it."

"Let me get this straight," he said, and then paused to bite into his pizza. The couch we were sitting on in our living room was in no danger of tomato sauce stains, as the color of the fabric was a deep arterial scarlet anyway. "You've got the day before, the day *of* Halloween, and the weekend following it as paid vacation?"

"Yes," I said around a mouthful of cheese. "I just have no earthly idea what to do for a vacation."

Sophia came out of the kitchen with a couple of beers and laid one down in front of me on the coffee table. I nodded my thanks, and she sat next to her husband after grabbing her own slice.

"Well," she said while arching her eyebrows, "I wish we could tell you what's going on in Dallas around then, but we're going to be out of town."

I flipped a dismissive hand in her direction.

"No problem. I have a month to figure something out," I said, and leaned back on the sofa. As I did so, the pain in my stomach fired up again. With a moan, I slapped a hand over the sore spot.

"You alright?" My only reply was a nod at Marcus, who shook his head. "So, what did you tell your boss about that, anyway?"

"The truth—that I went out on a date and pulled a groin muscle."

"Did you tell him *how* you pulled it?" he asked with a knowing leer.

"No. See, that's the kind of information one does not tell one's boss."

He chortled and continued eating his pizza.

"'Fuck me harder!'" Sophia said in a high-pitched, mocking tone.

"Quiet, trollop!" I growled.

"Not as young as you used to be, eh, old bean? What was her name, anyway?"

"It was Cassie," I grimaced. "God. You know you're getting older when you get in the sack with a good looking woman, and you walk away with an athletic injury." I tossed the crust onto the vacant half of the open pizza box and swigged some more beer. We all ate in silence for a moment, a comfortable quiet that happened from time to time in our household when we each had something to mull over.

"You know," Marcus said in a contemplative tone, "I wonder if it would be possible to take you on our trip?"

"To New Orleans?" I was slightly skeptical.

"No, he's right," Sophia chimed in. "It could work."

"It could?"

"Yeah! You're off the same days that we were going down there!"

"That would be fun. I could really use the break, what with the last year and all. But . . . I dunno," I said, thinking hard. "I might not have the money for it . . ."

"Pshaw! You have a little over a month to scrape together some lucre!" Marcus was literally rubbing his hands together at the thought, like some cartoon criminal in a black cape and top hat. "For four days, you only need about four hundred dollars anyway. Haven't you ever gone before?"

"You *know* I haven't. We talked about this last month."

"Well, hellfire and damnation, son, that settles it," he said, grabbing my knee. "You're coming with us whether you like it or not."

My phone's ringer always sounded like a video arcade game on crack.

"Hello."

"What's up, sexy man?"

"Not a lot, Jade. What's up in your neck of the woods?"

"I hate Ohio in autumn. It's horrible. But I have a new boy toy, and I also wanted to gloat."

"Fine. You first."

"You have something to gloat about too?"

"Better believe it."

"Okay, then guess where I'm going for Halloween?"

"An intervention put together by all of your friends?"

"Hardy har har. No, the Hematarium is doing a party on Halloween in New Orleans!"

"You're kidding."

"Not even a little! I get to go to New Orleans!"

"Hematarium . . . This is that group of vampire wannabes, isn't it?"

"Watch it, boyo."

"I know, you're all into that and stuff. Well, then, I have even *better* news for you. When are you going down there?"

"On the thirtieth. We're staying four days and I'm going to tear shit up. Fuck Ohio."

"Jade, how long have we known each other?"

"I'd have to think on that. Um. We met on the Erisian Fields email list back in . . . what, 1997?"

"I think so. Damn, it's been five years."

"About that, yeah."

"Well, it looks like I finally get to meet you in New Orleans."

Insert twenty seconds of dead silence.

"Say that again?"

"I'm going to New Orleans for Halloween as well. Looks like we'll be in the town on all the same days. I get to finally meet the infamous Jade of the Red Hair and wild-ass booty."

"Oh my god! That's fucking *great*! Holy shit! Where are you staying?"

As the air in Dallas stayed in the lower range of summer heat, October broke upon me like a wave of good fortune after a long run of *very* bad luck. Two weeks before I was to leave on vacation, I met Catrina.

I was drinking at a Gothic nightclub where most of the clientele wore leather and chains. In the gloomy interior of this watering hole I spotted a lithe, slender woman with long, walnut-colored hair, a tight brown velvet lounge dress that showed a generous amount of thigh, and the eyes of a jaguar. Tall and long legged, she physically appealed to me on every level that I normally looked at on a prospective seduction. The fact that she was in this nightclub, one of my favorite hunting grounds, was just too much for me to bear. I excused myself from a banal conversation with several drinking buddies, and sidled up to her as casually as I could.

She was fumbling in her purse with an unlit clove cigarette in her mouth. My arm snapped out in an eyeblink, and the lighter clicked to life a moment later. Not even flinching reflexively, she turned her head and took a drag, inhaling deeply as the tip crackled to life above the flame, with sensual, unpainted lips and smoky eyelids hooding her gaze. When her eyes finally rose to meet mine, the frisson down my back was electric.

"What's your name?" She spoke the question brusquely, not even a hint of thanks in her voice for the light.

"David." I gave her a touch of a smile, just enough to show my teeth. "And I don't need your name."

"Oh, no?" she asked, and I could tell she was feigning her offended air. Those thousand-watt eyes gave me the once-over, and she cocked her hip in the haughtiest posture she could. "Cute."

"I don't need your name," I growled, putting my face close enough to her ear to be heard over the music on the dance floor, "because you're fucking hot. I'm not going to forget what you look like, whether you give up your name or no. You'll give it to me when you want to."

"You're pretty sure of yourself," she laughed, but there was nothing flippant in her words. "Well, David, if I think you can handle me, I'll tell you my name. Care for a drink?"

We flirted the night away together. Catrina was a gorgeous example of woman, and every question of mine she answered raised two more. Her wit was sharper than the edge of a running bone saw, and she'd exuded a Predatory mindset in every eloquent, feisty sentence. By the end of our first drinks together, I knew for a fact that my libido was in dire need of seducing this tigress.

As the last call came about, we happily exchanged phone numbers, and I went home with that wonderful buzz of hormones one gets when beginning a courtship.

Unlike most of my carnal conquests, Cat was the kind of lady who wanted to make the most of the hunt between us. We called and emailed each other constantly, prying into the details of each other's lives. There was a lot to like about her—she rode motorcycles, had both a double black belt in Tae Kwon Do and a degree in English Literature, and we shared most of the same voracious appetites in life, from sexuality to fine cuisine, partying to literature. I was a little bit shocked to find that she was only six months younger than me. Her body looked nineteen and her brain came off as a well-educated, hungry, sensual thirty-five. After a few days, she stopped by to accept a dinner invitation I'd extended. A tomboy-turned-sex-kitten, she was wild and hungry in every way that mattered, yet refined enough to discuss philosophy and religion.

Our conversations laid down several rules. One of these was that Cat wanted to take it slowly, and not just leap into the sack (much to my dismay). There was a definite spark between the two of us, amplified by the evenings we spent together. A brilliant intellect is a powerful aphrodisiac, and this woman had wits as enticing as her trim, finely toned body. Which of us was stalking the other was an excellent question, and one that didn't really require an answer—we were having fun taking it slowly, as only two Predatory people can, teasing and wanting without actually indulging in each other. We came close several times, but Catrina whispered on each occasion that she wasn't quite ready to give herself over yet. Her last boyfriend had injured her emotionally, and she'd wanted to make sure that the hurt had faded before she put herself in a vulnerable position again.

Kissing on the couch, exploring each other hard with lips and fingertips, I felt my heart try to smash through my ribcage with desire. She was wearing a matching black shirt and pair of slacks made of fabric that felt paper-thin and left very little to the imagination under my touch. Her hands became claws at times, digging into the back of my neck, clutching at my sides, and when I kissed the hollow of her throat she gasped in a manner that made my cock go ridiculously rigid. The scarlet couch was the only witness to our want and hunger, as my roommate was at work and his wife was asleep in their room.

Her mouth found my ear, and traced the edge of one lobe delicately.

"Not yet," she whispered, and I could hear the longing in her breath. Although I wanted to ravage her hard, roughly, tear her clothes off in ragged tatters and throw her naked, nubile body on a mattress, I also knew when to back off.

"I can wait," I said, and it almost physically hurt to make those words come out. I soothed the pain by leaving several more lingering kisses on her collarbones, listening to the way her inhalation hitched as I did so, feeling the way her hands were trying to clutch me to her. My arms untangled from her embrace, and I snatched a glass of merlot from the table while she laid back and let out a sigh of exasperation. The gulp felt like swallowing a fist made of the distilled essence of grapes that some villain in Italy had grown while plotting the downfall of his enemy. A quick glance at my watch told me that it was disgustingly late in the evening, and that she would have to go soon.

"So," she said, digging into her purse and removing a single thin, hand-rolled cigarette that probably didn't contain tobacco, "Tomorrow is the big day, huh?"

"Absolutely," I said as she lit the stick with several hard draws and passed it to me. The thick, oily smoke tasted like something from Mexico, and I suppressed a cough before expunging the cloud from my lungs. "Time to check out New Orleans, and see what adventure awaits."

"I hope you have a good time," she purred, and her tone showed she meant it. "Do you think it will be all you've suspected?"

I frowned, took another hit, and passed the joint back to her. Her lips cradled it sensually, sucking the air of the room into the narrow tube of marijuana and down her lovely throat.

"I dunno," I said, washing the taste of ashes and dead leaves off of my tongue with another slug of wine. "Maybe it'll be disappointing, after all the fancy descriptions people have given me. I probably won't even get laid, and if the bars there don't titillate me a whit, I'll probably just hitchhike home the next day."

She expelled a plume of grayish-blue fog and gave one perfunctory cough to her fist.

"I hope it's worth it," she said through a quiet smile. "From what I've seen, Dallas is wearing you down. You need a break, and hopefully your days will be spent carousing with gorgeous little Goth girlies and drowning your pains in a storm of alcohol."

"Here's to that," I cheered, and we clinked glasses before continuing to excite one another physically (and nothing more). If there was one thing about Cat's Predatory side that I adored, it was that she shared my outlook on sex: As long as it's done safely, have at it. We'd made no exclusive promises since we'd met, and by the time she left me stoned and horny that night we still hadn't laid claim to one another.

My roommate knocked on my bedroom door on the thirtieth at ten am. Unfettered, I jumped into his car and finally pursued a city that I'd heard about all my life.

CHAPTER TWO

Compared to other road trips I'd been on in my life, the voyage down from Dallas was easygoing. I took the brunt of the driving, first talking with Sophia and navigating the rolling, mild hills of East Texas while David snored like a running wood chipper in the back. After a few hours the scenery suddenly changed to deeper bayou, thick stands of trees and dark green, murky plains. The change was so abrupt that the sign reading "Welcome to Louisiana" a few minutes later was woefully redundant.

"We're already out of Texas?"

"Yep," Sophia chirped. "You've never been here before?"

"Never," I said through a grin while my wide eyes took in the mossy forests that were zipping past the car at a fairly high rate of speed. It felt really good to be on the road again, traveling, eating up asphalt and shitting out spent miles.

After a couple more minutes, my bladder began to protest its increasing state of pressure. A blue sign warned me that a rest stop was ahead, and I piloted the hatchback into the off-ramp. As luck would have it, the area was also a Visitor Information center.

I had my first pleasant surprise as I entered through the swinging glass doors of the white building. Tottering over to the steel coffee dispensers, I overheard a conversation between an elderly man and his wife.

"Mais nous sommes en retard!" he exclaimed, obviously exasperated.

"Fermes ta bouche," she'd snapped in return as the two of them bumbled their way out of earshot. It took me a moment after they were gone, but a jolting realization rattled me in mid-stride: People in Louisiana really spoke French! I'd taken some years of it when I was in High school, a mistake for anyone who likes to learn a language that they will someday conceivably use. Now I heard large groups of strangers speaking *la belle langue* in public, and it put a grin on my face when I realized how much of it I still understood. It was musical, and brought home to me the fact that I was entering another world. I relieved my bladder in the restroom, and then grabbed some free java from the table near the door. Walking back to the car, I noted that Louisiana's air had a strange scent to it, so faint that it was barely on the edge of human perception—an earthy smell, like wet sawdust that had been left on a back porch for too long.

We continued down the route through sparsely populated areas. I did a relaxed eighty-miles-per-hour through the L-shaped byways of Louisiana while noting the cities we'd passed through rather quickly. Some had been towns I'd heard of all my life, and Shreveport left me completely unimpressed—it looked like Ft. Worth without all of the glamour (that is to say, none whatsoever). Others like Alexandria were mere drab conglomerations of concrete buildings, passing pickup trucks, and gas stations offering delicious, chemical-laden snacks and cheap cigarettes. Yes, the bayou was very interesting, but I found myself completely nonplussed by the bergs along the way. Visions of New Orleans danced around in my skull, leading me onward into the afternoon sun. All the tales I'd heard from my co-workers a lifetime ago were running through my mind, and images of impending debaucheries elevated my mood with each mile marker. Sucking down saccharine soft drinks and filtered cancer sticks, I kept a steady rate of speed while my roommate and his wife slept, until finally trading off the steering wheel at Baton Rouge and catching an uneasy nap in the back seat. Around seventy-thirty pm, Sophia shook me awake as we passed the city limits of New Orleans.

The superdome in the distance looked like a giant demonic tortoise overlooking the pits of hell. A cemetery the size of a small city whisked past my window, crammed full of ancient headstones the color of a dead man's teeth.

My grin felt like it was going to split my face in half.

"Now, to find the hotel!" Marcus looked like a proud father at the moment of his child's birth.

"What's the name of the place again?" Sophia was rummaging through her black leather handbag, digging into a melee of lipstick, keys, and other weird shit that women keep in their purses.

"'Prytania Palace,' I believe," my roommate announced. "I still can't believe we found a vacancy so close to the Quarter, and at such an unbelievable price."

"Aha!" Sophia pulled out a heavily abused sheet of folded paper, with a map and directions printed on it. She read off the address aloud, and her husband nodded.

"It's a loft? How is this going to work?" I asked. My teeth found purchase on the calloused knuckle of my right index finger, a bad habit I'd acquired over years of smoking in a society that was trying to outlaw my vice in public. "I mean, do you guys want upstairs or downstairs or what?"

"All in due time," Marcus chuckled. "We've never stayed at this hotel before either." He piloted through a sudden snarl of traffic, aiming for an off-ramp that was labeled with street names I'd never encountered before in my life. "So, my dear compatriot, what do you wish to do this first evening in the Quarter?"

"I think I told you already," I said, itching for a cigarette but refraining until I could smoke outside the car, "that I'm not much one for an itinerary."

Marcus snorted, though whether in approval or disdain I could not tell. "You just run amok in a new town, that's it? No plans?"

"Exactly," I said. "Don't worry about me. I'd like it if you two could show me around the Quarter a little bit tonight, and then I may disappear for a while. Don't get nervous if I don't make it back to the hotel for a night on this trip. Call the cops only if I don't rejoin the two of you on Sunday."

"Well, you *do* need to have drinks with us at least once," Sophia chimed in.

"Agreed, but you guys know my appetites. I hope you don't find it rude of me if most of my time here, I'm nowhere to be found."

"You're the captain of your own fate," Marcus laughed. "I've seen how you are at a party, and I know you can handle yourself. Still," he said, turning momentarily to fix a somber stare on me, "Don't let it be said that I didn't warn you. I'm sure that NOLA isn't the kind of demented whirl that you'll find too heavy for your brand of hedonism." He pronounced the abbreviation like the name of a woman, "Nola."

As he turned back around to continue maneuvering the little car, I felt my grin split just a little bit wider. My teeth were in the open, and I stifled a chuckle. Oh yes, I was ready for anything the town could throw at me. I filed his little warning away under *Yeah, Right* and leaned back, still gnawing on my finger.

On Wednesday, the thirthieth of October, at nine pm, I hefted my two small traveling bags of clothing and hiked them up to our shared room off Prytania St. We'd found this place as a last-ditch effort, since all the hotels in the French Quarter had been booked solid by the time we'd decided to go. Our surprise had been mutual when we'd found a hotel a mere half-mile from Canal Street with vacancies and reasonable rates. As we entered the joint my worst fears kept tugging on my brain. I just *knew* that we'd have a room with no air conditioning, a family of cockroaches whose small civilization had progressed to the culmination of religion under the beds, and our neighbors in the adjacent rooms would keep us awake at all hours with noisy, unnatural sex acts, heard through the paper thin walls. At the front desk I handed over my share of the cash for the room, a surprisingly small amount for a four-day stay.

After check-in, however, I was pleasantly shocked to find that the loft we'd paid for was actually very nice. It was on the second floor of an antique-looking building, and the walkways were flanked by lush, vibrant foliage that had run rampant across any spare soil it encountered. The door to our room looked old enough to have been opened by soldiers fighting under Old Hickory, but the lock on the handle was electronic—the kind that opened after you swiped a credit-card type key through its reader. Once inside, all three of us whistled at the spacious unit. Most of the amenities of the room were far better than we'd expected, with walnut-stained paneling and two king-sized beds—one above, in the loft area, and one below. True, a microwave and college dorm-sized cube fridge did not exactly live up to the advertised moniker of "Working Kitchen," but I wasn't in NOLA to impress people with my skills of cooking pasta. Marcus and Co. immediately claimed the loft bedroom, and I wished them well as they ascended the tight steel spiral staircase to the next level. It wasn't that they were unattractive people. Marcus was about six-feet-tall, with a better physique than that of most men in their early forties. His hair was neat and short, and his male pattern baldness worked well with his goatee giving him the air of a college professor. His wife was twenty-six, an age discrepancy that had sparked no small amount of chatter in our social circles, but they were quite happy together. Sophia resembled what Betty Page would have looked like if, instead of a modeling career, she'd pursued life as a cook in a French restaurant and put on a little extra muscle and curve. Although they were far from physically repugnant, I still couldn't find it in myself to risk walking in on Mr. L.'s naked ass pounding the missus a good one after a night of scheduled drinking. The upstairs loft would make it difficult for such a thing to happen, as I couldn't imagine why I would venture up there. My bed and chest of drawers were both downstairs, as was the bathroom, sink, and everything else aside from their sleeping area.

I unzipped the bags I'd brought and unpacked the way I normally do on any vacation longer than two days: upending everything onto the mattress and sifting through the clothing one garment at a time before putting it away.

"Hey, Plebian!" Marcus called from upstairs.

"Speak!"

"A handful of rules need to be laid down before we get started!" I could hear the two of them emptying their luggage in a flurry of assorted odds and ends. The whisper of fabric, the squeak of PVC, and the jingling of chains were aural incense as all three of us slid drawers open and flung wide closet doors. "First of all, no throwing up in the room!"

"Agreed, although I'm a little bit shocked that you would even have to speak such a thought aloud. When have you ever seen me puke?"

"I seem to recall a certain *drinking contest* that a certain *someone* got into a few months back when we threw a party . . . "

"Humph! You're never going to let me forget that, are you? Fine, I'll try not to puke on the carpet. The bathroom is right down here anyway."

"Secondly," he continued, "No room service! The prices will undoubtedly not be worth it, and the French Quarter has finer comestibles than anything that a mere hotel can offer!"

"Agreed. Go on."

"Thirdly," Sophia called out, "No strangers staying the night!"

"What?"

"You heard me," she said, taking the stairwell back down into the area I was unpacking in with a plastic makeup case in her hand. "We came down here a couple of years ago, and the two of us met a very pleasant, sexually vibrant chick at one of the pubs. The morning after the three of us went to bed together, we found that she'd let herself out with all of our cash and several of Marcus's shirts."

"That bitch," her husband growled from above.

"We don't mind if you bring someone back here," she said while she arranged an army of cosmetics by the sink, "but after you've had your way with her..."

"Or him!" my roommate called from above, snickering.

"...Just be sure to see her out, okay?"

"That's cool," I said, hanging up the last of my shirts. "I really don't know if I'm going to get laid while I'm here anyway." This statement brought snide chortles from the both of them. "What?"

"Dude, you got laid at a funeral a month ago," Sophia giggled. "A fucking *funeral*."

"So what? It's called 'consoling the widow,' where I come from."

"I'm just saying that you shouldn't play innocent with us. You're in New Orleans now, a place where every single woman is looking to get some." She ducked into the bathroom, depositing some toiletries into the shower stall. "I have a funny feeling that we've led a bull into a china shop, as the saying goes."

"Whatever," I mumbled, noticing that the tank-top I was wearing reeked of the day's trip.

"This leads us to our final rule," Marcus called out. "Although we can be forgiving if you break it, we'd prefer that you *didn't* fuck anyone on our bed up here."

I ignored their laughter and pulled on a fresh shirt, then stepped outside to have a cigarette as they finished unpacking. Hefting my PDA, I wondered how much writing I was actually going to get done on this trip. It was steel-gray and roughly the size of a large slice of bread, this miniature computer, but its diminutive size was misleading. Its software included a word processor, a phone book, and many other little capabilities that I'd been using for months. I'd nearly purchased a collapsible keyboard for the gadget before leaving, but had opted to save the money and instead tap out the words with a stylus if I really had to. (A decision I would later regret to no end.) If even half of what I'd heard about New Orleans was true, I would find plenty of inspiration for poetry, or maybe even a short story or two.

After activating the backlight on this wafer of technology, I exhaled a plume of smoke and leaned back with my eyes closed. The night air of New Orleans had already begun working on me—a bizarre mix of smells, some of which were identifiable, like car exhaust and fried foods. Others were not so easy to place, but evoked abstract and strange connections—purple satin, the acrid wisp of drunken tears, the smell of something that glittered and shone and always hid, laughing and running, just around the next corner. I opened my eyes and spent several minutes focused upon testing the microscopic digital keypad, realizing that I already felt a need to start writing. Opting to save up the creativity until after I'd partaken of the legendary French Quarter, I slipped the little display back into my pocket, stomped my cigarette with a weathered black boot, and went inside to see what was keeping my erstwhile compatriots.

Although they'd had a good forty-five minutes since we'd arrived, he was still only clad in boxers, and she was halfway done up in black PVC. The two of them looked like refugees from a cyberpunk horror movie, standing side by side at the large mirror above the sink.

"So," I said, with a sinking feeling, "Are you guys ready to go?"

"Soon," Sophia muttered as she applied eyeliner to herself.

"Yeah, hold your horses, miscreant," Marcus added.

Fuck. If there's one thing on earth I didn't want to do, it was to wait any longer. My gut dropped a little bit more as I realized they were both preparing in the fastidious and elaborate manner that most Goths did before going out—a process that usually took hours, as the scene in question was all about freaky garb and the wearing thereof. They were both consulting each other about which makeup, which accoutrements, what jewelry to wear, and I was possibly looking at another half hour before they'd be ready to actually *leave.* Clad only in slacks, a black t-shirt, and a bandanna with a jolly roger embroidered on the front (for, after all, any night could be a good Pirate Night), I was raring to go out and explore this strange new world I'd been dragged into. Unlike most Goths, I had no need of primping and preening all birdlike when I could instead spend those wasted minutes having a good fucking time.

Instead I patiently paced the floor and swore at them while they tried on various clothing. Sulking on the bed, I rearranged my possessions while waiting, pausing only to snarl abuse in the direction of the lingering bastards. Six pairs of socks. Three pair of pants, not counting the black corduroy slacks I'd driven down in. Two tank tops, one of which I'd already retired from service due to the journey. A suit jacket for my costume. Two men's thong underwear, which was one more than I expected to need—I rarely wore the stuff, preferring the "Hang Loose" theory of undergarments. A black box of twelve condoms, of which I hoped to use at least one before the trip was over, contrary to my earlier protests. A pair of custom sunglasses, provided to me at great peril and last minute planning by an acquaintance of some fame. A stick of eyeliner... well, even if I lost it, I was sure I could find more *somewhere* in New Orleans. Cologne, deodorant, and a handful of various herbal supplements—Ephedrine (nasty, but legal, stuff), Ginseng, Vitamin B supplements (hangover prevention ahoy!), and multivitamins. My black felt fedora, and (of course), my spiked leather jacket.

On the outside, it's a lovely thing, this modified black motorcycle cop's leather. Picked up out of a Pawn Shop in 1995 for the scrotum-shriveling low amount of $25 American, I had promptly put rows of steel points across the shoulders and lapels. Not long after that, due to a mosh pit incident, I'd removed all the spikes, inserted some thicker leather pads under the holes for reinforcement, and put them all back in with no further fears of wild and crazy teens at a concert careening into me and taking a spike with them as they bounced away, bleeding. If this jacket could talk, it would be the worst character witness a prosecutor could use to cement my downfall in court. It has outlasted memberships in two bands, travel in five states, and being worn by an owner intoxicated on pretty much any substance the DEA could name. It has also protected my skin in bar brawls, turned pretty blonde heads in shopping centers, kept me warm on strange city streets, and hung over my shoulder in hot Dallas nights. The lining is full of more holes than a syphilitic body-piercing fanatic, but the outer shell is still sleek, black, and uncompromised.

While I was twiddling one of the spikes, Sophia strode over and presented herself with a flamboyant "Ta-da" gesture. She'd chosen a black skin-tight bodysuit that left absolutely nothing to the imagination, and knee-high boots that sported a horde of huge silver buckles up the sides. The soles of the footwear were stacked two inches thick, with four-inch heels. Her long, ebony tresses were tamed into a solid braid down her back, the end of which was held in place by a band of leather that had tiny white skulls printed on it. The smoky circles of shadow around her eyes and arterial lipstick she'd applied made her look like a B movie vampire queen, but in a manner that was actually quite attractive rather than gaudy.

"What do you think, mortal?"

"Tres bien," I said, giving her a comical and tiny round of applause. Marcus grabbed her from behind to administer a lascivious squeeze, and made a growling noise. He was sporting his regular club wear: A turtleneck, wide-legged gabardine pants, and a pair of loafers, all of which were the prerequisite black. A medallion shaped like a German iron cross hung from his neck on a chain, and he'd also slapped a beret onto the balding top of his head.

"You're wearing *that?*" Marcus sniggered after giving me the once-over.

"What's wrong with it?"

"You look like a damned pirate."

"And you have something against pirates?"

"Well, I suppose it's fitting that you should look like someone who's interested in booty," he chuckled.

"I don't need to take any shit from a guy whose clothing makes him look like a raging Bukowski fan."

"You wound me!" he replied sarcastically. "Such a critique from a man whose fashion appears to have spawned from one too many rides at a theme park!"

"Fuck you. And lose the goddamned beret. It's silly."

"I like the beret," his wife said, patting the top of the hat. "I think it looks very dashing."

"You would. C'mon," I said, standing up and leading them by the hands. "Let's blow this taco stand."

We stepped out onto the street corner and hailed a cab with no wait. I'd never experienced this before. Hailing a cab in Los Angeles is a fucking joke. In Dallas, you have to call a cab and sometimes wait hours before they arrive. In the noisy and gray evening streets of New Orleans, we just stuck a hand up and the cab was *there*. It was like a scene from a strange movie about New York.

The interior of the car stank of old cigarette smoke and used beer. The driver was a large black man in a greasy white t-shirt, and Marcus ordered him to take us to an address that he was familiar with. From Prytania St., we followed St. Charles up to Canal. The ride was strange, my mind taking in a million forms of visual stimulation. The streets, aged and comfortable aisles of concrete and stone overgrown with ivy and moss, slowly evolved into bright things, multicolored and filled with people. Lights of every hue beckoned from the buildings around me, and the noise of a city in full bloom slowly permeated the interior of the sweaty, abused cab. Marcus announced each interesting landmark as we passed it; The surging tide of tourists on Canal Street, the vacant and barren stalls of the farmers market, the various different avenues of the French Quarter and all the stores therein, each one shuttered and locked with iron gratings at this ungodly hour of nearly eleven pm. My excitement built slowly, the anticipation of a debaucherous and drunken night that I could almost see lying dead ahead, a brick wall that I intended to smack into at a dead run. My pulse was thudding hard, even before I'd had my first drink, and I could feel the beast in me rising, much in the way it had on prior vacations.

I could already feel a sensation that it would take me almost four days to fully comprehend. It was like tingling on the back of my neck, but from the inside, as if a warm and gentle touch were being applied to my spinal column with fingers of pink fog. I wrote the feeling off as a symptom of excitement as we carried on toward the heart of the French Quarter.

We exited the cab and against my protests, and the two savages bodily dragged me into a restaurant. My roommate was a severe diabetic, so if he didn't eat when his body required sugars, he was courting death. I swore and ground my teeth—I was on a diet, damn it, and didn't need a fucking *eatery*. No, I only wanted to enter a nice dark bar and get stinking drunk. At the same time, I didn't feel comfortable stepping back out into these unfamiliar streets until he'd given me some information with which to set my compass.

Sophia and Marcus ordered their food. Inside, the place had walls that were an interesting mix of wood paneling and centenarian gray brickwork. As a speaker system piped in jazz at a low volume, the waitress came to my side at our flimsy table, and looked at me expectantly.

"Give me a shot of vodka and . . . do you have Guinness?" I asked with the same fervor that a devout orthodox Jew might ask for kosher beef. She nodded. "I'll take a pint. That sounds like a good enough dinner to start off with."

I smiled and lit a cigarette while watching her retreating ass wiggle in her tight black jeans. Marcus was smiling at me with his eyebrows raised.

"She's a cutie."

"Yeah," I said, sipping some of the ice water that had been provided, and turned my gaze to the spacious windows. The street outside was packed with freaks, people in black and spikes, my kind of crowd. "Where's the nearest club?"

"Easy there, tiger," Marcus said soothingly. "It's right next door, and we'll be within the place in two shakes of a rat's tail."

Suddenly the crowd outside the window shifted. The Goths and punks were replaced by a new mob that seemed composed entirely of teenagers, all of them dressed in rag-tag, filthy garments in dire need of repair. Each of them sported backpacks, some of which were barely kept from bursting at the seams by duct tape or twine, and many of them had long, unkempt dreadlocks falling down around their faces. At the same time, I noted that their skin was cleaner than that of the average homeless person, and their posture belied a strange, feral aggression as they walked by.

"What the fuck?" I murmured, turning fully in my seat to watch the progression of the strange horde.

"Oh! Those are the Squatters," Marcus stated, leaning back in his chair. "Strange lot, aren't they?"

"What *are* they?"

"Runaways mostly. They travel in a large group, and their social structure is interesting. I've talked to them once or twice. Bright kids. They look out for one another, and their group affords them protection above and beyond what a normal squad of ragamuffins lives in."

A blonde girl of about fourteen in a shapeless, gray sweatshirt and tarnished jeans brought up the rear of the group as they began to fade from my line of vision. Sensing my stare somehow, she snapped her eyes up through the window to meet mine. Her gaze spoke volumes.

Don't fuck with me. Don't fuck with any of us. We look out for our own, and hell take anyone who would bring pain or discomfort to my brothers and sisters. Attack any one of our number, and we will all retaliate in a pack. Our teeth are sharp, sharper than the blade in my pocket or the steel in my eyes, and your flesh is soft as butter.

Then she was gone, and the waitress placed our orders before us with nimble hands. I turned back around in my seat, my mind still rattled by the onslaught of information it had just witnessed. Shaking my head, I began my planned bender from hell by hoisting the crystal-clear shot glass. Marcus and Sophia did the same with their glasses of water.

"Eat, drink and be merry," I intoned loudly, "for tomorrow we die!"

"Huzzah!" my roommates answered, and I slammed the ice-cold vodka down my gullet. It hit my tonsils like a fist of anti-freeze, and the feeling marked my official dive into party mode.

They ate and made small talk with me as I nursed the beer. Guinness has a very smooth aftertaste, almost like a chocolate milkshake without the chocolate. Or, for that matter, the shake. Ten minutes later I slurped the last remnant of foam from the pint glass, and waved the waitress back over to the table. I ordered another one and was informed with impeccable sorrow that I'd just imbibed the last one that they had stored behind the bar.

Thieves! Fire! Murder! Without Guinness, a pub became merely a place that people came to in order to sit on their fat asses and drink swill! I sullenly ordered brown ale, and felt the need in the back of my mind begin to voice itself. Fuck this sitting around shit—I needed to stretch my legs, get into a nice club, dance, drink, and *move*. Like a fuzzy-faced protagonist in a black and white werewolf movie, I could feel the change slowly happening. The Predator in me was growing hair and fangs. I needed a hunting ground, a place to carouse and be a general nuisance to anyone with morals.

After a mind-splittingly long time, Sophia and Marcus pushed their plates to the side.

"Are you ready to have some fun?" He leaned toward me with a leer. The alcohol was singing in my blood by then—I wasn't quite what I'd call "drunk," but felt a good buzz.

"Motherfucker, I'm ready to hit this place like a bomb," I snarled in return, my own smile toothy and voracious.

"Then let us explode." We rose and piled money on the check until it was paid in full, and I bolted out the door like a proverbial goosed wildcat, making a beeline for the Goth club next door. The line was short to get in, mostly bogged down by a bouncer who scrutinized every ID card like a jeweler appraising a diamond. I entered the oh-so-black-that-you-fucking-can't-bear-it interior, and my shoulder came lightly into contact with someone standing to my right.

"Sorry," he said. I looked up and found myself facing a young man with russet hair, about my height and wearing only a pair of gray jeans, combat boots, and scarlet body paint on every inch of his exposed torso. He'd completed the look with both a red tail sewn onto the seat of his jeans and a pair of plastic horns glued to his forehead. The dark-brown goatee appeared to be natural.

He was smiling the same way I was, as if he wanted to find a gorgeous lady and bite her on the ass by way of introduction.

"Steep cover charge," I grumbled.

"No, not really. There's a second bar upstairs," he said, pointing to a staircase just next to the bouncer. "Cover charge gets you into both, and either one is pretty good."

The hulking brute at the doorway inspected my identification card and took my ten dollars without so much as a Neanderthal grunt. My first step inside the darkened interior submerged me in an ocean of dancing, drinking, screaming, laughing freaks. I muscled my way up to the bar with a complete lack of interest in those I brushed aside.

I'd been hoping that on my vacation in this famous city of sin, I would find Gothic nightclubs that were so far above and beyond the norm that my very toes would clench in excitement upon entry. The downstairs room was very much nothing of the sort. In fact, as I watched the sea of black-clad little shitheads storming around me, I realized within minutes that this place could have been a Gothic nightspot in any major city. Same old black paint on the walls. No change in the gritty dance floor, which had a drink spilled in one corner and was missing some floor tiles in another. The bartender was your typical corset-bearing babe who would gladly punch you in the nose if you tried to get her number. A minor peep-show was happening behind a glass aperture in a small room, but after growling my way to the forefront to get a peek, all I saw was a run-of-the-mill cute Goth chick tied to a chair while some shirtless, pale, ribsy freak shaved her labia with a safety razor. I snorted and turned my back on the display. Such activities might titillate Bob and Edna from Dogfuck, Iowa, but I was used to hardier fare in my entertainment than some generic gloomy girl getting groomed. The beer was the same as I'd swilled in most of the places I had frequented in my regular, everyday nightlife. And, of course, the DJ was playing your average old mix of The Sisters, Siouxsie, and The Cult, interspersed with a handful of three-minute imported German tracks that all sound like the singer was trying to emulate Hitler's public speaking voice. The actual space allocated to the dance floor was tiny, and the entire room would have fit twice into my favorite Dallas nightclub.

After five minutes of watching people in black vinyl flail about like monkeys on crack I had to go upstairs. I'd come five hundred miles to go to the same thing I could get back home? What the hell was this happy horseshit? A horrible suspicion had taken root in my mind that aside from the spooky façade, New Orleans was going to be just another city.

The staircase was narrow, poorly lit, and long. As I emerged from the screeching wooden steps, I nearly bumped into a portly guy dressed like a Turkish landowner. He sported a mustache, Fez, and monocle with the same white linen suit I'd seen in adventure films about archaeologists in Egypt.

What the hell?

My feet, still unaffected by the single beer I'd only halfway slaughtered since entering the first bar, took a hard left through a doorway. I had to shove a bead curtain aside, and suddenly I'd entered a scarlet scene, weird and unearthly.

A band was playing, with a woman pounding old middle-eastern rhythms on a floor tom, single cymbal, and snare drum. Accompanying her was a man blowing into an instrument I could neither identify nor see through the bizarre crowd of dancing heathens in the room. With the voice of a 1940's lounge singer, a lovely waif was wailing lyrics of which I could make no intelligible word. The melody licked your ear and tweaked your nipple, then grabbed you by the hips and made you want to fucking *dance*.

My pulse rate shot through the roof, my eyes nearly fell to the floor with an audible *Ker-Plunk*, and my mouth warped into an incredulous grin as I surveyed the crowd. No Gothic club, this—the scene that was slowly being burned into my retinas was too bizarre for any mere crowd of PVC-wearing angstmongers. Women with wings, girls with heads sporting peacock-like sprays of feathers where their hair should have been, men dressed in outlandish silks and scruffy worn leather . . . each person I looked at brought a new amazement. Tall or short, fat or thin, each individual in this slightly cramped room sported a look or style that would not, *could* not be found in the universe that I live in. Here was a lady dressed as a Vegas showgirl, complete with sparkling hose and top hat! And there, a man in a pale peach caftan and turban was talking to a woman who could only have been a rogue gypsy dancer! A black man the height of a small tree with long shiny braids, in an impeccable tuxedo and opaque sunglasses sat at the bar sipping a martini, and when he smiled it was like looking at the grim reaper taking a holiday!

For the first time in many years, I actually took a step backwards in shock while the vision settled in my brain. Caught completely off guard in a good way, my mind was trying to come to grips with a very strange thought: *This was no scene I had ever witnessed before.* I'd been so accustomed to the uniformly black crowds of Goths, the baggy and homogenized garb of the technophiles, and the denim crowds and predictably depressing music of the Blues bars in Dallas that I could have walked into any of them with no compunctions or introduction, grabbed a beer, and been comfortable if the night allowed it.

But in this small, strangely cramped pub, with crimson couches and dim amber lights, I found myself completely, deliciously bewildered. This was the most wild urban jungle I had ever witnessed, and as my gaze drank in the throng of fifty or sixty human oddities surrounding me I felt a terrible urge to tear off my shirt, bare my teeth, and howl at the fucking moon in this field of alien beasts.

Instead I put one foot in front of the other and walked up to the bar. The bartender, a thirty-something lass wearing a green leather corset, white gauze skirt, and feathery red hairpiece, was giving off the smiling, tired aura of experience that would have been at home on an experienced Madame in a Western. I very politely asked her for vodka, with a Guinness to help the shot do its job—unlike most places of alcohol worship, I could not bring myself to give her my usual bravado and show of teeth. There was no way in hell that a mere city boy would have been able to charm or intimidate this one—no doubt she ate young men such as myself for a snack each night, and would shit our bones out into a small bucket at home in the morning; little undigested, dry pieces of ivory that would rattle against the dilapidated steel container with a musical noise.

As a belly dancer took to the dance floor, swiveling beautifully round hips to a tribal rhythm, jewels in her navel glinting like tiny stars from the night sky, I struck up a conversation with several of these bizarre denizens. They laughed at my naive questions, but were happy to set me straight on some of the rules of New Orleans. The laws here were different, and I was truly a stranger in an ape-rapingly strange land. After a couple of interesting facts, one of them startled me utterly and I had to stop for a moment and clear my head. The alcohol in my skull had finally decided to do its job, and my thoughts were a wee bit fuzzy.

"Wait," I said in a state of mild shock, "You're telling me that I can order a *beer* and a *shot of vodka* in *this very establishment*, take it outside, across the street, and into another bar that I have *not* ordered a drink in, drink it there, and nobody will be even mildly upset?"

The person I was addressing was a tall, clean-shaven man of exotic racial origin, as thin as an undertaker and dressed twice as sharply. His alabaster, hairless face lent him an almost androgynous look, and I had a strange mental image of this particular fellow eating a repast of tree bark late at night, sitting on a rock and devouring it with crunching noises. He nodded, the oiled and tightly curled locks of black hair on his forehead barely moving.

"As long as you get it in a plastic cup and don't take it out of the French

Quarter, nobody cares," he confirmed in a voice that was as smooth as frozen milk.

Incredulous, I found only dispassionate agreement in the faces of other people who had joined the conversation. This group of miscreants was obviously trying to trick me! Let's all fuck with the tourist, get him good and arrested while he's so inebriated that he can barely see straight! Then we'll drive back to Dallas and piss on his CD collection! Well, I wasn't going to take this lying down. No sir, *I was onto their little charade*, and I knew exactly how to defuse such a fucking mockery! Grinning like the cat that ate the Canary, the Goldfish, *and* the four-month-old baby, I slapped my hand down on the counter and, per my request, received two plastic cups! One held vodka, the other . . . hell, I think you can guess what dark beer was in it. Hoisting my ill-gotten gains and without a single word of rebuttal to the mocking bastards around me, I careened out the door with a somewhat steady stride and down the staircase, past the bouncer. As each step left the bar behind, I steeled myself against the inevitable cry of "Hey! You can't take that out there!" Only silence greeted me, and I knew that he too, the goddamned *bouncer* was even in on this horrible sham! What a way to greet tourists! Fucking *assholes!* I wasn't going to stand for it, and it was time someone taught these treacherous cretins a lesson! I used my foot to prop open the door of a bar after I'd crossed the street, a quiet little place with garish, multicolored paint splattering the walls. A silken strain of Dixie jazz floated into my ears as the door wafted shut, and I found myself being looked at by a very quiet handful of people. No nightclub, this—no, this was a place where people came only to poison their livers and chuckle over bad jokes. The bartender, a slim and stunning black woman in a lavender v-neck sweater, raised an eyebrow at my entrance. I froze in front of the door like a rabbit before the headlights of an oncoming Chevy Nova at midnight, realizing that I'd just brought in two drinks *from another bar.* I had surely screwed the proverbial pooch. My bloodshot and vodka-tinged eyes locked with hers. For just a moment, all went utterly and completely quiet. Off in the distance, a dog barked.

And then the lovely young Nubian princess smiled, winked at me, and went off to fill a pint glass for a customer on the other side of the bar. The jazz music resumed. A single bead of sweat slid off my cheekbone, and I found that I had no idea what to do next. Keeping a hawk's eye on the temptress behind the counter, I downed the vodka as quickly as I could, ricocheting a tiny bit of it off of my upper lip onto the tip of my nose. The bartender didn't even glance my way, although the more I noticed the lovely curve of her ass, the more I wished she *would* look at me. As I drank the darker, smooth fluid from the other cup at the bar the bartender walked over, polishing a glass.

"You just get in?" she asked in a perfectly musical accent. I was puzzled for a second—she had seen me enter the bar, after all. What kind of silly question was that? Was this a trick?

"Oh," I said, a tiny flashbulb in my skull going off, "Yeah. First time here, actually."

Two of the patrons, a nondescript but friendly-looking couple next to me, turned around at those words, eyebrows raised.

"Your first time in New Orleans?" asked the woman. I nodded. Her guy clapped a hand on my shoulder, grinning amicably.

"Well, welcome to our city," he said in a very calm, non-partying tone of voice. By now the drinks were rampaging through my head like a herd of wild buffalo, and I clapped his shoulder in return, mostly to keep myself on the barstool.

"You live here?" He nodded. I was astounded that someone so calm could reside in a place that offered so many alcoholic liberties. Part of my brain was trying to speak up, saying *To these people, it's just another Wednesday night, fucko.* I ignored it, smiled vapidly at the two and attempted against all odds to think of something else to say. Absolutely nothing came to mind—my head was full of sloshy brains, and the muscles in my neck were starting to loosen up to the point that I felt myself nod like one of those stupid plastic dogs certain people put in the rearview mirror areas of their cars. With nothing to reply, I gulped the rest of the Guinness (stupid!) and grinned again.

"What are you drinking?" the guy asked, pointing at my now empty cup. I told him, and he ordered me a pint on the spot while his wife took a white loop of cheap beads from around her neck and draped them over my own, smiling with the grin of an angel.

"Welcome to New Orleans," she said, and I felt truly honored, albeit drunk as hell and feeling dizzy.

At that point, my memories of that night became jumbled and scattered like a house of cards that has been smashed with a baseball bat. I remember talking to the couple at that bar, walking with them to another establishment, and drinking a whole *hell* of a lot more alcohol. One clear memory was the astonishment I experienced when, right after ordering my umpteenth beer, I glanced at my watch and discovered it was 3:45 in the morning. In Dallas, I could set my watch by Last Call. Here, there was no such of a creature. Sometime during the night I went back to the scarlet room of bizarre people, sat down and pulled out my PDA. In the dim lighting and furor of the various strange denizens, I tapped out the following while attempting to force my eyes to focus:

Thurs—4:05 am
French Quarter

Mein Gott.
 Incredible fucking city. New Orleans has an almost palpable air of dirty places and intoxicating skin. I'm sitting in a bar rife with flesh and filthy, whorish perfumes, dizzy from the heady ambrosia and beer that so many poets and ne'er do wells have described in their prose. My vision is blurred, my nose aroused by the scent of decadence so thick that one could reach out and grab it with both fists. I can barely move. Bent over this lcd display, seeing double, I wonder how I'll make it back to my room alive. Around me, half naked women cavort. The bowels of hell have opened, and succubae beckon. The night is ripe with female curves and the bitter taste of slow-brewed ale. The clock strikes three! All lovelies to me!

 I wander.

 My beads have been twisted by a demoness. My mind is spent. I shall wander adrift until the sun peaks, and then off to mine bower. So speaks the chosen one!

 I cannot, in any way, remember exactly how I got back to the hotel that night.

CHAPTER THREE

Halloween, 2002. The sun tilted above the Louisiana haze, a thick marine layer of moisture that looks like thin clouds on the horizon and lazily raised the air to a comfortable level of warmth. People went home or woke up, and went either to sleep or to work, respectively. All the while I snored, my face embedded deeply into a pillow that stank of perspiration that rolled over my scalp's stubble.

I woke at about one in the afternoon in rumpled, sweat-stained bedding. My eyelids scraped open through a crust of dried fluids. This action was immediately regretted—my head was filled with angry wasps, and my tongue felt like I'd spent the evening scouring old beer kegs clean with my mouth. I groaned like a dying man, rolled out of bed, and noted that although I'd managed my way out of most of my clothing, my pants were still on. They smelled like fresh vomit. Further unpleasant study of these slacks brought back a vague memory: on my knees in the bathroom of some anonymous bar late the previous evening, puking my guts out. How lovely. With unsteady legs I stepped out of the soiled trousers, kicked them beneath the spiral staircase, and made my trembling way to the bathroom. My bladder felt the size of a beach ball. I tottered, still slightly buzzed from the prior evening's debauchery, feet screaming from too many paths walked in drunken rambling. I remembered that at some ungodly hour of the night I'd decided to walk off the buzz. The attempt had been valiant but ridiculous—that much beer would have gotten me to Chicago on foot. How many hours had I wandered the strange and unfamiliar concrete roads? I had no memory of the sun coming up, but that wasn't an indication of anything—my recollections of the night were fogged in a black mist that I couldn't penetrate. I grabbed one of the cheap, white terry cloth towels off the rack in the bathroom. Knees quaking, I turned the shower on as hot as I could endure. The heat helped a bit. Leaning against the fiberglass wall of the stall, I slowly felt my brain congeal into something I could use. An annoying sector in my head tried to remember how much beer I'd swallowed, how many shots of vodka I'd tossed down my gullet, but it was no use—I honestly couldn't remember. The thumping beat in my temples was arguing that it had been an awful *lot*. After a while I felt like movement was once again possible, and grabbed a fresh blade off the side of the tub. It was time to do my hair.

While banishing the stubble from my head with the razor, I soaked under the spray of water and gained what further composure I could. By the time the stream coming from the showerhead was running down to pisswarm, I felt like a human again. A half-dead, tortured and traumatized human to be sure, but human nonetheless. With a towel around my waist, I ventured back to the lovely sink/makeup area the hotel had so thoughtfully provided to finish my ablutions.

My hands rifled through my smaller duffel bag, and I made a horrible discovery: I had forgotten to pack my toothbrush. This made me cranky, much in the way a savage and large dog that is trained to kill will become cranky when you pull its tail too hard. I could hear my roommate and his wife sleeping upstairs, and wondered if they'd been there when I'd returned at . . . uh, whatever time I'd gotten in.

I desperately gargled a mouthful of toothpaste in an attempt to destroy the foul flavor, but this did nothing to remove a thin film of scum I could feel across my gums and lips. I spat, wiped my mouth, and applied deodorant.

Stumbling back to the bed, I opened my closet door and removed the costume I had decided upon weeks before. A fresh pair of black slacks, cut loosely to allow more comfortable movement, slid up to my waist. I cinched it with my belt, and then pampered my feet with a pair of fluffy, fresh socks that I'd purchased expressly for this trip.

I was wrestling with the laces on my boots when a creaking noise came from behind me, followed by a yawn.

"Bonjour," Marcus croaked as he trudged down the stairwell clad only in a pair of indigo silk boxers. "Good to see you made it back here alive."

"Barely," I grunted, and tightened the knot in my laces.

"What did you get up to last night? When Sophia and I turned around, you'd disappeared, and we didn't see you again until we returned to the room this morning."

"I remember drinking. Then I remember walking around a lot. Much more than that, I couldn't tell you."

"We figured that would be your answer," he chuckled, sitting down on my mattress while I pushed one arm into my suit jacket. "So, what do you think of the city so far?"

My fingers turned the lapels of the jacket right side out, and I shook my head.

"Its amazing. This town is like a big playground for the demented, a god damned amusement park for adults with adult appetites."

"Yes, isn't it just?" He peered at my getup and raised one eyebrow. "Ah, so you're already getting into your costume?"

"Damned right. I went to all of the trouble to arrange it, I might as well wear it every chance I get."

"What are you dressing up as, again?"

I rummaged through my briefcase, and then extracted a comic book. It landed at his knee with a soft slap, and he brought it closer to his face.

"'City On Fire'?"

"That right there is one of the best graphic novels ever written. You do yourself a grave disservice by not reading it."

"I told you I don't read comic books," he murmured, flipping through the first few pages idly before his fingers stopped on one panel in particular. "Ah." He held it up and compared it to what I was wearing. "So you're this chap right here . . . "

"Croft Derwood, at your service," I said, grinning as I slapped the black fedora onto my smooth pate and gave a theatrical bow. Marcus's brow shot upward, and he nodded with a prim grin.

"The resemblance *is* astounding. Who exactly is this character?"

"'City On Fire' is a story that's very noir. Croft is a freelance news reporter who runs with a dangerous crowd, writing stories about both sides of a mob battle that's raging in his neighborhood." I lifted the strap of the attaché case over my shoulder, and adjusted the red handkerchief poking out of my breast pocket. "He's my favorite individual out of the whole series. Very aggressive, and not above committing a crime to get to the heart of a story."

"Hmm." My roommate flipped through a few more pages in a disinterested manner. "Sounds almost intriguing enough to compel me to read this pap."

"I swear to you, it's great," I insisted.

"Tell me why this Croft fellow wears a suit jacket over his bare chest."

"It's his trademark style, along with these," I said, producing a pair of custom-made sunglasses. The black wire rims held two silvery, diamond-shaped lenses.

"You went through all that trouble back home for *those*?"

"Hey," I said, putting them on, "Nobody carried them. I found the last pair for sale at a comic book shop in Arlington. Now the costume is complete. What do you think?"

"Oh, you definitely look like this individual, without a doubt," he said, comparing my attire to that printed on the page before him. "You even obtained the white hatband and the pocket square. Impeccable reproduction on your part, and the facial resemblance is uncanny."

"Thank you," I said, bowing again in full regalia.

"You both wear that particular leer that speaks volumes about a man. Namely, that he has very little class." I let the quip slide by without retort as he scrutinized one of the pages. "Ah, and it appears that you both use the word 'fuck' copiously. What kind of ridiculous name is Croft?"

"What kind of name is Marcus? Why not a simple 'Mark'?"

"In every case," he said, flipping the comic back toward me across the bedspread, "Do you honestly believe that anyone will recognize your outfit?"

I cracked open the front door, and stood in the doorway to light a cigarette.

"Frankly, I don't give a flying shit," I muttered around a butt in my teeth as I lit it. The smoke seemed to draw into my lungs, and then burrow up into my brain, banishing the edge from my headache. "Today's Halloween, chum, and it's my favorite holiday."

"Your favorite? How incredibly Goth of you," he joked.

"Hey, I grew up in poverty. Most people think Christmas is the best time of year, but I fucking hate it. All of my yuletide memories as a child are centered around watching other kids play with their brand new toys, and being too fucking cold." I blew a couple of smoke rings into the breeze where they were stripped into nothing. The wind had a distinctly sweet smell, a fragrance of the purple and pink flowers growing from a tree down the hall.

Crape Myrtle, I thought, and then paused. *How the hell did I know the name of that tree?* I tried to remember where I'd read or heard the name before, but my mind kept drawing a blank. Someone must have told me the night before, although I didn't recall getting in any conversations about fucking *plants*, for chrissake. After a few moments, I wrote it off as just another piece of trivia I'd heard somewhere, one of the bizarre little confections that my brain likes to hang onto for no apparent reason.

"So why Halloween, then?" Marcus's question snapped me back from my reverie, and I leaned against the doorjamb with the cigarette clutched in my teeth.

"I'm surprised you even have to ask, old bean. I love this day because it's the one time of the year when everything I delight in is worshipped openly. Children are painted up as goblins and demons, and free candy is theirs for the taking. It teaches them that they should have one holiday centered on vices and abundance. We might have been too poor for good Christmases in my family, but you're never too poor to throw on a bed sheet or some makeup and get free sweets." I ashed the tip of my smoke into the air, watching the roasted flakes fall away like snow.

"Why am I not shocked that you delight in the corruption of today's youth?" he chuckled.

"Plus for the adults, it's even better. Parties where everyone dresses up morbidly, and everyone has a good time while the weather outside kills all the plants . . . this kind of day only comes once a year, and I try to make the most out of it every time."

"I see," he said, his voice straining as he stretched his arms above his head. "So you're not into the whole 'All Saints' Day' aspect of it, or the Wiccan take on Samhaine?"

With a derisive snort, I spat a wad of congealed crud from my throat over the edge of the stairwell, but it failed to hit any pedestrians that might have been walking by.

"Agnostic to the bone, my man. I'm neither catholic nor a hippie." The cigarette butt also flew over the railing, with the same unfortunate lack of effect as the phlegm.

"Well, I hope you haven't forgotten the Night Without End Vampire's Ball this evening," he said, walking over to me. I realized without warning that I was completely prepared to go out for the rest of the day. A wad of cash was nestled in my wallet, and there were no further preparations needed. My feet itched to be moving.

"It sounds interesting, but I don't want to paint myself into a corner right now," I grinned. "C'mon, it's Halloween in New Orleans. I want to see what my options are."

"I understand," he said, closing his eyes and breathing in the perfume of the air. "Sophia and I have already purchased our tickets, so we're definitely attending. If you find nothing else to fill your evening, I suggest you be back here at 8:45 sharp." He opened his eyes and gave me a hearty handshake.

"Tell you what; if I don't return by eight, consider me AWOL and head out by yourselves." I tipped my hat and strode out the door, waving at Marcus. "I'm off to find out what this place has for me!"

"Bonne chance!" he called out, and closed the door.

Even though the sunlight seemed bent on drilling a god damned hole through each of my eye sockets, I was very surprised to find myself in a balmy 70 degrees Fahrenheit. Hangover be damned, I felt good. A light breeze sifted through the exotically twisted limbs of the trees around me, and I noticed for the first time that the air of New Orleans felt no other I'd ever experienced. The humidity seemed folded into the air by some giant ethereal chef, whose wire whisk made every lungful into a creamy, moist soufflé. I thought about lighting a second smoke as I departed, which was an old tradition I'd picked up years before—When going out, start with a cigarette.

Halfway down the cement stairs of the hotel toward the front office, an enticing aroma permeated my nostrils and yanked any thoughts of nicotine out of my head. I followed the scent as only a junkie could, fixated on getting my daily dose of poison, and stomped into the hotel office with one thing in mind.

"Good morning, sir!" The tall, Hispanic-looking man in a starched white shirt waved gaily at me from behind the counter. I completely ignored his greeting and trudged to a rather beautiful sight: A flimsy folding table held one big steel decanter, with a pump mechanism built in, and a pile of Styrofoam cups. The cardboard sign in front of the entire glorious setup read "COMPLIMENTARY COFFEE." I gave a moment of thanks to whatever gods might exist and snatched up a cup. My greedy finger pressed the button on the dispenser and the fluid that came out was seductively dark and thick. No mere dime-store java, this. As a member of the ranks of the Caffeine Dependent, I understood that really good coffee had nothing to do with how much milk and sugar went into it. No, it was about how evenly a cup of Joe could balance the bitterness with that earthy, rich flavor that I loved and worshipped. It was also about how much of a kick the coffee had—too much caffeine, and I got off to a shaky start on the day, not enough caffeine and I wouldn't wake up until the fourth or fifth cup. I tipped the blazing-hot liquid past my lips and prayed for something that would slap my face fully awake and help ease my hangover.

Coffee in NOLA, I discovered, was a funny thing. It was awful, *truly* awful, the brown sludge that the denizens of that town were willing to spill down their throats, torturing their digestive systems. To call the beverage *bitter* was the same as calling the sun *hot*. It was so ridiculously bad that it was almost *good*. Thick, blacker than the inside of a dead cat and twice as foul in flavor, it wrapped a hairy, sweaty, brown fist around my tongue and tortured it for a second before splashing past my tonsils, a noisy and bitter guest that my stomach would have to deal with. Coffee this bad was usually something you drank if you had sins to pay for, or you just liked doing terrible, cruel things to your taste buds.

(Before long I grew to associate that smell, that burned earthy aroma, with the lifeblood of New Orleans. If I close my eyes and breathe deeply I can still smell it. Right now.)

Armed with a second cup of vile, noisome fluid, I stepped out into the parking lot of the hotel. The public transportation system reportedly ran down St. Charles Avenue all the way to Canal. My feet took me to the corner, and it was a little surprising to see what this side of New Orleans looked like in the sunlight. No huge crowds of drunken merrymakers, no visible pubs at first glance. The shops were quiet, simple rectangles of cement and glass, not too modern, but not ancient either. Traffic on the street could only have been described as *lazy*. Each passing car trundled by at a languid thirty-five-miles-per-hour or so. A median of green grass ran between the two opposing flows of traffic, and it was there that I eventually waited, by a dilapidated yellow sign that indicated a Streetcar Stop.

After I'd waited around for a couple of minutes, I decided to use my unfailing Public Transportation Summoning Spell. Without attracting undue attention from the two fellows who were also waiting for the car to show up, I reached into my jacket and removed a magical Sacrifice Stick. I touched some flame to it. The magic, as always, worked—no sooner had I taken my third drag off the cig than the streetcar appeared four blocks away, making its meandering way towards us.

A giant alien caterpillar, the brown and rusted behemoth rolled toward me with noises that you would be hard pressed to find outside of a steampunk movie. I'd seen streetcars in films, but nothing prepared me for my first ride on one. As soon as it rolled to a complete halt, I noticed that the entire mechanism had gone utterly silent, save the creak as its doors shuttered open. The seats, as far as I could tell, were about halfway filled with a wide spectrum of riders, leaving plenty of room for new passengers. Gold lettering on the side of the mechanical beast noted that this car had been in operation since 1918. I marveled at the concept for a second. In 1918, Los Angeles had been a relatively small seaport, the motorcar had not yet been widely accepted by the public, and most houses hadn't had electric refrigerators. Yet in New Orleans this car had gleamed brand new back then, clean and efficient, and had carried people around the city.

I smiled, took a dollar and a quarter out of my pocket and stepped on. A strangely modern cash acceptor stood bolted to the front of the interior. I paid the fare and gave the weathered weary black man in uniform a grin before walking to the rear of this eldritch machine. Moments later the car lurched forward with a loud grinding noise, and we were off. The ride jolted every few seconds, but in between lurches was remarkably smooth. Standing near the rear of the cab, one hand wrapped around a leather strap in the ceiling, I watched the streets slowly evolve as we passed through them. The older, more solemn houses of the neighborhood I was staying in turned first to industrial buildings, then dilapidated and often abandoned office structures. Rocks or bullets had smashed out about half of the filthy windows on these, and a small scrap of a cheap white curtain fluttered out of one in particular, like a flag of surrender for a man who had once worked there and failed miserably at his job.

The scenery became more eclectic. Camera shops nestled parallel to Cajun food joints, music stores smack-dab adjacent to travel agencies, car rental establishments slapped next to everyday fast food huts... suddenly I felt like I was in the downtown of almost any big city in California.

By the time I reached Canal street, a familiar sensation was already coming over me, and it wasn't a great one: *loathing of tourists*. There were droves of fucking tourists in every direction. Morons in denim shorts and yellow polo shirts, sporting big ugly straw hats, cameras around their necks, and ridiculous hiking backpacks strung from their shoulders. I'd grown up in a city where tourists came in hordes to gawk at Mann's

Chinese and Grauman's Egyptian. I knew by instinct how the locals of New Orleans must have felt. Tourists suck. They walk around acting like morons, buying things that they can probably purchase in their own hometown, but with the name of the city they're visiting emblazoned on it in gaudy pink cursive writing. Part of my mind patiently mentioned that *I was also a tourist here*, but I was having none of that jive. *I* wasn't going to go buy a fucking pink t-shirt with a crawdad on it. *I* wasn't going to pose in front of some stupid Mardi Gras store, snapping off photos for the grandkids. No, I'd gone to other cities for my vacations, but I would sooner eat the shit out of a live hippo's ass than join the ranks of mindless robots I knew only as *Fucking Tourists*.

The streetcar pulled to a stop on the corner of Canal Street, so I stepped off of the hulking, ancient mechanism and put my foot down on the sidewalk.

I peered through the silvered lenses, checking out my surroundings. On each side of Canal, tall buildings of deep red and filthy gray brickwork stood like sentinels, keeping God knew what at bay. Across the building walls, billboards touted various brands of alcohol, strip clubs, and car manufacturers. The grime on the structures and the pristine surface of the huge advertisements provided a strange contrast, like putting a clean white tuxedo jacket on a soiled hobo. All around me, crowds of people and cars milled in various directions, creating a metropolitan murmur in my ears. I walked slowly, taking it all in the way a connoisseur would sip at a wine. My expression was relaxed and my step easy. I detected a wild mix of accents around me; Southern drawls, the twang of people from the East coast, and the lovely, buxom sound of *French!* I made a note to try my rusty skills at some point on an unsuspecting bystander. The shops that lined the avenue were wide open, belching forth Zydeco music from tinny speakers in their walls. I sneered at a display of flimsy, non-impressive Mardi Gras masks, which were being held upright by a poorly preserved, small stuffed alligator in a window. The gator's dull, glassy eyes seemed to say, "Fuck you, shitlips. You think I like being stuck out here, holding up cardboard masks day in, day out? I wasn't even allowed to rot, like most dead gators do—now I'm some kinda thing for you bastards to gawk at. Not even very old when some asshole shot me. I mean, *look* at me. I'm just a little gator, dead too young, stuffed full of Styrofoam and sewn up like some ghoulish party favor. So fuck off."

I stopped at the next corner, lit a cigarette, and decided to check out the

French Quarter. One small problem occurred to me: I had no idea how to *get* there. Sure, I'd wandered around the place for hours during the previous evening, but I had taken a cab there and had no recollection of how I'd returned. For all I knew, it could have been miles away in any direction. Just as I was turning to ask a grumpy old man in a sweatshirt and shorts for directions, a sign caught my eye at waist level, two feet away. *French Quarter,* it said, with an arrow pointing across the street.

After legging it past the stopped traffic at an intersection, I was face to face with a small liquor store hopelessly surrounded by camera shops. Once inside, I snagged a new toothbrush, some breath mints, and a fifth of good rum, all of which I paid for quickly and deposited into my briefcase. The saleswoman had been yet another tired shopkeeper, and she'd confirmed that all I had to do to get to the Quarter was hook a right at the next intersection. Shrugging my satchel, I began my trek anew.

I was halfway through the next stoplight in the middle of a jaywalking violation when a grinning bald man accosted me. Not bald as in "head shaved," but bald as in "friar Tuck looking head" kind of way. He wore a bright Hawaiian shirt and Bermuda shorts, and his teeth clenched a vile and putrid cigar as he trod along in the opposite direction, staring off into the distance as I passed him. He suddenly stopped in the middle of the crosswalk, grinned at me, and pointed one hairy finger right at my chest.

"*That* is the best fucking costume I've seen all day!" he said in the same tone of voice that I'd once heard an off-duty paramedic use to describe a stripper's ass at a nightclub. "What's up, Croft?"

"Thanks," I said around a cigarette, and smiled like the Devil himself. I rounded the corner.

I entered a tourist shop long enough to pick out the ugliest, nastiest New Orleans t-shirt I could find. It was not a proud moment, but I realized that I couldn't have passed up anything that was for sale at $2.99, especially not a black t-shirt with the gaudiest neon print of a Masque with feathers and beads, and the words "French Quarter" emblazoned across the front. I bought one in size XXL and stuffed it into my briefcase as quickly as possible, as if it were a videotape of child pornography. I had a souvenir.

Back on the street, I wondered what actually delineated the Quarter from the rest of the city. I'd walked five blocks before going into the tiny shirt store, and it had occurred to me in mid-stride that *I was suddenly in the French Quarter!* Spinning on my heel, I took in the streets lined with a plethora of different architectural fashions that now surrounded me, two or three-story houses in varying shades of white, gray, yellow, mauve, or light green. Every style had been present and accounted for in a display of French Quarter bravado, whirled together without reason or rhyme: Classical townhouses perched next to Creole Cottages with their sharply canted roofs, the narrow front porches of warm, humble Shotgun Houses stood alongside a few American Double Galleries, grand in their stature and serving beer. Each separate sidewalk tile was unique as well—cracked, the pieces tilted at slightly odd angles, an obstacle course for the intoxicated. I dimly recalled dealing with such footing during the previous night's debauchery, but could not remember tripping on the uneven surface. I did know now that I'd probably covered a fair amount of space in my prior night's walking, since my feet hurt and my legs were in pain. It felt like I'd hiked a good twenty miles in my drunken state. At the same time, each step along the walkway seemed to ease the pain a little, and also increased the sensation I'd noted before. That warmth on the nape of my neck had returned, nothing incredibly unnatural, but at the same time a sensation I'd never experienced. The closest approximation I could give is that it felt like a warm, gentle beam of the sun was shining directly on me, not blazing like the Texas heat does, but instead spreading a lovely, relaxing glow between my shoulders and my head. At first I wondered if it were the onset of a fever, but I didn't feel even slightly ill. After a few minutes, the feeling was so pleasant that I decided to stop worrying. I walked.

The city began to truly show me what she was like. Our first date had gone poorly, compared to what she showed me that day. The architecture bloomed with each new building. I felt like this strange place, this city compiled of designs of wildly varied time periods, might even be a rare area that the gods and time itself had forgotten about, left to become something wondrous on its own. My eyes were overwhelmed. It was as if someone had found a control dial marked *"Human Experience"* and cranked that fucker to ten. The crowd around me, unlike the ones I'd seen in other places, seemed to be primarily happy and joyous, albeit a touch intoxicated. I wasn't sure if I wanted a drink yet, so I just kept walking around, looking at the strangely relaxed chaos.

It was unlike a crowd I had ever seen. An elderly couple straight out of a film about Miami followed closely behind punk Mohawks of bright blue. All manner of dress and style was being flaunted mercilessly, with no regard for the proximity of polar opposites. A group of pot-smoking hippie types lounged on the benches outside a church, while not five feet away a fat old white woman sat and played electric piano while belting out jazz tunes.

The music was everywhere. I stopped several times in the middle of a sidewalk, on a corner of two of the narrow, one-way streets, to listen. The first thing I noted about the French Quarter was that I heard music everywhere. Not just some guy honking on a saxophone either—*real* music, from people who really knew how to play, and most of it was the most beautiful jazz I'd ever heard. I felt like I was walking through an aural buffet as I stopped every so often to snack on another lovely sound, whether it was the spicy Acadian notes of a small accordion, or the smooth and silky flavor of a cello coming from just inside an alley. And it was during this first small bit of walking and wondering that the presence began to speak through my brain.

I did not actually hear a voice at first, but the little moves the city made around me, the wind that whispered in my ear may as well have been a woman standing just over my shoulder, murmuring a guided tour. The mixed conglomeration of various delicious smells in the air was like a perfume, a symphony of pheromones that plied my mind with information. Each house and smashed sidewalk tile was the skin of a real being, something that began to whisper so quietly in my head that I barely felt it, but became louder with each step. I felt like I heard someone, something that spoke in the sweetest and most relaxing tone I had ever felt in my life, not words but thoughts injected right into the center of my mind, the closest to utter telepathy I had ever experienced.

Look over there. The man in the black silk suit, his violin weeping notes to splatter across the cracked sidewalk. See him? He is one of mine.

I smiled at the musician as I walked by, and took note of his incredibly smooth, waist-length dreadlocks and dark chocolate complexion that was offset by eyes whose irises were the color of steel. He grinned back, flashing a set of strong, bright teeth so big and perfect that he almost looked like he would take a bite out of anyone who came too close.

And here? Read this bronze plaque. Understand how old I am, child. Understand that what you are seeing has been going on here, uninterrupted since time immemorial.

Without having taken a single drink since the previous night, I felt a calm, intoxicating buzz settle over me as I read the historical marker. Part of my mind started to object—by all rights, I should have been feeling like a dead dog from the hangover, and my logic center started to tell me that *something was very, very wrong with this situation.*

But the warmth spread across me, light beyond the perception of human nerves, told that part of my mind to go fuck itself. I didn't care what was causing this strange new feeling—I liked it.

I soon found myself half a block from Bourbon Street, and decided to turn around. With my hatred of tourists, I refused to go there before it was absolutely necessary. The most infamous street in the Quarter for drunken college students was *not* my idea of a party, unless I was allowed to bring a rather large fully automatic weapon and fire into the crowd.

You will *go there eventually,* the vaporous presence in my mind conveyed, and I almost nodded in reply as I walked. I felt high on some hitherto unknown drug as I meandered. Each footstep brought yet another wonder into my vision, and that voice became stronger in my mind.

And here? Here a French pirate killed three men in one morning, dueling beneath this tree.

The milling crowd around me swirled and became a surreal cross section of humanity. It flowed down the same paths and streets that had supported crowds for literally hundreds of years. My eyes felt like they'd been filled with so many sights that they couldn't possibly have taken them all in, like small cups held in the current of a fast-moving stream. Trees covered in moss and wrought iron fences and statues and the ever changing shattered cement tiles of the sidewalk, smiling, walking, yelling, whispering people all around. I paused in front of a strange building of brick and wood, by a sculpture done in an almost modern style, so very, very old.

See how the statue holds his arms high, not upward but out at my streets? See how he praises me? Look on me, and understand, traveling one. My body is old stone and metal, my pulse is the stumbling intoxication of thousands and thousands of revelers. My breath is a humid breeze with the scent of flowers and wine and mildew.

As I walked, my legs loosened up again. The aches of wandering faded away, and I felt more stable. Too distracted, too overwhelmed, I welcomed this strange phantom in my head without any question at all, and that it became more and more powerful as the minutes flew by was of no consequence to my thoughts.

A place of whores, a place of thieves and murderers, rapists and criminals. Once upon a time walking these streets you would have been crooned to, called at, Trav-

eler. The lusty and well-versed women of my brothels would have stirred your loins and whet your appetite. They are gone for the most part, and those that remain are not the finely painted ladies of before, with their silk ribbons and perfect hairdos. The houses that once served fine carnal relief are gone . . . but you can still find any manner of sexual fulfillment in this place, Traveler. Can you feel it already? There are many in this city looking for pleasure of the flesh, and you can find it without even trying.

And I felt it, hot damn but I felt it. Like a sheet of slow-moving warmth through the air, it saturated me. Part of me wanted to walk faster, grin, and begin hunting for someone to smile at, dance with, and take home. But my pace did not, *could* not increase, strangely enough. Even though my appetites had been aroused, I couldn't raise the tempo of my lazy, relaxed stride—I felt like a car that had the accelerator and brake mashed to the floor simultaneously. I was still floating on the pleasurable heat in my brain, listening to the way the presence was speaking through my very bones.

Never in my life had I felt the awe that so many had described when they gazed upon a mountain range or the Grand Canyon and said, "it was like looking at God." Sure, such things could be immense, or breathtaking. I'd once had the pleasure, during a ski trip, of looking out over the snow-drenched Rocky Mountains at eleven thousand feet above sea level, and that view had been amazing. At the same time, I hadn't looked at those peaks and thought that I was having a holy experience. But as my feet found their way on the uneven concrete and pavement of New Orleans, as I listened, tasted, smelled this city, it was the first time that I really understood. The realization hit me with an ecstatic shock: I was in the arms of a goddess, and she was speaking to me. I felt her in my mind. No mountain peaks, those tarnished and dirty brick walls, but the feeling was the same as looking into the sky and seeing heaven as clear as daylight. The presence in me was that of the city, and it was no anonymous monologue, either. She spoke directly to me. Led me. Lured me. Tempted me.

And perhaps, the little paranoid voice in my mind piped up, *it's planning to kill me*. After all, I *had* just assumed that this ethereal being in my skull was kind and benevolent. I'd never run into a higher power before, but the idea that a great being would automatically be kind and merciful was bordering on foolishness. Many were the old folk tales and legends of other cultures where a God or Goddess was actually cruel and scheming.

While I thought this, a fluttering, tingling sensation occurred across the back of my shoulders and neck, and I realized that the city was laughing. It was a golden feeling of heart-lifting comfort that spread through my limbs, not unlike the sensation I'd experienced when taking Ecstasy in the past, but more fleeting.

But do you think you are so special to me, Traveler? Do you believe that I would go to great lengths to plot your death? Hardly. Many have died here, more than you can imagine. Do you think I had to lead them in any way? People perish here of their own vices and actions, and rare it is that I have any part in it.

For some strange reason, the thought was reassuring. I walked on, carefree to the core, my eyes still drinking deeply of the surroundings. The presence began to communicate to me strongly. Before it had been a mere feeling on the edge of perception. Now it was as if I had another being in my head, one that let its own thoughts flow over mine like a breeze. I welcomed it fully, and each step brought the rapturous hum in my nerves to a higher level.

Can you even imagine everything that has happened on Decatur, mortal? Can your mind understand even a tenth of how many times people have eaten, mourned, rejoiced, fucked, shat, cried, fought, laughed, and died on this street? No, you cannot. But it has been happening for a very long time before today, and it will not stop for a very long time after tomorrow.

I was stuck in a hypnotic tapestry of the human experience. It occurred to me that I didn't really care whether or not this city was plotting my demise. My every sense was filled with wonder unlike any I had felt since childhood . . . Perhaps not even then. The city showed me *life*, not merely distilled and put on display in a bottle, but grown freely on the vine. From the musicians on the street that filled every alleyway with ringing echoes of notes, to the laughter of tourists from so many faraway places coming together to order drinks. Before I knew it, I had spent two hours doing nothing but looking at the people around me and walking, listening to that soft, warm, ancient presence in my ears.

It was about four when I remembered Jade. Thoughts of meeting her startled me from my reveries, and the presence quickly to a low, humming feeling that sang a slow, relaxing melody through me. I looked around—the street I was on was unfamiliar, but I vaguely remembered crossing Bourbon Street a few blocks back. I wanted to find Jade, but had no idea where to begin. Wrapped in my preparations for the trip, I'd completely forgotten to call her before leaving Dallas. I wasn't even sure if meeting her was going to even be all that great an experience. The few pictures she'd sent me over the years had shown a woman of slightly heavier than average build, with long and impressive red hair. Cute face, but she could have lost a few pounds. Mentally, her messages and phone calls had painted a picture of a Predatory woman whose hungers in life were as debaucherous as my own. Although it would be fine to cavort through the streets with her, I didn't expect to find her that attractive in person. The Internet was funny that way—it only gave you a glimpse into a person's mind, not much more than that, and meeting an online friend in person was usually a bit of a letdown.

I thought about finding an Internet café to get her cell phone number from my email. Surely she was in town by now, and if I didn't hook up with her at some point in this vacation, I'd be disappointed. Unfortunately, I didn't have even the foggiest notion of where I could find a computer, and I wasn't even sure that there *were* cyber-cafes in this strangely alien city. Hell, I hadn't even seen a television since I'd arrived, save the cold, dead unit in our room.

In a flash, I remembered that I'd possibly written her phone number in my electronic organizer, and my hand reached into my pocket . . .

Don't.

I paused. I still did not literally hear a woman's voice in my head. It was more of a feeling than anything, wordless and yet it conveyed itself perfectly. Ordinarily I might have been incredibly shocked to hear someone, something else in my skull giving me a direct order, or felt fear, or paranoia, or at least amusement. But for the last two hours I had become used to the presence, and now I had no problem with listening to the soul of the city, this goddess.

This was, however, the first time it had commanded me.

Why not? I thought as my hand tentatively brushed the aluminum case of the PDA. *I want to meet her.*

You will. Don't worry. Walk, and live.

After a few moments of standing on the street corner and waffling, I decided to try going by the order. The choice was made with no small amount of trepidation. Part of my brain tried to scream out that this was madness, utter madness, and that I had very foolishly turned my back on any chance I might have had to meet Jade. Still, my hand left my pocket, and I walked on as the spirit continued to tell me about the city.

And over here, a man once died in a car accident with a mule-driven carriage. The animal was pooling blood in the street, the carriage smashed, people horrified and screaming. The man was a simple bystander, neither a passenger nor driver.

This wall was once touched by a man whose fingers played the saxophone more beautifully than any other ever will. He left me, went on to great fame and fortune in the outside world of man's music, playing the sweet harmonies that would share some of what he felt in me, and when he knew he was old and going to die, he came back here and died in me. He rests in one of my cemeteries forever.

And over here . . .

And in that alley . . .

Long ago on this street . . .

It was a constant flow of information from a being that sang the words through me. I continued to wander, following this siren's song with legs that felt energized and worn. And so I never pulled out the electronic gadget, and I never looked inside to discover that I did not, in fact, have Jade's phone number anywhere in the little digital storage unit. I did not venture anywhere near an Internet café the entire time I was in the city, and I had no way to contact the girl from Ohio.

In a city of millions of strangers and miles of roads, as I ambled back up Royal St. in the sun not five minutes later, I stopped at an intersection full of people and saw Jade across the street. Although I'd only seen a few pictures of her, there was no mistaking her face. She was a little bit shorter than I had expected, and the sight of her was so abrupt that I almost tripped on the concrete. Long, red hair, pretty face, and she'd apparently lost no small amount of weight. I stood on the sidewalk facing her, and my brain said *holy shit*. There she was.

I can give you so much more, said the presence in my head, and I grinned like a wolf in a room full of legless chickens.

Thank you, I thought back, and stared pointedly at the lovely young thing I'd somehow been shown the way to.

Behind small sunglasses, she noted my gaze without recognition, and then spoke nervously to a taller, auburn haired female friend next to her. I merely continued to smile and stare, suddenly a little unsure if I'd been sent to the right woman. If not, then I was making a big mistake. One does not smile like that at strange ladies on anonymous streets unless one wishes to taste pepper spray. Fuck it—the smile stayed on my face for another five seconds. I could always duck, or run like hell if I'd been looking at the wrong woman.

Suddenly the redhead froze, then a huge grin spread across her face.

"Oh my *God!*" she yelled. Heedless of traffic, she bolted across the street to grab me in a very warm, luscious embrace. A puzzled expression came over her friend's face as she checked both ways, and then followed. "Oh my God," Jade repeated as I lifted her off of her feet, chuckling as I did so. "David! What are you doing here?"

"I told you I was going to be in New Orleans," I said with an exaggerated tone of nonchalance.

"Yeah, but how did you know where I was?" she asked. Jade's smile had an interesting effect—although her face was attractive already, her smile made it absolutely stunning. Pale, gorgeous skin the color of cream, with the smattering of freckles that only natural redheads seem to have.

My mouth opened, and I started to tell her what had happened. Then I stopped.

"Just found you, I guess," I stated as evenly as I could. The presence in my mind let out a chuckle, and lapsed back into humming its strange, languid tune, as if aware that I might not want to be distracted at the moment. Part of me wanted to tell Jade what I'd experienced all day, all of it. The non-stupid side of my mind, however, realized that such a story might not be the best thing to recount upon meeting a woman unless I wanted her to think I was a raving fucking lunatic.

Her back was muscular under my hands as we embraced. The top of her head came up to my lower lip, and I buried my nose in her tresses. Her skin gave off just that one tiny bit of sweet, animal musk that I'd learned to recognize in certain women. I didn't even have to say a word or ask a question to know that I was in the company of a fellow Predator. There was no way that I was going to risk scaring this one off with bizarre tales of a city that was speaking in my fucking *head*—not when I could just as easily keep it to myself, and walk with her for a few days. We turned back down St. Charles Avenue, which, she explained, was the street her hotel was on. Jade walked slightly ahead of me, bubbling over with pleasure at our unexpected meeting. I admired a really delicious set of firm thighs through the denim of her black jeans, and the way her rather generous breasts pushed against the knit fabric of her top. Her voice was musical, and as we walked I could only think one response to the city: *Thank you.*

The city just continued the subdued melody, and the three of us continued down the sidewalk.

Jade introduced me to her friend Melanie, whose presence I had barely registered.

"Charmed," I spoke softly, and bowed my head in a tiny nod as I shook her hand. Melanie was taller than me by about a good three inches, and her posture was mannish. The vibe I got from her was sheer aggression, like the aura of a rough bouncer at a topless bar. Melanie's skin was cool to the touch, and I could tell that she was still rattled by the way Jade and I had met.

"How do you two know each other?" Her voice was strong and husky, and also a disapproving. She didn't seem to like me very much, for some reason.

"This is the guy I was telling you about on the plane," Jade said happily, turning back toward me. "I tried calling you right before our flight boarded, but you were already gone."

"Then this *is* a stroke of luck," I lied. "How long have you been in town?"

"We checked into the hotel last night at about eleven, and then went and got some drinks. God, I fucking love the Quarter," she murmured as the three of us stopped at Canal and waited for the traffic lights to change. "Melanie and I and the rest of our group got too trashy by the end of the night. We didn't even wake up today until an hour ago, and we just had the best goddamned oysters on earth."

"It did nothing for my hangover," Melanie growled, rubbing her temples.

"Yeah, me neither."

"I know the feeling," I said as the light turned green and our feet hit the asphalt of the crosswalk in matched strides. "My head's still feeling somewhat soggy as well. You ladies want to go get a Bloody Mary?"

"Sure!" Jade blurted, and looked at Melanie querulously.

"Ugh," the taller woman spat. "I hate tomato juice. No, you kids go ahead without me." She rubbed her temples and grimaced. "I need a fucking aspirin and about three more hours of sleep before the festivities begin."

Jade gave her companion a hug on the corner, and then we were two. As Melanie trudged further down the street, Jade hooked her arm through mine with a smile.

"Bloody Marys, then?"

"Let's," I replied, and we set off at a delightful pace. As we walked, the realization of how unreal it had been for the city to lead me to her grew stronger.

I didn't know that this vacation was going to get even stranger over the next three days.

CHAPTER FOUR

I purchased a disposable camera at one of the crowded and bizarre liquor stores on Canal, and tore the foil wrapper off with my teeth as I exited the shop.

"Hey, Jade. Stand over here." I pointed at the carved, black granite steps of the entrance to an office building, and she obliged without hesitation. She held her arms over her head and struck a pose like a Greek statue, thrust her hips to the side and gave me a demure smile. The camera snatched the moment out of the air and tucked it away to be printed off later.

"Always have to start off the roll with a pretty lady," I said jovially, and stuffed the plastic rectangle into my briefcase.

"Flatterer. Oh, hey, look," She exclaimed, pointing at an establishment down the block.

"Pay dirt!"

A sign above the door was visible from hundreds of feet away, with thick red letters screaming out "BLOODY MARYS/$10.99" at the entirety of creation. We strode swiftly, wolves moving in for the kill—nothing could possibly have distracted us.

"Ten bucks for a Bloody Mary?" I growled as I followed her into the joint. "Better be worth it."

The interior looked like a pizzeria, from the blue and white checkered floor tiles to the jukebox in the corner. The smell of pepperoni was strong, and a glance at the far side of the counter revealed a steel carousel containing four basic pizzas cut into triangles. A small cardboard sign on the metal contraption read "$1 PER SLICE" in blue marker. The scruffy, longhaired young man behind the counter looked slightly stoned. He gave us a smile that wasn't very friendly and leaned forward as we approached the cash register.

"What can I do you for?" His voice was gravelly, and the breath that crossed the countertop stank of used marijuana.

"Two Bloody Marys!" I countered, and whipped out my wallet before Jade could open her purse. "I got this one."

"Wail, much obliged, kind suh," she replied in a passable Southern Belle accent, and curtseyed.

"How spicy do you want them?" The twisted smile on the kid's face was ridiculously sexual, and his bloodshot eyes were unabashedly glued to Jade's well-proportioned chest.

"Hmm. Medium," she said bluntly, and then turned her back on the cashier. Abruptly deprived of boobs, his eyes traced her ass muscles through their tight denim covering as she retreated to a table by the window. Only when she'd situated herself across the room from us did the clerk turn his eyes to me, and I placed him at about twenty years old.

"What about you?"

There was no way in hell that I was going to give this kid the satisfaction of showing the slightest hesitation. I gave him my best feral smile, all teeth and nothing but hunger in my eyes.

"Make that fucker *hot*," I snarled, "And gimme a slice of the pepperoni while we're at it." My stomach had curled up in a whimpering knot, and it occurred to me as the kid bustled away clumsily that I hadn't eaten anything at all since a scarfed down package of snack cakes during the drive down.

Jade was lit a cigarette by the window and gave me a flirtatious wink. I snapped my teeth together at her, and then turned back around when the cashier handed me two enormous plastic tumblers with red, speckled sludge and ice floating in them. His grin was a little less crass now, and he tapped a finger on the plastic of the right-side cup.

"This one's hot," he informed me, and then pointed to the yellow words printed on the sides of the disposable cylinders. "You get refills for two bucks. I'll bring your pizza out when it's ready."

"Many thanks," I said gruffly and paid the number he rang up, plus a dollar tip. The two drinks must have held a full quart between them. I carefully strode over to the table that Jade had claimed.

"Holy shit," she breathed as I plunked hers down in front of her. "That *is* a ten dollar Mary."

"Got that right," I smirked, and slid into the chair next to hers. I removed the bizarre sunglasses, dropped my hat onto the far corner of the table, and set my briefcase carefully out of harm's way. When I looked up, she was holding her drink up to make a toast.

"To finally meeting." Her free hand ran swiftly over my scalp, a cross between a caress and a friendly rub.

"And to New Orleans," I added as we clicked the rims of our cups together and took our first sips. The drink washed upward through the straw and spilled over my tongue in a wave of chilly heat.

"Damn," she said, putting her cup down and shaking her head for a moment. "That's . . . good, but . . . "

"No kidding," I gasped, unable to ignore the pain, and quivered my head in an attempt to dislodge the abrasive flavor of the fluid. "What the fuck, I think there's *horseradish* in here." I took another sip. "And about a gallon of vodka. I think this is the strongest Mary I've ever had."

"Mmm," she crooned, a sound that made the hairs on my arms stand on end with quiet lust. "So, you're in town the same days I am?"

"I think we both leave on Sunday, right?"

"Indeed. That's just awesome. We need to hang out some and party."

"No problems here," I said, noting that the cashier was walking over to us with a steaming plate.

"Dude," he said as his greasy hand deposited the food in front of me, "I just realized. You're dressed like Croft Derwood, right?"

"You got it," I said casually.

"Wow, man, that costume is just, like *kickin'*."

"Thanks." We watched the stoner retreat in silence, and Jade giggled. "What?"

"I was wondering what that getup was. Nice chest, though." Her eyes dropped demurely to her drink as she wrapped her lips around the straw. The directness of the compliment was not lost on me.

"Same to you," I smiled, and bit into the pizza as she playfully slapped my arm.

"Goof. So, what are you doing tonight?"

"I'm not sure," I said after swallowing what was possibly the best mouthful of pizza that had ever danced across my tongue. "It's Halloween in New Orleans, and there's bound to be some parties tonight. What's this thing you're working at?"

"Well, you know I'm a member of the Hematarium."

"I don't hold it against you."

"Anyway," she said, rolling her eyes, "We do a fancy dress and costume ball every year in New Orleans. It's a big to-do, and people come from all over the world to attend."

"They're all 'vampires,' I take it?"

"Most of them. A lot of planning goes into this, getting live bands and the reservations for the gig and all that. This year we've rented Gallier Hall."

I shrugged in an admission of ignorance. "What's that?"

"It's one of the big old Southern dance halls here. Right across from the hotel I'm staying at and such."

"So you've got it made for tonight?"

"Not really," she said, twirling the straw through the ice cubes in her plastic cup and sighing. "I have to work the front door, taking tickets and such. It kinda sucks. I mean, I'd really like you to go, but I'm warning you that I'm not going to be able to play around or anything."

"Hmm." I mulled the idea over. On the one hand, I really wanted to hang out with this chick. At the same time, I wasn't sure about being surrounded by a bunch of poncy strangers acting like rejects from a horror novel. "We'll see. If nothing else, we could meet up after the ball's over, or something."

"Yeah, we could do that." Although she masked it well, I detected a tinge of disappointment in her voice.

"Besides, my roommate already wants to drag me to some other shindig called the Night Without End Vampire's Ball anyway."

"You're kidding," she giggled, and the look in her eye gave me the answer before the question had even been born.

"Oh, hell. Let me guess . . . "

"The ball I'm working at tonight . . . "

" . . . Is the Night Without End Vampire's Ball!" we finished simultaneously, and chuckled together for a second.

"What are the odds?"

"At least that settles it," I said as I polished off the last bite of crust and wiped my hands on a napkin. "If you can't drag me there, then he will, so I might as well surrender."

"Good," she said, and squeezed my forearm for a moment. "Rachel was just talking about how we need more volunteers for setup. Consider yourself conscripted."

"Hey, hold on a second now . . . "

"You'll get in for free."

"Where do I sign my name? Need it in blood?"

She giggled. I liked her laughter very much for several reasons, one of which was a trademark secret I'd known for years: In the world of seduction, making a woman laugh can go a long way. If you can bring that kind of joy to a lady with just words, then her body is halfway to your bedroom already.

"Don't worry," she said as she lounged in a feline posture, "There's no really hard work involved. Mostly we need people to help arrange decorations and such."

"I won't be preparing any vats of virgin's blood or anything?"

"Hush, you," she said, giving me a mock warning glance.

"No frisking the attendees for wooden stakes and hammers?"

"*Shut it*," she commanded with a grin. "You know we're not like that."

I started to wave a dismissive hand, but something made me pause. Maybe it was time that I learned more about this weird religion Jade was part of, especially since I'd be rubbing elbows with them all night.

"Can I get some clarification on what this scene's about?" I asked as I fired up another cigarette. The harsh smoke complimented the fiery zing of the drink perfectly.

"I thought you weren't interested?" She seemed actually surprised. I didn't blame her—in our online discourses, I'd dodged the subject of religion many times. The words in my emails had communicated that I accepted that she was following some new strange belief, and nothing more. I'd never really asked about it previously.

"Humor me. If I'm going to rub elbows with these people all night, I don't want to go in cold."

"Okay." She sat up and laid her chin on one hand as she leaned closer to me. "What do you want to know?"

"First off . . . let me get this straight. Members of religion think they're vampires?"

"Yes." Her acknowledgement was even and direct.

"You're a vampire?"

"Yes."

"My pizza must have been killing you."

"Very funny," she smirked.

"It had about ten pounds of garlic in the . . . "

"We're not creatures out of some B-movie," she stated while she ashed her smoke and gave me another warning look that wasn't altogether playful. I shut up. "Bram Stoker did more harm than good with his stupid little book. Vampires are human beings whose hunger has awakened, and the benefits are nothing like what you've seen in films."

"Okay . . . so you're not immortal, at least?"

"Nope."

"Heal supernaturally fast?"

"Nuh-uh."

"You can't see in the dark? Fly? Turn into a bat?"

"None of the above," she smirked, butting her cig in the ashtray. "But we do gain some magical ability, and feed off of humans."

"Hold it." I propped my boots on a vacant chair and raised one eyebrow. "You *what?*"

"We feed off of other people," she said in the same conversational tone.

"What, you mean, like, blood?"

"Sometimes," she said, glancing around the room. I had the feeling that she didn't want to look me in the eye. "Blood has energetic properties that, under the right circumstances, give us power and pleasure."

"Right circumstances?"

"Usually in rituals or sex play," she said. Part of my brain clicked into understanding. I'd read about blood play as a sexual fetish before, but had never felt any interest in it. In a world with HIV, Hepatitis, and other nasty diseases out there, the last thing I wanted to do was to touch someone else's blood. The only exception I made was when I was in a fight.

"Okay, I get it. Real vampires get off on playing with blood during sex. You mentioned something else?"

"Psychic energy," she said, and lit another cigarette. It occurred to me that New Orleans seemed to make people into chain-smoking chimneys, myself included. "We feed off of the . . . well, I'm trying to summarize here, but we collect and use the power other people give off in passionate moments."

"Aha." I tapped my fingers on the table for a moment. My smile stayed placid as I studied the tabletop, but my tongue tasted indecision. As an agnostic, I'd run into many people of many different religions, some of which I'd studied. Unlike most atheists I knew, I'd never tried to ram my convictions down the throats of others. At the same time, I'd often had to stifle a reflexive disdain, especially when I felt someone else's religion was complete horseshit.

I looked at Jade, and repressed the urge to voice my misgivings. She was intelligent, witty, and good-looking. Who was I to pass judgment on her personal belief system?

"And the Hematarium is a group of vampires?"

"From all over the world," she declared. "The internet has been a blessing for us, allowing vampires from everywhere to contact each other and lend support."

"I see." My straw sucked air. I rattled the ice in my cup. "Wait right here."

"Refill mine, too?"

"Sure!" I trotted the woefully vacant cups to the counter and had the stoner replenish the Bloody Marys, then scuttled back to the table.

"You're not going to make fun of me and my friends?" she asked, and although she worded the question flippantly, I could hear a veil of trepidation in her voice.

"Nah. I can't."

She smiled, and I sucked some more thick, clotted fluid down. My head was feeling worlds better, but the vodka was also battling with my ability to think clearly.

"For one thing, you're just making a minor mistake that most Predators do when they're younger."

"Come again?"

"I haven't even come the first time yet."

"Hardy har har. Predators?"

With a sigh, I tried to lay my thoughts out in order, but it didn't work. The vodka was inducing a really great buzz—I wasn't yet too drunk to walk, just slightly past the ability to drive.

"That's just my word. I'm pretty sure that it's not in common parlance, because people like us don't really have a *club*, per se. There's no prepackaged moniker to give us a sense of community, because we really don't have one." I tugged a splash of Mary down my throat, and drummed my fingers on the table, trying to find the words. "How old are you again, Jade?"

"Twenty-five last June, and that's a rude question," she smirked.

"Yeah. Most Predators at your age have been part of a gang, or group, or private group for about five years. It all starts in the teens, usually."

"What, exactly, starts in the teens?" she asked, drawing a line through the condensation from her cup with one fingertip. The line pointed from her to me.

"The Predatory instinct. It's a . . . well, a *hunger* of sorts. But it goes way beyond eating." Her eyes locked into mine, and I saw only questions without guile or sarcasm. "It's on all levels. We find the pleasures in life and fucking immerse ourselves into them. Pure, abject hedonism, with very little regard for laws, self-preservation, or morality."

"See, *we* call that 'being awakened'. Most real vampires start feeling the hunger in their late teens or so."

This time, I couldn't help it. My hand made the arrogant, dismissive gesture.

"Fuck that noise. You weren't 'awakened.' There's no real point in making up bullshit words to describe something so basic. Sure, maybe the whole blood play thing is erotic as hell to you, but that's no different than what turns other Predators on. You don't need to try to be something mystical and spooky to wallow in your vices. Some of us prefer sex, others drugs, and yet others enjoy illegal activities. Societies for our kind have existed forever, and all they do is give Predators a slew of pointless rules and guidelines. These things get in the way of the real pursuit of living fully. Whatever the case, in their teens a Predator learns that in our modern times, excess is easily attainable and sustained. At least," I said, pausing before the straw of my drink, "relatively so, when compared to prior human history."

"Okay," she said in a low, slightly dangerous voice, "go on. What makes someone a Predator? They just like to eat and drink and be debaucherous a lot, or what?"

I swallowed a chilled gulp, noting uneasily that my drink *did* look like blood.

"It's not that we enjoy excess. Everyone enjoys tying one on every so often, but it's something they do once in a blue moon and tell anecdotes about later. Our kinds of people enjoy excess as a way of life—*that's* the big difference. Unfortunately, this has a side effect that most people don't enjoy the concept of pursuing."

"What's that?"

"It tends to shorten our lifespan. Tell me," I said, and leaned close conspiratorially, "If I said that after the ball that there was a kilo of Bolivian flake cocaine and three gorgeous Asian call-girls in my room, would you accept an invitation to retire with me for the night?"

She licked her upper lip and smiled, showing so much tooth that she looked utterly lethal.

"Sounds like a party," she growled. I could tell that she wasn't faking the interest.

"See, that's the response I'd expect from a real Predator. Most people would joke about how much they'd want to come back with me, but they're bluffing. In reality, the majority of the population would balk, and duck out of any such offer due to fear, or distaste, or what have you."

"I think I understand," she said, and her right knee pressed against mine under the table. "You've described a lot of the vampires I know."

"Nah, not really. Think about it. How many of these 'vampires' do you regularly hang out with?"

She thought about it for a second, inhaling deeply. I liked the effect it had on her chest.

"About twenty," she answered.

"Okay, now tell me truthfully—how many of those people are truly debaucherous, and not just hanging out because they want to be around people who *do* burn this brightly?"

Her brow knitted and she rocked back in her chair a little bit, pondering.

"About four," she said quietly after a moment's concentration.

"See, that's the problem with groups like these 'vampires.' They attract Predators, and yes, a young Predator will gladly join a community that they initially perceive to be made of their kind. The problem is," I said, taking another sip of my drink, "Such crowds attract lots of wannabes."

"Tell me about it," she murmured with a tone of distaste.

"Once you get a little older, and I'm *not* trying to be condescending here, you will probably leave the group and realize that I'm right."

She snorted and fixed me with an incredulous gaze.

"Oh really?"

"It's true," I replied, and took her hand in mine very gently. She didn't stop me at all. "I just want you to know that I will not think less of you. You told me about this before, and I didn't hold it against you then, did I? Many of our kind join a gang, or a vampire group, or a bunch of Wiccan 'pagans' out of a need to belong. Once you get over it, you'll find out that there are Predators everywhere. You'll even be able to come up with your own word for us, and recognize us on sight. Some of your friends probably *are* our type, and if you walk into any Blues bar, you'll find that plenty of other people like us, but we don't need a community. It's the curse of being a Predator—knowing that there are lots of us out there, but we are happiest when we're able to run free, not tied down by some congregation of fuckheads who want to make up rules and regulations. Predatory humans run best with one another for short times only, and usually prefer to be by themselves."

She gave my hand a gentle squeeze before she disengaged, but I could tell that she wasn't entirely sold on the idea. And yet . . . from the look in her eyes, I could see that my words had taken root, and that somewhere down the line she would indeed admit that I had been right all along. It felt good, mostly because a man named Carl had given me the same speech many, many years before, and now I'd passed along the information to another up and coming Predator.

"So," she said with a grin as she hoisted her purse with one hand and her drink in the other, "*Do* you have the hookers and blow?"

I stood up and retrieved my attaché from behind the seat.

"Would you be more likely to come home with me if I said 'yes'?"

"Hmm," she said, and bit her lower lip at me. "I'll have to ask Matt if he's cool with it."

"Matt?" I wrapped one arm around her waist as we exited the establishment. "I thought you didn't do boyfriends."

"I don't," she said, and returned the embrace. "He's just a friend and lover from time to time, but I kind of came here with him, to a degree. He has no problem with me playing while I'm on vacation, but our understanding was that he had first call on my whereabouts tonight."

God fucking dammit, I thought, and the humming, quiet melody in my head seemed to perk up and pay attention.

"And here I was planning on dragging you by the hair back to my room this evening."

"Ooh, I like that idea," she said, and bit me lightly on the shoulder. It sparked a pleasant shock down into my loins, and as we approached the crosswalk of Canal, I realized that I was both drunk and *hideously* attracted to Jade. "We shall see," she said softly, and I met her gaze for an instant. The air between our eyes damned near crackled with lust. I'd been afraid that my lecturing might have turned her off, but she had obviously taken my warning in stride.

As the dying sunlight glowed across the brick sentinels of Canal Street, we crossed the road with the light steps that only two people interested in fucking each other's brains out have. The hum in my mind was like a constant, wonderful mental massage, and I knew that the night was going to be one hell of a good ride.

CHAPTER FIVE

The structure was massive, stately in its size and looming presence. It grabbed my eyes and wouldn't let go as it dominated my view of the street.

"Here we are," Jade cheerily piped, and then noticed the look on my face. "Is something wrong?"

"Not at all," I mumbled, and put the custom shades back into the pocket of my attaché. My feet refused to move an inch from where I stood as I let my vision play all over the building. "Just . . . what is this place?"

"Gallier Hall," she said, walking over to the carved stone stairs in front of us and resting one foot on the first step. "It's beautiful, don't you think?"

It was a striking 19th century structure with Roman Doric stone columns and an iron fence across the front, several stories tall and nearly wide enough to claim half a city block. In my home area of Southern California, all the houses had been composed of stucco and drywall, wood and plaster. I'd never even seen a house made entirely of brick until I'd migrated to Dallas, and such architecture gave me a strange feeling whenever I encountered it—that unlike the disposable homes of my childhood, there existed houses that had no fear of earthquakes. The building gave me the same feeling of awe on an even deeper scale. I saw not a scrap of wood in its creation, not so much as a single panel of stucco. The walls were all marble and granite, forever unyielding.

"How long has this been here?" I wondered aloud, craning my neck backward to stare at the tops of the immense columns. No mere façade, this—it took my breath away quite literally with its pale, solid permanence.

"Hell, I don't know," she said, giving me a bemused look. "You like architecture?"

"It's a hobby of mine," I murmured, and slowly ascended the steps to grasp a wrought iron gate. The metal was cool in my palms, and past the padlocked bars I could see a courtyard. Each of the thick stone pillars was rooted between potted plants, and a pair of bronze statues with graven togas flanked a massive entryway. "This is beautiful . . . "

"Quit drooling and get on over here," she said, walking over to the corner of the building. "You'll get a better view of it all once we're inside."

She led me to an open door and we ducked through the diminutive wooden portal. The foyer looked like the waiting area of a hospital, except for the huge wooden staircase to our left that leapt up one floor. As I navigated the steps to follow Jade, I realized that I felt great. Not just good, or happy, but excited and jubilant. This vacation was turning out to be an incredible experience.

The interior of the building was just as spectacular as it had appeared from without. Once past the staircase, I found myself in a hallway to end all hallways. It stretched for over a hundred feet in either direction, and you could have drilled a marching band four musicians abreast without brushing their uniforms against the tall pink walls. I followed Jade, who seemed to know where she was going, and between each of the many gigantic doors hung huge paintings of grim old white men. Not reproductions, but each one a real paint-on-canvas original as big as the hood of a car. It felt as if I were in an old movie about the Civil War, and any moment the hallways would echo the sound of an approaching platoon of Robert E. Lee's men, racing through the building in tattered uniforms to secure positions against the damned Yankees.

Instead I heard the sound of an echoing CD player that buzzed forth the machine-gun beat of a German band, and the squeak and patter of rubber-soled tennis shoes on hardwood as we approached yet another doorway. Inside was an utterly bare dance floor, with a crystal chandelier the size of a wagon wheel hanging over the center of the room. About five or six people rushed around the spacious ballroom, their arms burdened with piles of silk fabric or boxes. Another man stood on a ladder by the wall and precariously stapled black drapes to cover the towering window panes. A voluptuous brunette in jeans and a rock band t-shirt seemed to be the center of all of the activity, and as we approached I began to hear her giving out orders in a tired, frantic voice. Her pigtail braids jolted and jerked as her head snapped back and forth to give commands.

"Has anyone seen Frank? God *damn* it, where is he?"

"Rachel, where do you want the pin-lights?" asked a squat, balding man with a goatee and arms so burly that he could have crushed unopened tuna cans in the crook of his elbow.

"One over each doorway, and I need them to be centered on . . . oh, for *fuck's sake*," she snapped, gesturing at the chandelier. "Where's the damned glitter ball?"

Glitter ball? I mused, and crossed my arms patiently as Jade attempted to get the woman's attention. *Vampires like glitter balls?*

"I'm doing it in ten minutes," another young man called out from across the room.

"Okay! Fine! Dylan, where are you?"

"Right behind you," a taller, lanky kid said nonchalantly. "I tried to raise Frank on the phone, but he didn't answer his cell. You still want me to go for . . . "

An older blonde woman with her hair twisted into a bun stuck her head into the room and snapped her fingers.

"Rache! We need you out front! They need some signatures!"

"I'll be there in just a couple," she said, not bothering to turn around at the sound of the other woman's voice. "How long on the sofas, Silvie?"

"Maybe fifteen, twenty minutes," replied a woman in the corner, who was arranging huge pillows into a pile.

"Good. When you get done, I want you and Dylan to see about the equipment in Room B. Until then," she barked, turning on the tall kid, "Go ahead and start setting up the Vanity Room, Dyl. Everyone else, you know what to do." She huffed, and turned to leave.

"Hey, Rachel," Jade said behind the flustered woman. "Wait up a second."

"*Fuck!* What now, for the love . . . " the words snipped short as she whirled around with her fists clenched, and Jade flinched backwards. "Oh, Jesus, honey, I'm *so* sorry," she said, and the two of them hugged as only old friends do. "You would not *believe* some of the bullshit I've had to endure today."

"Rachel, this is David. He's that guy I told you about that I wanted to meet, and he's offered to volunteer."

The curvy woman grabbed me in a bear hug, and almost lifted me off the floor in her enthusiasm. I staggered backwards, too drunk to keep my footing under the onslaught of her gratitude.

"That's great! God, I need all the hands I can get." Her arms let me go, and I tried not to lurch too hard as I regained my balance. I knew that I was pretty buzzed, nay, *drunk* even, and that in the past I'd been able to hide my inebriation easily from others (the ability to do so had always proven more of a curse than a blessing) as long as I wasn't completely obliterated. "Okay, here," she said, hustling over to a large cardboard box next to a pile of electrical cords. "The glitter ball's in there, with a bunch of plastic tie-downs. Think you can hang it up on the chandelier?"

"Uh, sure," I stuttered, "You have a ladder, I hope?"

"Right over there," she said, pointing forcefully at the opposite side of the room. "Okay, Jade, sweetie, I need you to come with me. I've still got to find out what the *fuck* is keeping Frank, and I might need you to go back to the rooms and get a few things." She took Jade's arm and guided her out the door. "Plus the band's late, and I swear, I will wear their fucking nuts on a necklace if . . . "

The threat faded away as they walked out of earshot down the hall. I was left in the cavernous room with several total strangers, a big-assed box, and a ladder. Although I knew what I'd just been ordered to do, my brain was still somewhat foggy as I tottered over to the steel ladder and laid down my attaché. It was fifteen feet of pressed and bolted aluminum, and extremely light as I hoisted it over my shoulder and trudged back to the chandelier. I managed to unfold it and set it into place without actually smashing any of the hundreds of hanging crystalline teardrops, and then pried open the box. Inside was a disco ball, all right. It was slightly heavier than a bag of flour, and a black, donut-shaped motor hung from the top with a solitary steel ring at the end. I hefted the basketball-sized contraption in one hand, and very nearly dropped it onto the hardwood floor. Yeah, this was going to be a fun escapade, I could already tell.

Ten minutes later I shakily descended the rungs of the ladder, and it occurred to me that I'd just done something ridiculously stupid. The ball hung from the tip of the chandelier in a surprisingly centered manner, considering how many times I'd nearly plunged to my broken-necked death from atop my ladder. Beads of alcohol-enriched sweat rolled down my face, and I dried my forehead on the sleeve of my jacket. My legs felt shaky from the combination of vodka in large doses and adrenaline jolts in small but frequent ones. What the hell had I been thinking? I was in no condition to get on a fucking ladder!

Still, the glitter ball *did* look really cool, hanging fifteen feet off of the floor.

"Nicely done!" As I turned around, Rachel came back into the room carrying an armload of power cables, and dumped them to the side. "I like it. Okay, I need you to run this power cord along the wall and staple it in place, then string it up to the ball. Oh, and another thing," she said, and removed a small plastic card from her pocket. I accepted it curiously, and discovered that it was a staff badge on a lanyard, designed to be worn around one's neck.

"Do you mind if I . . . "

My query was cut off as a scrawny waif of a man entered the room. He was about five-feet-tall with short-cropped hair that had been bleached the color of cotton, and he might have weighed one hundred pounds if his black denim shorts, combat boots, and sleeveless gray shirt had been soaking wet.

"Yo, Rache," he called out in a raspy voice as he trudged toward her with all the energy of a damp mop. The badge around his neck looked like a flapping rope on a flagpole. "How's the preps going?"

Rachel's face underwent a transformation akin to that of a clear day turning into a hurricane. Pure, seething rage spilled across her features, and with a motion much quicker than anything I would have expected from a woman of her proportions, she grabbed the emaciated man by the arm, pulling him with her as she exited the room. I followed for a few feet, eavesdropping on the snarled curses emanating from Rachel.

"I'm gonna fucking *kill* you, Frank! What was the delay? Too much meth last night? Fuck!"

"Hey," he whined as she continued hauling him along the hallway. His feeble attempts to pull free were pathetic—her hand was welded to his bony arm.

"We've got one band cancelled, another one that lost a couple of speakers, and you didn't leave me the fucking numbers of the DJs, you asshole! Then you come in here, two hours late?"

"There was a . . . "

"Get on the phone *right now* and . . . "

Their voices dwindled away into muted echoes of anger and simpering. I looked at the electrical cord that she'd piled in the corner. There was a good forty feet of extension there, and an industrial-strength staple gun. I looked at the ladder, still propped up under the chandelier. A quick survey of the ballroom showed me that by some fortuitous stroke of luck, I was all by myself. I gave the ladder another baleful glare, grabbed my attaché, and headed out into the hall.

I ran into Jade again almost immediately in the cavernous hallway. A young, stately man walked alongside her. Dressed in a 19th-century black tuxedo, top hat, ebony cane and white kid gloves, he was slightly taller than me and lanky. A pair of large, black contact lenses completely obscured his pupils, and his facial features were mildly Hispanic. As they approached, he put his arm around her shoulder and gave her a friendly squeeze that Jade shrugged out of—not in an unfriendly way, but in a manner that showed that she wasn't in the mood for such close contact.

"David! This is Matt, my friend from new York," she beamed.

"Greetings," her partner crooned, and smiled to show off a pair of theatrical-grade false fangs. He stepped toward me, just a fraction of an inch farther than could be considered amicable. One glove came off, and his hand gracefully extended in greeting. As I took it, several thoughts entered my mind in quick succession:

So this is my competition?

This man is no Predator.

His body language . . . he's tried to make a total claim on Jade already. I just fucking know it.

I squeezed his hand, perhaps a little bit too firmly, and he disengaged posthaste.

"Charmed," I replied and felt my hackles rise beneath my jacket. Something about this dude already rubbed me the wrong way. It might have been his ridiculously pompous costume, or that he was obviously vying for the same woman's affections that I was, but I decided right then and there that I didn't like him one little bit. My smile showed lots of tooth enamel as he stepped back and faced Jade.

"Are you ready to go?"

"Yeah," she said, and moved closer to me. "I wanted to let you know that I'll be back later. Matt and I have some things to talk about. You gonna be here?"

"To tell you the truth," I said softly, "I'm a little drunk right now. Going to go walk around for a half an hour or so, and try to clear my head."

"But you'll be back? You're not going to ditch out on this, are you?"

I slapped the fedora onto my head, and gave her a wink.

"Wouldn't miss it for the world. Have fun, you kids. See you in a few." I turned my back on the two of them and walked away, whistling. As I descended the staircase to the main exit, I turned and looked out of the corner of my eye at the two of them. Matt was saying something to Jade, and the hand gestures between the two of them weren't entirely comfortable. With a grin, I got the hell out of there.

Back on the concrete sidewalk I set out across the street to a public park, where a large metal plaque informed me in French that I was looking at Lafayette Square. I read it with no small amount of pleasure—maybe it was the arrogance implied by the choice of language on the inscription, or perhaps it was because the melody in my head was getting stronger. Once I was finished with the sign, I looked up and down the street in the glow of the sunset and wondered which direction I should go. The presence spoke again, for the first time since I'd met Jade.

Are you displeased with the Hall? it asked. I shook my head, looking around the street corner where I'd paused.

Nope. Just a little inebriated, I replied, checking the silver face of my wristwatch. It showed 5:08 pm, and the party wasn't due to start for another four hours. *I feel a need to stretch my legs and walk this off. I'm on vacation, dammit. If I'd known that I was going to be on a ladder that high up, I'd have stayed sober.*

The city chuckled inside my mind, and I felt gentle warmth spread throughout my bones.

Very well, Traveler. Walk [with/through] *me.*

And so I set out again, with a light step and a lovely harmony that played through my soul as the city showed me more sights. Each footfall was like a tiny, brushing kiss from a beautiful woman against the back of my neck, and I found myself in love with the entire world for a time. In the dying late autumn glow of impending twilight, she began once again to urge me onward, not desperately or with any amount of force, but rather plying my mind with a siren's call. At each intersection I left the decision of direction up to her, and every time I was shown some new marvel, from the subtle to the gaudy, and my camera began to snap off photos with crisp clicks of the shutter as the presence in my mind became clearer. Her words were spoken directly into the center of my brain, and the tone in her voice was a smile. So far this city had shown me so much, given me such an experience that I trusted her completely, so without paying heed to any possible danger I waltzed through her streets and let my eyes be filled.

Stupid.

The whole time, I'd assumed that New Orleans was a place of joy, of love and cheer and debauchery. The city spoke to me, a wholly new and ultimately bizarre form of pleasure unlike anything I'd ever dreamed. Anyone else who had lived in this city could have told me that she was also a goddess of sadness, terror, mayhem, destruction, and cruel to the bone when she wanted to be. But I knew nothing of these facts, and so I caroused brainlessly through the early evening, drunk on vodka, laughing quietly and filled with wonder.

Right after I'd snapped a picture of a railcar I sobered up on a random street corner. The city had gone quiet for a minute, and it left me very clear headed.

A glance at my watch showed the time to be just past six. I'd been gone from Gallier Hall for an hour, and probably needed to head back. I turned my head to the left, and then to the right. My eyebrows knit together as an ugly truth hit home.

I had no fucking idea where the hell I was.

My eyes scanned everything in sight, up and down the street. Somehow, my intoxicated ramblings had taken me to the stone and glass front of a hotel that I didn't recognize. It was a posh, high-dollar deal with valets that parked and retrieved cars like a busy line of worker ants. A black doorman was flagging down cabs, his wool suit dark and sinister, like some kind of demon on the river Styx trying to summon the ferryman to pick up souls. The sun was entirely down, and although I could see the stretching streetlights up and down the block, I had no idea which direction to head. It was as if all memories of how I'd arrived had utterly vanished.

After about thirty seconds of glancing around and feeling the panic build by small increments, I felt a fluttering sensation in my mind. The feeling of sparkling insects running through my body was somehow off, less pleasant, and I realized as the tingling faded that the city was laughing *at* me.

Little help here, please? I asked wordlessly.

Is there a problem, Traveler? The tone of the question was teasing and cruel, and part of my mind found it odd that something so ethereal and awesome could speak to a person with such sarcasm.

I walked to the corner and stared at the metal placard bolted to the top of a pole. The name on the sign was completely unrecognizable.

How do I get back to the Night Without End Ball? I lit another cancer stick as fear ran through me. Thinking hard, I couldn't even remember any of my wanderings for the past hour. I peered up and down each direction of the intersection and hoped for the lights of Canal. No matter where I gazed, there was nothing but more pavement flanked by brick buildings that stretched off into the distance. I hadn't been this lost since I'd done too much acid one night in my early twenties, and had woken up dazed and bewildered at a friend's house in San Diego.

You don't know the way to the Gallier? Lilting, spiteful, malicious, the presence in my mind was definitely mocking me.

No, I thought in exasperation, *I don't.* My paranoid mind raced, thinking about what would happen if I couldn't get back. At the very least, my chances with Jade would be shot to hell, and I would have risked my life with the hanging of that fucking glitter ball for no reason. The staff badge around my neck would be utterly worthless.

I'd made one specific intersection my touchstone during all my time walking—Canal and St. Charles. I glanced about in frustration, unable to figure out which way I was even facing, and the pit of my stomach felt like a rusty elevator dropping inexorably toward hell.

The doorman of the hotel sensed my consternation and lumbered over to me. The man was immense, the size of a linebacker and clad in a full-length woolen overcoat that made him look like some kind of royal guard. His mustache was perfectly trimmed, and a pair of immense white gloves covered his hands.

"Do you need help, sir?" His voice was smoky and low, the sound of charcoal dust being blown across an iced pond.

"Yeah. Where's Canal Street from here?" I tried to keep the fear out of my voice. The doorman whistled in a manner that did nothing to assuage my fears.

"You go down *that* way about seven blocks," he said, and pointed behind me. "Then hang a right. You'll see it from there, sir."

"Thanks for th . . . wait. Did you say *seven blocks?*"

"Yes, sir. Seven streets down that way, and turn right on Royal." He smiled and touched the brim of his cap to me. "Have a pleasant evening, sir." The doorman spun on his heel, an action that momentarily turned him into a revolving mountain, and then strode back to the front of the hotel.

"Thanks," I called after him, and then started off in the direction he'd indicated. None of the buildings around me even brought up a memory from five minutes before. It was as if my alcohol-induced stupor had completely wiped my thoughts away, as sharp as a knife slicing through spider webs. I sucked nicotine through my clenched teeth and cursed myself for getting lost.

You want to see [Memory of Jade's face flashed in my mind] *again, don't you?* The thought was so forceful and strong that I almost tripped in mid-stride, as if the city had put its mouth close to my ear and yelled.

Yes, I thought back angrily. My teeth nearly bit through the filter of my cigarette in annoyance as I stomped and frantically searched for any familiar rock or streetlamp.

I have a test for you, Traveler! The entity spoke powerfully through my body.

What, it's not enough that I'm fucking lost and you're not giving me any help? I thought bitterly.

If you find Gallier Hall in time, you shall have her tonight! She will be yours, if only you find the Hall in time for the Dance! Yours to lie with, and yours to have!

Dumbstruck, I paused long enough to take a deep draw on the crimped cigarette before I asked for clarification.

And if I do not find the place in time?

Without preamble, everything around me went deathly still. The brick walls, dark alleyways and flickering restaurant signs all had taken on a subtle malicious cast. There were no other people in my vision and I couldn't hear any music. It felt like I had been plucked out of my universe and deposited in an empty one, a separate New Orleans, a colder place where I was by myself. The streets were devoid of cars as I waited, and the loudest noise was that of my heartbeat.

A grinding noise began to churn, far underneath my feet. The sidewalk rumbled, and at the same time I felt the presence inside me grow cold.

Then you will never see her again, Traveler. The words hammered through me like spikes of iced steel. There was an inherent threat implied, one that I could not fully grasp. A truly horrifying glimpse winked past the corner of my mind, of a place filled with corroded engines and pipes, where warmth had been banished since time out of mind. It was a place where dead things still moved; a dark, lightless area of suffering and terror, destruction, disease, and the hollow, cold bodies of loved ones coated in diseased semen and smooth, veined tentacles and things with horribly sharp teeth, and sick, and filth, and rot, and decay. The city was merely a skin, a thin layer that had been placed as a barrier against the thick foulness beneath me. That veil, I suspected, had the ability to open up and swallow me whole . . .

Or maybe even swallow someone *else*.

The vision evaporated as if it had never been. A wave of sounds crashed down on me, and the warmth from the humming in my body returned. My hands moved to brush down the hairs on my arms through the fabric of my jacket. They were still standing on end, even though that horrific glimpse had lasted less than a few seconds.

I shook my head and took a trembling drag off the cigarette.

No, thank you, I replied. *Your terms are too steep, and* . . .

Then the city really *did* laugh. It was a thunderous, massive vibration that flooded through every fiber of my being and overflowed my skull, as if I were standing directly beneath train tracks as an old steam engine rolled by. I leaned against a brick wall, curling my arms to my chest, bowing my head and cringing. The sensation was not exactly painful as much as it was incredibly uncomfortable—I felt as though my entire body might blow apart at any moment, molecule by molecule. It went on for about ten seconds before fading. The next thoughts that the city spoke turned my blood into ice water.

That was not an offer! You have no choice! The test is already begun, Traveler! The clock is running down! The reward or the punishment, it is all up to your path! Now MOVE! To Gallier Hall!

Fresh peals of its terrible laughter rang through my body as though I were a bell that a giant muddy fist was gleefully smacking. I *did* move, walking as fast as possible without jogging. *Fuck me*, I thought repeatedly, tearing down the street like a marching automaton. My boot heels ate up the sidewalk one cracked and weathered square at a time, but my stride didn't seem to be fast enough. I was living a horrible nightmare, and a slick sheen of clammy perspiration formed under my hat that occasionally spilled a thin line of moisture into my eyes.

After seven blocks I turned to the right with the city still goading me on, using cruel taunts that defied the English language. Basic mental images of the Hall, its Doric columns rising vastly, each thicker than a tree trunk . . . Jade's face, her smile glimmering like a tiny, dimming beacon . . . And every so often, a flitter of that foul, horrific *something* beneath the city streets that made my skin prickle with gooseflesh. Two blocks away the glow and bustling crowd of Canal Street came into view, and I finally ran toward that welcome spine of the city. The streets blurred beneath my pounding feet, the attaché smacked against the small of my back, and I had to use one hand to secure the fedora from the rush of air around me.

I burst through the throng of costumed tourists onto the intersection of Royal and Canal with a war whoop, elated and happy. My cry of success hadn't fazed anyone in the laughing crowds. It was a large group of people for so early in the evening, every one of them bedecked in Halloween finery. The bright lights of cars and shops lit up the sidewalk, reflecting off of a wide variety of revelers in their best spooky and colorful duds. I stood, marveling and thankful to be finally back in familiar territory. As I did so, the feeling of elation died in my chest, strangled to death like a canary in a sealed plastic bag.

Yes, I was on Canal Street and Royal. No, I had no idea how to get to Gallier Hall from there. I had a vague inkling that it was on St. Charles, but didn't have any idea of how to find that street.

My fist knocked against my forehead in an attempt to knock a memory loose, but it was no use. Jade had led us there before. Of the trip, I had no recollection outside of her shapely body, damn my libido. I struggled, wild-eyed and despairing, to remember any clue at all that would guide me to my goal. Despair finally sank its hooks in. Frantic, I walked up Royal again, praying for a sign that never came, some distinct lamppost or section of sidewalk to orient myself by. After several blocks of searching it occurred to me that I might be on the wrong side of the street, but the thought was preposterous. Surely, I hadn't crossed Canal in my wanderings. No way. I'd remember *that*. But the doubt began to grow, and as I walked toward the French Quarter I realized that every instinct was screaming No! Go Back! Wrong way!

Everything except the city, of course. She was in my head, chuckling like a little teasing bitch. She was *getting off on this!* That whore. That cunt. That fucking foul hussy with disease and rancor for blood.

I didn't realize that I was speaking these words aloud until two fat faeries in their late fifties turned around. The closer one whacked me on the forehead with a magic wand. Not hard enough to sting, but the shock jolted me out of the profane internal dialogue.

"Watch your mouth, whippersnapper!" said the one who had struck me. She was in a yellow taffeta dress that had seen better years, and her tiara was askew. A cloud of whiskey fumes flowed from her mouth, and she managed to look both indignant and humored at the same time. Her rumpled gray hair flared out in snarls, and her wand was a cardboard star stapled to a thin dowel of cheap wood.

"Yeah! We've got virgin ears and such!" said her friend in the scarlet dress, the hem of which was filthy from dragging on the sidewalk. This one's tiara was in place, but her short, butch-dyke haircut made it look ridiculous. She was a little bit more menacing than her companion, and it occurred to me that if she wanted to kick my ass, I could make worse decisions than to *run like hell*. The thin cellophane and coat hanger wire wings on their backs were ridiculous little things, but the arms of these women denoted that they probably spent their non-costumed evenings tossing bales of hay back and forth like volleyballs.

Then the one in yellow bopped my head with the stick again, and the two of them giggled in a lighthearted, intoxicated manner. With as much flourish as I could force, I bowed deeply from the waist.

"My most sincere apologies, ladies of the Fae realm! I did not realize that ears as beautiful as thine own were being assailed by mine words of frustration," I said in the most theatrical English accent I could manage after the bow was done. "You see, dear ladies, I am lost, and the city has me at my wit's end."

The one in red giggled again.

"Ooo, isn' 'ee a pretty one," she said in a cockney inflection that actually worked rather well. "Think 'ee moight please the Queen, eh?"

"Non," said the yellow one in a *dreadful* impersonation of a French accent. "Ee eez, how joo say . . . too skeenee."

"Nay, good faeries," I said holding my hands far apart, as if to show them I had no weapons. "I'll not go to your lands. Tell me, do either of you lovely creatures know where Gallier Hall is?"

"Oo, a flatterer!" hiccupped the one in Red. Her companion pinched her arm playfully. "Right, that's down on Lafayette. That way," she concluded, pointing *back* the way I had come. "You can't miss it. Just take St. Charles . . . "

"I seem to have lost the street in question," I stated humbly. "My path has meandered hither and yon along Canal, but I cannot find St. Charles at all."

"Non, thees eez St. Charles!" said the one in yellow. "Eet stops bee-eeng Roy-ale on zee othaire sahd of Canal! Oui!"

I looked beyond the traffic at a street sign, and swore under my breath. She was right. I was walking on Royal, but it turned into St. Charles on the other side.

"Thank you, Ladies!" I said, and backed away for two steps to a final round of their cooing giggles. Then, at my fastest walk, I fled back across the crowded stream of costumed drunkards, beyond one side and then the other of Canal St., and into the relatively quiet roads of St. Charles. Soon I passed Jade's hotel again, and my stomach fell a little bit further. Something inside told me I was, once again, going too far down the road. I cursed under my breath—it wasn't hard for me to imagine those two dykes, later this evening, would shrink in size to the height of a thimble and traipse down a sewer vent in some dark back alley, emerging in another strange universe of daffodils and green skies, rushing off to giggle and report to Titania about how they'd gotten another tourist lost. Fucking faeries! I continued into the darker, less populated blocks of St. Charles, and dread loomed at the thought of having to return to Canal. How had I gotten into this clusterfuck? *Never again*, I thought, *will I ever believe that the universe contains nothing wondrous and strange*. Although agnostic, I silently prayed to anything at all, any gods out there that I would make it to the ball safely.

Time ticks by, Traveler, came the presence in my mind. *Pray not, for there are no others here that listen to you.*

Shut the fuck up! Just shut up! My thoughts were angrier than I normally would have directed to a supernatural being, but I didn't give a damn anymore. Stuck in a strange city, the cruel mirth of a strange and mind-boggling creature in my head, I no longer gave two shits about being polite to what was possibly a hallucination. I desperately jaywalked through the next two intersections, wishing that I had never listened to the thing in my skull.

My footsteps were quailing again, and I felt absolutely at the end of my rope when, lo and behold! Several blocks past where Jade was staying, I found myself quite suddenly and shockingly back in front of a certain white, columned, beautiful and majestic Dance Hall! My watch told me that it was just past seven pm, which left me another two hours before the ball began.

Well done, said the city. *You have passed the test, Traveler. She will be yours.* And then a delicious sensation came back, one that felt the way a fresh rose on the vine smells. The city was pleased with me again as it sang a gorgeous, irreproducible tune through my soul.

I slumped against the giant stone steps of the Hall, took off my fedora and rubbed my eyes. Around the corner, I could hear the preparations being made at the entrance I had fled so rashly two hours before. Part of me realized that I could now go inside, help set up, and then have another carefree night of debauchery. My Predatory instincts should have blazed to life, but something gave me pause.

My fingers uncapped the bottle of rum after I'd freed it from my attaché case. I took one silken, fiery swig to clear the last remnants of terror from my throat. The breeze had no effect on my lighter as I fired up yet another cigarette and pulled out the electronic doodad. A solitary twig on the steps became a stylus, and I began to type. The city whisked its gentlest fingers of breeze around my bare scalp. Her breath smelled of dandelions as my twig danced over the keypad, nature met technology, and the words spilled into text.

Thursday
7:05 pm
Night Without End Ball

In a moment of sweaty sobriety, I write these words under the incandescent fire of the New Orleans streetlights. The stone steps beneath the overworked muscles in my legs smell remarkably pleasant. It's a vapor of peace and dusty permanence. A gentle breeze is playing with my cheeks, flirtatious caresses from a city I now know is a deviant and hellishly cruel whore when she wants to be. The Night Without End Vampire's Ball will commence shortly, and soon these same steps will be crammed with poncy ninnies, dressed to the nines and their heads full of ridiculous gothic garbage. I will mill amongst the rat bastards like a hyena traipsing through a pride of cheap cardboard lions after what I've been through tonight. Silly they may be, but a party is a party, and I'm always prepared.

I just can't get over the idea that I'm in some kind of danger.

CHAPTER SIX

I laid my attaché on the immense floor of the ballroom and covered half of it with my fedora. Several new people had procured ladders, and were busy doing the job I'd been assigned earlier: stapling electrical cable fifteen feet above the ground, in such a manner that the cord was hidden by the doorjamb. I located Rachel's ladder in one corner, and she looked quizzically down between sharp clicks of the staple gun.

"Hey! Where'd you get off to?" Her voice held no annoyance, merely curiosity.

"Dancing with a demon bitch and trying to find my way back from hell," I said in a quiet voice.

"What?"

"I was drunk," I flatly smiled, "and had to go sober up a little."

"Oh. Okay. Hey, feed me some more cable."

For the next hour, we detailed the room with various strange items. After the glitter ball was plugged in and each canopied corner looked like an inviting area to lay down in, complete with large piles of fancy pillows, we turned our attention to the lighting. Rachel was pleasantly surprised to discover that I knew how to adjust a theatrical spotlight, and after I'd centered the narrow beams on the spinning disco ball, I stood amazed as a thousand points of white and red light danced in a lazy spiral on the floor. Further lamps were strung, and the city spoke more information to me.

This ballroom has seen many such functions, Traveler. Gallier Hall once kept the heads of the city, and some of the galas that took place within these walls would have stolen your breath away. The women then were as beautiful as they are now, and the men, although more stately, were all men who did not fear the things your people do. To this day, when the great Mardi Gras Parade floats down the street, the King of the Parade will receive a toast from the mayor in front of this Hall each year, a ritual in honor of what I am, in a way. You are standing in a living piece of history, and some would call this place one of my temples. Enjoy the feeling, Traveler. Remember this temple well.

Everything went off without a hitch, and before long the time had arrived to get dressed up. After easing into my jacket, I checked the skew of my hat in the mirror of the bathroom. A perfect rendition of Croft Derwood grinned back at me.

Various black-clad people in elegant dress roamed about the hallways and two bartenders behind a vast array of tables rummaged like crazed bees in a hive. I spotted Jade as she walked toward the courtyard doors, a delicious sight in an elaborate, jet-black Victorian gown and coiffed hair.

Yours, the city spoke in a warm tone as I quietly approached the redhead.

Pipe down, I thought back. The city tingled and giggled as I approached Jade from behind, put my left arm around her waist, and planted a fast kiss on the back of her neck.

"Hey, you," she cooed and turned around with an impish smile.

"That dress is marvelous, darling," I said, and put a hand on each of her hips. She blushed a little and smiled wider to show off two fake fangs while resisting my attempt to pull her closer.

"Behave," she said, "I have to go start working the front in a bit."

"Care for a quick bite of something?" My hand opened the attaché case just enough to let her spy the bottle of rum. Surprised, she furtively glanced over her shoulder before taking my arm.

"I think I need a cigarette," she said aloud, and then tittered as we went down a short flight of stairs and out into the courtyard, where the giant ionic columns stood. We each lit a cigarette and hid behind the massive columns, sharing pulls off the bottle.

"This is going to be one hell of a party," she muttered, and handed the fifth back to my waiting hand.

"How many people do you think will show up?" I slugged a gulp of the alcohol, and it tore a streak of crushed fire down my throat.

"Probably a few hundred. Phooey. I have to work the front door while *you* go have fun." She accepted the bottle from me, and nudged my foot with the toe of her boot as she took a swig, and then capped the bottle. "You'll at least stop by and say hello during the night?"

"As long as your New Yorker doesn't decide to get jealous and have Renfield attack me."

"Very funny. I happen to like his costume, but..." She frowned. "I *really* hope he's not trying to claim me for the entirety of this trip. He said a couple of things earlier..."

"I will do my damnedest to stay out of his way tonight," I said as evenly as possible.

Yours, the city remarked from the back of my skull.

Shut up.

As she handed the rum back to me, I caught Jade by the wrist and brought her to me. I put her forehead to mine and growled, doing my best impersonation of a wolf. She returned the sound without flinching, and hers resembled that of a large cat as she skinned her ruby lips back to expose teeth. My skin felt electrified from being this close to a powerful Predator, as excited as if I'd put my hand on the hide of a live wolf.

"I really want to kiss you," I whispered. Jade gave me a quizzical frown.

"You know I don't kiss," she said, staring me dead in the eye.

It felt like a slap across the face.

"What?"

"I don't kiss," she said, and tossed her spent cigarette out into the street. "I've never liked doing it. It makes me uncomfortable. I told you that a long time ago online, remember?" She ran the fingertips of one hand along my inner thigh for just a moment, pressed her body close and tilted her head back to give me a half-lidded stare.

"Well, ain't that a bitch," I growled. Hot dancing sparks ricocheted off my skin where she'd touched me.

"Don't worry," she breathed as she backed away from me. Her mouth pulled into a downright evil smile of carnal hunger. "I like to do *lots* of other things." She beamed at me, and I couldn't tell if the rushing sensation in my mind was from her touch, the implication of her words, or the alcohol splashing through my bloodstream. "I have to go do the door duties now. Have fun, and I'll see you around tonight."

Yours, the city repeated firmly as I watched Jade's retreat.

Many thanks, I thought back with a wry smirk.

I spent a few minutes relaxing and watching the cars drift by on St. Charles, and then glanced at my watch. In twenty minutes the attendees would arrive and the party would begin, so I decided to take one last look at everything before the ballroom became packed with throngs of vapid assholes.

Turn about, Traveler. I have something for you, the presence in my mind suddenly urged.

On the other side of the hallway, opposite the two bartenders who were madly organizing their plastic cups and bottles at the makeshift bar, I spied a trio of young ladies (none of them breathtaking or painfully beautiful, but all three attractive). They were setting up a folding table with some large green bottles and plastic cups. I strode up fluidly, albeit with a fairly intoxicated grin, and glanced at the bottles.

"We're not ready yet," snapped one of the chicks as the other two bustled away for parts unknown, and I held up my palms in apology.

"Sorry, I was just curious," I said, and pointed at one of the emerald green flasks. "Is this what I think it is?"

"Yes and no," the same girl replied, stooping to grab another stack of cups, and then taking a deep breath before arranging them in a neat formation to one side. "Sorry. I'm a little frustrated. Problems with this gig." Her black hair was clipped to chin length, with shorter bangs in the front, and her skin was olive in complexion. She held up the bottle I'd indicated. "It's not Absinthe."

"Looks like it, but that stuff's illegal in the States," I said, nodding.

"It's called *Absente*," she said, and turned the label so that I could read it in the dim lighting. "The illegal ingredient in Absinthe is Oil of Wormwood . . ."

"Yeah. Mildly hallucinogenic and also pretty poisonous, if memory serves," I said.

"Well, this stuff uses extract from a legal version of Wormwood." She put the bottle down and ran her fingers through her hair in a cute gesture of stress. This action satisfied my curiosity about whether or not she was wearing a wig. "It's called Southern Wormwood, and it's a little less bitter than the regular stuff."

"Does it have the same effects?"

She smiled at me enigmatically and went back to arranging cups.

I pulled out a ten-dollar bill and held it at waist level with the edge almost tucked behind my belt.

"I know you're not set up," I said, and leaned in closely as she noticed the filthy lucre, "But how much would it run me to try some *right the fuck now?*" I gave her a good Predatory smile, and she glanced around as if watching for the other women to come back at any moment.

"That's the problem," she said. "We had a misunderstanding with the management of the ball, and we can't legally charge for the alcohol. All we can accept are tips." She pointed to a large empty glass jar to my right.

I blocked the view of any bystanders with my body and slid the money across the table toward her with one hand and a wink.

"Whaddya say, girl? Care to give me the first nip of it? I won't tell if you won't," I said, watching the indecision dance around on her face. Without warning, her hand snaked out and the slip of cash was gone.

"I shouldn't be doing this," she snapped as she worked behind the tablecloth in an activity that I couldn't see, about a foot below the level of the linen. Her hands flashed into view occasionally, and I guessed that a sugar cube was about to be executed, lined up over a cup of vile green fluid by a steel straining spoon, its doom looming in the form of a water pitcher. Seconds later she thrust a low plastic tumbler out as if it were something incredibly nasty. Her eyes refused to meet mine. "Take it. Don't let anyone see." Then she walked away, leaving me alone at the table holding a cup of stuff that looked suspiciously like radiator fluid. I quickly hid it inside my jacket before anyone could come by.

I meandered down the hallway like a gangster about to pull a gun, but nobody on staff challenged my route. Acting casual, I sneaked my ill-gotten liquid booty into the darkest ballroom. The spacious area was now pumped full of electronic music provided by a single black-clad DJ and his prerequisite gigantic speakers, while speckles and swirls of multi-colored light danced along the walls and floorboards. It also happened to be the room I had set up earlier in the day, and my feet took me to the most deserted corner, where I was distanced from a small passel of staff members in full regalia. Their costumes were all immaculately contrived suits and dresses in the style of the 18th century, and whenever one of them told a joke, the rest would bray laughter and bare a dozen theatrical fangs. They'd quite obviously gone to great lengths to make themselves look like refugees from a horror movie—a disgustingly unoriginal idea for people who had proclaimed to be real vampires anyway.

Dumbasses, I thought behind my smirk, and tipped a sip of the jade drink into my mouth.

Not so. Revelers are always free to worship me, said the presence as a heinous and revolting tang flooded my head. It gripped my tongue with a ferocious hatred, a vile and bilious flavor. I had only tasted it once before when my friend Carl had smuggled a shaker of bona fide Absinthe home from Jamaica. My lips clamped together valiantly as my gorge rose, and my cheeks crammed the mouthful of evil liquid down my throat. This stuff made the most horrible cough syrup seem like lemonade, and as soon as it left my oral cavity the aftertaste was a second malodorous rape of my tongue. I leaned against the wall and shuddered as sweat broke out all over my body. *They may worship, and I will always welcome them*, the spirit in me repeated. *Look at them. You find them so silly, and it is true that their ways are often ridiculous. They think themselves magical, but much like you, Traveler, there is nothing special about them. What they lack in originality, they make up for in worship, and it pleases me that they are here. You have your own ways that are ridiculous as well, Traveler. Do not be so quick to hate them so just because they act silly.*

The music in the room swelled and the people around me became more vibrant, more colorful. I let out a breath I hadn't been aware of holding. The cup in my hand was still woefully filled with reeking, powerful fluid—my sip had barely reduced it.

Okay, I thought. *What else should I do to worship you as well as they do?*

Dance. Laugh. Love. Joue au festival, Voyageur, et embrassez-moi.

I hoisted the plastic tumbler into the light of the window without giving a crap who watched, bowed my head and shut my eyes with a madman's grin.

D'accord, I thought back. *Je vais.*

Then, quick as a flash, the cup arced to my lips, my head tilted all the way back and I chugged the rest of the noisome neo-absinthe, much to the dismay of my tonsils. My breath halted for a shivering half minute, and I let the beat of the music take hold of me. The voice of some German industrial singer made my boots stomp, my arms move, and my hips do that thing they do when the music is kicking ass, man. The room slowly filled with other dancers, all bedecked in wild and bizarre clothing.

And slowly, my body and mind succumbed to nothing but exhilaration.

At 9:26 by my watch, I was sheened in sweat and my diamond-shaped glasses were fogged over. It was time for a cigarette, and I was already lit up like a house on fire.

The hallway that had earlier been spacious and empty was now stuffed full of hundreds of partygoers. Two areas of obvious congestion were easily identified. The first was near the top of the staircase, where every new arrival to the party stopped and called out to friends. The second area was, of course, the bar, where the bartenders behind the table looked like they were involved in a hysterical, violent dance of fulfilling drink orders.

With elbows akimbo and no small amount of violence, I jostled my way past the head of the stairs, fixated on getting outside to have a nicotine dose. As I left the thickest blockage of human bodies, someone grabbed my arm. I whirled with my fists ready, but the hand on my elbow belonged to someone I just couldn't punch.

"You decided to come after all!" Marcus was dressed as he usually did when he attended this kind of function, in an impeccable 18th century black velvet waistcoat and an embroidered white silk shirt. The aristocratic air that he always carried, like a thick fog that traveled wherever he went, made his getup work perfectly.

"Hee hee," I said, holding up my Staff badge. Marcus's face did a slow, thorough and helpless crumble of shock.

"How in the *hell* did you manage such a thing?" he stammered. His wife, dressed in a skintight black vinyl bodysuit, also showed her amazement by giggling and holding her mouth open like a barn door. I shrugged with a chortle and took a swig of beer.

"What are your duties?" his wife asked, excited.

I held up my beer, took a second gulp from it, and wandered off to leave them bewildered and laughing.

Outside, I smoked and drifted around. My camera snatched some photos of the best costumes. Many people had come out for Halloween in garb that must have taken hours upon hours to put together, getup that was extremely pleasing to the eye. One woman in particular caught my attention like a fishhook. Although she was fairly short in height, her body was also very proportionate and shapely. Had she been two feet taller, she would have been a perfect candidate for supermodel stardom. Her sandals were leather, with thin straps winding up deliciously curved legs, which were bare and quite lovely. The nakedness of her flesh stopped right around miniskirt level, thanks to about five or six small animal pelts draped through a wide leather belt. The white, brown, and orange furs continued around her breasts as well, creating a Cavewoman Bikini effect that really worked with her flat, rippling stomach. Her face, however, was where her costume efforts really had paid off. With a touch of prosthetics, not enough to even look like she was wearing any, and painstakingly applied makeup, she'd turned herself into a perfect blend of human and leopard. Piercing amber eyes peered out from under spotted brows, which appeared to be a tiny bit pronounced. Her upper lip was cleft in a feline manner and ever so slightly rounded. A wolf's skull and more furs created a headdress that completely obscured her tresses so well that I could not have told you what this lass's hair color was, and every bit of exposed flesh was faintly spotted like a wildcat with body paint. Her costume brought to mind some strange, forgotten race of creatures from the prehistoric era, a fantastic blend of biped and leopard, whose small tribe may have flourished, advanced, and died out before the first human being ever picked up a stone knife.

"Wonderful costume," I remarked. "Really quite stunning."

"Thank you," she replied with a grin. Her teeth were not the Dracula fangs that everyone else wore, but big feral spikes of natural-looking tooth, the kind that could tear a deer's throat out with no effort. "I was going to say the same."

"Aha. You're a fan?"

"Absolutely. 'City On Fire' has to be one of the best graphic novels ever penned by Rick Ulster," she said in a smoky voice. "You know, you *do* look an awful lot like Croft, beyond the costume. Especially in the face." Her arm came up and she ran one catlike talon lightly from the hollow of my throat to the tip of my chin. A floral, subtle scent emanated from her skin, and I realized two facts; First of all, her eyes seemed to be naturally a beautiful, tawny color. Secondly, she was hitting on me.

"What's your name, love?" I asked, and moved a little bit closer. Her body might have been small, and the level of her forehead only came up to my collarbones, but she was also very tasty looking.

"Shandra," she purred, and ran the talon back down my exposed sternum.

"David. Pleased to make your acquaintance." I snatched her lingering hand up, and bowed to plant a soft kiss on the inside of her wrist.

"Are you having fun at the ball, David?" Her eyes were on fucking fire when I righted myself, although I could no longer ascertain whether the effect was an indication of attraction or caused by the mixture of rum and Absente running through my veins.

"I'm having an inordinate amount of it." Her proximity gave me a wonderfully warm glow, and I let some of that feeling flare through my eyes. "Do you live here, perchance, or did you come to New Orleans for the party?"

"I've lived here since 1993," she spoke gently, and placed a hand on my forearm. "Your face is unfamiliar, and I'd remember it if I'd seen it before. Where are you from?"

"Dallas, but I grew up in California."

"Ah," she said, and laughed. I could no longer tell if her teeth were fake or not—they looked very realistic and lethal. "So quick to make such a disclaimer!"

I knew then that if I wanted, I could have her. The laugh, posture, and the familiar glint in her eyes all projected that she was looking for physical pleasure, and that I could probably have it without much asking. The more I looked at her painted skin, the stronger the inclination to take the offer became. She was very attractive, and I could have done much worse than taken her home that evening to wash off all the paint on her body in a shared shower (or, perhaps to find that she wasn't wearing any, mere seconds before she devoured me with an inhuman snarl).

This one is not for you.

The thought brought me up short, like a dog running at full speed that finally ran out of leash.

You already have won the Prize, Traveler. This one is not for you tonight.

At that moment, four young men in matching costumes made of furs and skins burst onto the courtyard, laughing and making jokes.

"Shandra! There you are!" one of them called over.

"Hey!" she replied with the wave of one taloned hand. "Excuse me, I have to go talk to these guys. You going to be around later?" she asked, and ran her nails down the curve of my ass. I flashed my badge in explanation, but my smile felt like it was slowly sliding to the ground. "I'll talk to you inside," she finished, and then scampered off to join her friends. With a sour feeling, I watched the way the furs covering her perfect butt bobbed as she greeted her compatriots with a feisty round of hugs and busses.

Not yours, the city said more firmly.

Whatever. I stomped my cigarette and wandered back inside to dance my frustrations away.

Thursday/Friday
12:40 pm
Night W/O End Vampire Ball

The ball is populated with more easy, horny tail than you can shake a proverbial stick at.

I was, however, led to believe that this would be a truly debaucherous orgy. What a contemptible lie. One can only hope that the winnings of an earlier bet will be paid in full.

I finished tapping words into my PDA and tucked it back into my pocket. Covered in a thin sheen of cooling perspiration from dancing for the last hour, I gazed at the crowd and decided to go outside for some air.

A couple of ravishing female fire dancers did their thing in the evening breeze. I leaned against one of the giant stone columns and relaxed. I'd piled on a few more beers, and my legs felt like rubber from all the previous dancing. My mind was pleasantly numb, and my eyes were lost in the twirling fire batons of the dancers when a tap on my shoulder startled me. I spun on one heel as Jade smiled and pressed her body against mine.

"What's a nice girl like you doing in a place like this?"

She licked her lips and wrapped her arms around my shoulders.

"Who told you I was nice?" she whispered in my ear, and then nibbled my neck briefly.

Yours.

Excitement zinged through my body, and I growled. My teeth grazed her skin for just an instant. She pulled away with an unspoken question on her lips.

"Care to come back to my room?" I asked, without having to fake the husky inflection in my voice. She blushed a little, but didn't retreat any further.

"Dammit, I told you I don't know if I can tonight," she murmured. "Matt probably expected me to go with him . . . " The look in her eyes belied a desire to accept the offer.

"Understood," I said calmly through clenched teeth. "But tomorrow night?"

She smiled, bit her lip, and ran one hand down my inner thigh before walking away. Her wineglass hips swayed seductively with the grace of a stalking lioness.

Yours, the city reiterated.

Bullshit. You heard the lady, I countered, frustrated. I had really been looking forward to taking her home.

Believe, Traveler, the presence said patiently. I snorted, then finished my beer and tossed it into the garbage.

I wandered about, danced, and felt fairly out of sorts. Shandra, the leopard girl, passed me in the crowd and gave a come hither look. Squaring my shoulders in happy preparation to hunt, I prepared to go thither.

No, Traveler. The one you want will be yours tonight.

I paused in the hallway, and then continued my path away from the feline girl, cursing internally the whole way and feeling a bit unsteady. There was no rhyme or reason to it, but I decided to take a chance that the city might be right. Higher powers at work or whatnot.

My watch told me that the ball would only continue for another half hour. A mob had formed at the bar, patrons who waved desperate handfuls of cash and demanded alcohol. The bartender spied my Staff badge and waved me over.

"Hey, Troy just got a final beer run done," he panted. "Can you help bring some beer up?"

"Sure," I replied. *Who the fuck is Troy?*

"The van's down there," he said, and pointed out the front doors of the dance hall. I followed the direction he'd indicated down the stairs past several stumbling partygoers. Once outside, I met a tall character in a cheap black trench coat. About six feet two inches, and heavier in build than I was, his long and light brown hair whipped around in the breeze. He opened the rear doors of a rental van that was parked immediately (and illegally) in front of the entrance.

"You're Troy?"

He automatically proffered a hand in greeting.

"Yeah." His eyes traced the badge around my neck, and he grinned. "You are . . . ?"

"David. I'm a friend of Jade's," I said while moving to the back of the van. "The bartender told me you needed help."

"Oh. Cool. Take the beer up," he said and hoisted a case. The huge man hurried back inside before I could say another word.

I glanced down at an unexpected box of Rolling Rock. With a gleeful giggle, I tore open the top and grabbed two cold ones, which were immediately deposited into my attaché case. My hand slapped the flap loosely back in place, and I carried the box up to the bar where the attendant didn't even notice the discrepancy. His attention was absorbed by the demands and hurried requests of the cash wavers, all of whom needed alcohol *now*.

I ducked behind one of the giant courtyard columns and uncapped a beer with a mad cackle. Every face around me was starting to take one of two expressions—haggard and ready for bed, or lit up like flame and wanting more of the party. Alas! The party was almost over! I pressed the chilled bottle to my forehead. My appetites were more than a touch aroused and I wasn't sure which side of the crowd's spectrum I fell towards.

I pounded the quenching beverage and dropped the evidence of my theft into the trash with a hundred identical bottles. There is a rare and delicious kind of low-level madness that occurs when I have too much to drink, and I was swimming in it. The fete was winding down, and many of the strangely costumed denizens flowed through the front exit to their cars and a fleet of hungry cab drivers. A sinking feeling began to form in my gut as I wandered. Funny thing—I hadn't seen Jade when I'd gone on the beer run, even though her working area was directly adjacent to the front entrance.

A second check downstairs confirmed my fear. I leaned against the vacant admittance tables, lowered my head and cursed soundly for a minute. The entire area was deserted. She was gone. I'd missed her, and no matter what some fucking disembodied *thing* in my head had said, I was going home alone that night. I felt petulant, and more than a little disappointed.

Yours, the city reassured me, and I let out a bark of laughter that tasted like ashes.

Shut the fuck up. I don't know what you are, or why I'm imagining this, but she's gone. She went home tonight. Yeah, I can have her tomorrow, but five long years I've waited to meet this woman. This is cruel. It would have been disappointing enough if I'd met her and she'd had previous engagements, but you led me on you . . . you bodiless, lying thing.

I beat my fist on the table just once, but hard enough to make the legs squeak. Now I had to go back to a hotel room and try to go to sleep, by myself, without anyone else to keep me company. How harsh was that?

"Hey."

The voice zapped my heart with a purely lecherous, hopeful feeling. I turned slowly, not daring to assume the identity of the speaker. Jade leaned against one of the doorjambs with a lit cigarette and a crafty smile.

"Hey yourself," I said, bewildered. With my luck, she'd just caught a smoking break to say goodnight before heading back to the hotel with the wimpy little fucker I'd met earlier. She walked over and put an arm around my waist.

"Matt found something else to go home with, so I told him I was going back to your place tonight," she murmured into my ear. Her warm breath made all the tiny microscopic hairs on my earlobe stand at attention, and I had to choke back a cry of shock. Strangle it, really.

"Are you serious?" I asked as evenly as I could while my brain sang hallelujahs. Her smile became even wider, gorgeous and hungry, and she looked me in the eye with a languid nod.

"Tonight I'm yours," she said.

Yours, the presence in my mind echoed.

I had no reply at all for either of them, so I gave Jade a nice groping hug, crushed her to me, felt the luscious curve of her ass through the fabric of her dress and kissed her ear. My cock was rigid in anticipation and my mind swam with a strange kind of wonder.

CHAPTER SEVEN

We boarded the taxicab with hands joined. To this moment, I could not tell you what the driver looked like—my eyes were completely glued to Jade's startling green gaze, and our hands and lips found each other constantly in the backseat. We never kissed, and I will admit that it was something I dearly craved, but touching, biting, stroking, and scratching occurred in abundance. When excited, she made delicious sounds of hunger that I would never forget, a cross between a purr and a sigh, and the skin of the back of her neck tasted better than honey.

When we stopped, I tossed some cash at the driver and hastily pulled Jade out of the cab. The parking lot of the hotel was empty of any other people, and the front desk was deserted. Once again I felt the sensation of otherworldly existence, as if I were somewhere not on earth, but this time I felt no fear. Let the planet be empty, Jack. I got mine, in the form of a luscious redhead whose desires burned a stream of heat right up through our joined hands and into my brain. I led her to the room.

Through the trees lining the walkways (*Crape Myrtle*, the city said for the second time, and I realized where I'd gotten the information), back up the stairs to the hotel room, my mind was on fire and Jade's excited flesh between my fingers. I fumbled with the white plastic keycard at the door.

"Do you think your roommates are here?" Jade asked while attempting to peer through the blinds. Someone had left the lamp on, but aside from the telltale yellow glow through the window, I couldn't tell if the place was occupied.

"God, I fucking hope not," I growled, and slid the card into the lock. The light on the doorknob blinked green, and we went inside.

The room was blessedly vacant.

"Hello?" I called out as we entered, just in case someone was in the bathroom or hiding behind a bed. There was no reply at all. The air of the room itself was still and calm, as a place only feels when it is fully deserted. I set my belongings next to the bed, and immediately began straightening the sheets out. I'd left them in a hideous state, having forgotten that my roommate always left the Do Not Disturb sign on the doorknob due to an aversion to having maids in the unit unattended.

I don't like to think of myself as a womanizer or "player." At the same time, there are some pretty basic rules that keep my life clean and healthy, but my bed adequately stocked with willing lovers.

—I always keep condoms on me at all times. Always. Although it sounds ridiculous, you really never know when you might need one, and in this day and age it's better to have one and not need it than need one and not have it. I never, ever leave the house to even go to the supermarket for sundries without at least one little square wrapper tucked safely into a discreet pocket.

—There's a small stash of things I usually keep near my bed, just in case. Latex-friendly lubricant is a must have. Something to drink is also a good idea, a little touch to a sexual encounter that makes for happier bedmates. Massage oils, a couple of silk scarves, and (if in a place where smoking is permitted) an ashtray are all excellent accoutrements.

—If going out for a night, no matter what my plans are, I make my bed neatly and crisply. A wise man, whose identity I have since forgotten, once noted that a woman will not normally be disposed toward the idea of getting into an unmade bed. It's advice that I have taken to heart.

—A small stereo at the very least should always be nearby, to help set the mood. As long as nothing cliché is playing, like Barry White or R&B, most lovers enjoy having a soundtrack.

And there are other little things to do, keep around, or remember. If a person really wants to seduce a lover, it's no different from any other undertaking. Careful preparation usually pays off.

Jade excused herself, and headed to the bathroom. I frantically made the bed, but then a quick survey of the room left me with a disapproving frown. I had none of my usual items at hand, aside from condoms. The area was completely devoid of anything that could play music. Upon examination, the cube fridge *did* have a couple bottles of water that my roomie had apparently purchased, and I swiped one for the nightstand. The toilet flushed; I sighed and shook my head. It would have to do, and that was that.

She came back into the soft glow of the lamplight with her boots in one hand, and I noted that she was somewhat shorter than I'd expected. Some men have a penchant for ladies within a certain height range, but my tastes didn't disqualify any woman over such a trivial matter.

"God, my feet are killing me," she said, and dropped onto the mattress. I looked at the boots she'd set on the floor, and whistled. The heels on them were tall, about four inches.

"I bet," I murmured, and then took her left foot in my hands. My fingertips began to apply pressure in various practiced ways.

"Oh . . . oh, my god," she said, and fell to lie fully on her back as I hit a couple of pressure points with a nice hard, circular motion.

"I have to let you know," I said slowly while my fingertips worked the bottom of her foot, "My roommate and I have an agreement that nobody is allowed to stay all the way through the night and sleep over here except us. I hate to say this and all, but I thought you should know before . . . "

Her eyes closed and with pleased noises, Jade waved a dismissive hand.

"Quite alright. I have to go back to my hotel room once we're done anyway. I didn't bring any of my stuff, and Matt would worry." She put down the foot I had been working, and lifted the other one to my hands. "God, that feels good."

I grinned and kissed her heel, then lingered over her Achilles tendon, still rubbing with my fingers, and letting my teeth graze her ankle through the thigh-high stockings. She let out a cheerful little sound, almost a murmur but with some hunger bleeding into it, and her eyes opened to give me a half-lidded, feline stare. One of her hands stroked my arm, and I flexed. She explored my bicep with her fingers and smiled.

"Nice," she said. "Do you work out?"

"Not recently," I said, and put her foot gently down on the edge of the bed. "I was lifting pretty hard last year, free weights and such, but I haven't had time to hit the gym in a while."

"Hmm," she murmured and sat up to kiss my neck with languid ease. I gasped and raked my right hand through her hair, cupped the back of her head and pulled her against me. She gave me a nip with her false fangs, and I shuddered from the sudden erotic desire to clench my fist in her tresses, pull her back down on the bed, get on top of her, take her by force immediately and without mercy . . .

But I curbed the urges as I damned near always had to if I wanted the experience to be as enjoyable as possible. Instead I pulled her head back a little, growled, and buried my teeth into the thick muscle of flesh that ran from the nape of her neck to her shoulder. I put enough force behind the bite for her to really feel it, but not hard enough to break skin, clamping down and squeezing her flesh between my jaws. Her breath hitched as her hands clutched at me, not to defend but to instead pull me closer. In lieu of kissing her lovely red lips, we did a little dance of teeth for the next few minutes, biting and tasting each other's skin like mating tigers, letting our hands wander without actually fondling each other like teenagers.

While my nerves were busy singing a high crystalline note of desire, I slowly and forcefully stood her up with me next to the bed. After I'd circled to stand behind her, I began to unlace the dress, surprised to find that it was actually a corset and skirt whose patterns blended together seamlessly. She was intoxicating, and my hands shook a little in excitement as I helped her out of her top, then crushed her to me from behind. Moving against her, I let my hands stroke the delicious and nicely-formed curves. I was not a breast man by any means. "Breasts is breasts," in my opinion, and all women had them, be they petite and barely pronounced, with tight, pert little pink buds in the center that catch your eye and make you want to nibble, or massive and intimidating, like two large globes of rounded, straining flesh that move in an enticing manner once unfettered. No, I was a leg man through and through.

Jade's breasts were large, not gigantic but definitely of a size to be reckoned with. They hung ever so slightly from their weight, with aureoles on each the diameter of a quarter. I avoided these little pink buttons of flesh—most men focused on a woman's nipples too much, from what my lovers had told me. Instead I dragged my fingertips along the smooth curve where her softer flesh met her ribcage, biting the edges of her shoulder blades, listening to her quiet cries and gasps. My hands slid smoothly down her stomach and the tips of my fingers inserted easily under the waistband of her skirt. I pushed it to her ankles with no effort at all, which left her standing in front of me solely clad in stockings. She moved her hips in slow circle, one arc of which ground her naked ass against the crotch of my slacks, and reached up to pull my neck closer.

"Do you want me to leave them on?" she whispered rapidly into my ear. Her voice had achieved a state of husky arousal, as if she were holding back a feral scream, getting ready to pounce. In reply, I bent my knees slowly and left a trail of kisses down her spine. My lips felt the little shivers of desire course through her like iced lightning. I chose to stray down her right hip first, and I pushed her upper body over the mattress until she was leaning on it, her feet still on the floor, kissing the arc of flesh that denoted where her ass stopped and one lovely, muscular thigh began.

On one knee, tracing lines down her legs and enjoying the soft, silky skin there, I grabbed the top of her stocking in my teeth and pulled it downward in one fluid motion. I could smell her scent of arousal as I did so, and it was marvelous. Some women aren't very clean, and your nose can tell before you get anywhere near certain parts of their bodies. Jade smelled slightly musky, with an undertone that evinced thoughts of clean rain, and the salt spray of the ocean. I did the same to the other leg, leaving a perfectly naked redhead leaning against the bed, peering at me coyly over her left shoulder as I stood back up. She giggled, and I spat the stocking onto the floor.

"You're still dressed," she said, slinking onto the covers and lying on her stomach.

"Yes, I am," I said, as I crawled on top of her and proceeded to kiss and bite her lovely body, from her spinal column to the delicate curve of her hips to the soles of her feet. In return, she gasped, moaned, and sighed in all the ways that reminded me of playing a piano. If you know what you're doing when you handle a woman's body, they make *music*.

After a few nerve-straining minutes of such treatment, she suddenly propped her torso up on her elbows and gave me a stare from between dangling locks of hair that could have stopped traffic on a busy street. With an animal noise, she launched from her prone position and pinned me across the bed haphazardly. My head ended up over the open space off the edge of the mattress, and her hands clamped my wrist and shoulder, respectively. I had a good fifty pounds on her, but she was remarkably strong, and I didn't feel like resisting in any way, shape, or form. As she made the sounds one would expect to hear from a feeding wolf, she bit into my neck. Not the friendly nibbles one normally receives from a first time lover—these were hearty bites, demanding. Her lips met my flesh, her tongue tasted my skin. I was momentarily thankful that I'd shaved myself before heading to New Orleans. I'm not as hairy as some men, but the light smattering of black fuzz that grows all over me can make me annoyingly self-conscious when a lover is working me over. The thought quickly fled as the gyrations of her hips, the movements of her hands at my belt, and the fiery and consuming trail of heat left by her mouth made my whole body come alive. She moved her hands adeptly, fiercely, without pausing or lingering to kiss. Instead she unbuttoned and unzipped me with a single-minded focus. Within the space of a minute, I was as naked as she.

We tangled together then, both of us craving each other, both of us having to hold back. I wanted to plunge my cock into her, take her deeply and forcefully, to show no restraint whatsoever, but sadly enough the modern times we lived in didn't allow for such things. Her crotch danced over my rigid dick without actually touching, but moved close enough for me to feel the heat left by her passing. I sucked my breath in hard as her tongue found one of my nipples, clenched my teeth and let out a cry of pure desire and longing as she flicked and bit with aptitude.

She straddled me, the center of her heat resting on my stomach, and gracefully stretched her arms over her head, growling.

"I hope you brought a certain something with you," she said meaningfully. I chuckled, then rolled out from under her and snatched up the black cardboard container I'd brought with me. One thrust of my thumb split open the box, and I shook the row of condoms out with all the aplomb of a junkie receiving his fix. Impatiently, I tore one off without bothering to aim for the serrated line, ripping open the package and detaching it in one fell swoop. She lay sideways and watched me as I stroked the latex sheath on with a solitary movement, and then climbed back across the bedspread toward her. She laid back with her legs parted and her beautiful pussy exposed, inviting me in. Some women have sexual organs that are too well pronounced, making them look strange and alien, and others are too underdeveloped, making them look like a mere crease in the woman's groin. Hers were exquisite to look at, with labia that were smooth, shaven clean of pubic hair, and ever so slightly rounded, the tip of her clit a pink little nubbin of flesh peering out.

Grabbing her forcefully, I rolled to the side in a practiced maneuver. She let out a cry of surprise as she found herself on top suddenly.

"Hey," she breathed, and then started taking me in. With a sigh that was so pleasant it nearly killed me, she thrust down in a smooth movement, gliding down most of me to stop with only an inch left to go. I gasped, as the sensation sliced clear to the marrow of my bones, and then put my arms around her neck to pull her head down to mine.

"Don't push any farther," I murmured with a grin. "I think I told you about this game once."

"Yes, you did," she said in a voice strained with pleasure. "I've wanted to try it with you for a while."

When I was sixteen, I had discovered a very odd manual about sexual practices through the history of mankind. It had been chock full of historical facts about sex, and although there'd been pictures of all kinds of acts, both the regular pornography and the stranger kinds of visual notations, it had also been rife with information that I found absolutely fascinating. Chapters on chapters detailing the sexual practices of every nation on earth throughout the ages.

I'd masturbated to it mercilessly for years.

One chapter, however, had been so interesting and odd that I'd decided to try the art it had described. My girlfriend at the time had been intrigued, so we'd attempted it with the kind of horny abandon that two teens can show each other. It had blown our minds, and we did that specific sexual act over and over during our time together.

The art of Karezza, it seems, was a tantric kind of sexual congress, one aimed at prolonging the experience between two people. Scholars sometimes argue about whether it first appeared in India or Japan, but I don't really give a rat's ass. All I know is that it's fun, easy to do, and completely a mindfuck for anyone that you do it to for the first time.

To perform it properly, the man and woman engage in enough foreplay to be completely and utterly aroused. Not enough to hit an orgasmic peak, but a sufficient amount to leave them absolutely wanting each other. When ready, the man enters the woman as deeply as she will take him, and then the man *stays there*. Holding him inside her, the woman doesn't move either. Anything else goes—touching, scratching, kissing, biting, squeezing, flexing . . . it's all fair game, except for actually fucking. No in and out movement is allowed.

The payoff is that after some time, both partners feel a heightened sensitivity, and the urge to actually *fuck* like mad becomes stronger and stronger, building up like a crashing wave in the ocean, until you can't stand it any longer. Some of the most intense sexual experiences of my life have occurred during this game, and I will never tire of taking a lover to my bed and showing her this trick.

I held Jade for a little while, running my fingernails with medium pressure down her back, and then flexed my Kegel muscles. She gasped, then bit her lip and squeezed back.

"Nice," I managed to pant, and then slowly sat up, bringing her with me unexpectedly.

"Ah. Careful," she cautioned me as I curled my legs and gradually turned, then pinned her beneath me on the bed in a comfortable motion. Now I was on top. We sat there for an instant, and she smiled up at me with brilliance that would have startled the gods. Carefully and ever so slowly, I lowered my hips, felt myself push just a little bit farther inside her, filling her, and finally met that ultimate resistance that told me to go no further.

"Jesus," she breathed, her eyes shut, panting quietly.

"I'm not hurting you, am I?"

"No," she gasped, clenching her internal muscles again and shuddering. "God, that feels good."

"The feeling is mutual," I said quietly, enjoying the ambrosial feel of her, both inside and out. Her skin was like hot silk. "Damn, you're tight, woman."

After ten minutes of biting each other's necks and letting our hands explore each other, I could feel the nearly electrical current build in me, the pressure of an imminent explosion. I flexed internally, which elicited more delicious noises from her, but the action was mostly to quell my own urges. Kegel muscle exercises are a wonderful thing. I'd found many years before that practicing them daily allowed me to repress my orgasms far better than I could in my teens. Women don't seem to understand that, for men, it is very difficult to learn how to stifle the urge to come.

At thirty minutes, I felt like my cock was swollen to the size of a school bus, and she was actively trying to buck her hips beneath me. I instinctively started to kiss her, but remembered at the last moment her earlier warning and planted a quick smooch on the end of her petite nose. She giggled, her eyes glazed with pleasure.

"Hold still. Perfectly still," I whispered to her, and then decided to push my luck. For the next fifteen seconds, I slowly pulled myself back, slid inexorably out of her with the speed of a freshly wakened snake leaving his burrow. She moaned, quivering beneath me, her hands digging fingernails into my shoulders like tiny knives as I pulled away until I was barely inside her. I stopped there for a moment, silently clenched my jaw from the sheer exhilaration, and then began pushing back into her twice as slowly. She moaned harder, this time a sound of determined need, and tried to raise her hips to me, engulf me, swallow my flesh with hers. I held back, matched her undulations, entered her again at the pace of a burning candle until I was almost all the way buried. She gasped as I pushed back inside fully, the last half inch almost (but not quite) stretching her too far. She panted there, her alternately soft and taut flesh wrapped around me, and a tiny bead of sweat rolled from her cheek to the pillow beneath it.

"Oh, wow," she said, taking shallow, rapid breaths.

So I did it again, slowly, carefully, as I ground my molars together like tectonic plates. Again. And again.

After forty-five minutes, both of us were drenched in sweat, and she finally needed to give in and fuck. I could see the wild abandon and need in her eyes, and she licked her lips as we flexed and squeezed each other.

"I want you to come inside me. Now," she said suddenly in a voice tinged with sultry longing. Her eyes slammed shut, and her face looked suddenlydesperate.

"What about you?" I asked. My heart was being stunned with a thousand volts of lust.

"Fuck it," she gasped, trying hard to rock her hips against me. "Please. I'm almost there."

I decided to give in. It was too much. I could show physical restraint in bed, but no man is a god when a woman makes such demands, especially during your first encounter together, and when the woman was a saucy redhead whose body made you think of cream and fire. With a cry of reckless abandon I buried my face in her hair, clasped her hips with my hands, and began to move faster. She felt gorgeous and hot, so hot she burned, and she snarled and stroked me back, her hands dug furrows in my flesh, and she rose to me over and over. Jade began to make a low keening noise beneath me, and I felt her muscles tightening throughout her body like steel springs. She snapped into her orgasm hard, her arms and legs rigid and her breath halted as she shuddered beneath me. Before I could prepare for it I felt myself burst as well. The sensation flattened me like a speeding freight train, with the strength of a flash flood and the power of an avalanche. I tried to let out any noise I could, but my throat had seized up like a frozen pond, locked my breath inside my lungs. My pulse was a bass drum that thudded in my head until I thought it would shatter my skull, and after a few quaking thrusts I collapsed, fighting for air.

A little later, she began to stroke my back with one gentle hand, and snuggled peacefully beneath me.

"Mmm," she said in my ear. "Nobody's going to believe this back home." She referred to a strange group of online friends on an Internet message board system that we'd both been part of years before.

"Which part?" I asked, still feeling slightly atmospheric.

"This. Us. What we just did."

"Well, I'm still surprised that a woman I met over the Internet isn't fat, nasty, and twenty years older than she said she was," I said, and kissed the tip of her nose again. She giggled and held my face in her hands for a moment.

"I am so glad we ran into each other."

You're welcome, said the presence in my mind, startling me badly. It was stronger now, much more like an actual voice in my head than before.

"Me too," I said, and tried not to show how unnerved I was by the sudden interruption. Slowly getting onto my hands and knees, I disengaged gently from her and headed to the bathroom to deposit the now slightly filled latex sleeve into the john. Part of me still couldn't believe any of this. For years, Jade had been a Virtual Person, a mere collection of posts, emails, and phone calls without a body to put to the name. Having met her and had such a hungry and immediate sexual experience with her . . . it was a little bit overwhelming. After the toilet flushed, I pinched my own arm between a thumb and forefinger. Nope. Intoxicated, more than a little high on the rush from an orgasm, and also feeling a day of walking and dancing slam tinges of pain through my legs, but dreaming I most certainly wasn't.

"Hey, is this your water?" she asked from the bed.

"It is now," I replied, and walked back into the lamplight. "Have at it, lovely."

She uncapped the bottle and took a long pull off it as I climbed under the thin sheet with her, spooned up next to her and enjoyed the warmth of her flesh next to mine.

We laid back and cuddled, talked about a few minor details in our lives—her ridiculous and breakneck work schedule at two jobs, my happiness with the car I'd recently purchased, this and that. It was comfortable, and for the second time since I'd met her I found it fascinating that two people could be so familiar with one another just from electronic communication.

"So," I said as I took the water bottle and sipped a mouthful to wet my throat, "Where did you and Matt meet? Is he from Ohio too?"

"No, he lives in New York," she said as she grazed one side of my chest with her fingernails and lay her head on the other. "We met through the Hematarium, and he's kinda new to the scene."

"I could tell. He doesn't hit me as the kind of guy who goes for this kind of debauchery," I said.

"What do you mean?"

"Well, he's . . . I don't know. Stuffy. A little meek." *Jealous*, I thought.

She giggled, and nodded.

"Yeah, well, he's been raised kind of conservative. I think he might have been a little disappointed if I'd just toddled off with you tonight. But I did tell him I would go to New Orleans with him and the rest of the crew, and when he asked me if it was okay for him to go home with that other chick tonight, I decided that it was a perfect time for us to get together," she said, and kissed my nipple.

The touch of her lips fired another round of hot lust through me, and I felt my cock stiffen again. I chuckled, and then lifted the sheet slightly to look down towards my groin.

"Down, boy! Down!" I used as stern a voice as possible, but my penis had no ears for my commands. The little bastard stubbornly rose, and the scent of the lovely naked thing next to me didn't in any way help curb my erection. Jade cracked up, and then lifted the sheet herself to look.

"God, I don't think so," she said in an almost apologetic tone. "I'm a little tender already." She caught my look of disappointment, and cupped my cheek in one hand. "Aw, don't worry. We can do this again later."

"Yeah." I stared at the ceiling and argued with a nasty little libido that was demanding *more! Now! Damn it!* Then, a few seconds later, my eyebrows shot upward of their own volition as a new sensation began. "Hey!"

Jade smiled again, continued to use her fingers on me, and then returned her lips to my chest.

"What?" she said in an innocent tone of voice, and fluttered her eyelids at me. "You don't like this?"

"No, I do . . . just . . . "

"Then shut up and enjoy it," she said, and her hands moved across all the right spots on various parts of my body. I was impressed—I didn't normally enjoy mere manipulation by hand from a lover as much as I did actual sex, but she worked me like an expert.

After a few minutes, I was absolutely rigid and trying to not thrash about. Some men spoke about how they want nothing but virgins. I personally thought these men were fucking *idiots*. Inexperienced women were never welcome in my bed, and I'd rather have enjoyed one night with a lover who knew how to handle my cock without reading an instruction manual than a whole month of virgins. Our society holds to the common belief that anyone who takes pleasure in a good number of bedmates is probably *unclean* and *promiscuous*, a word I still find funny in its dirty connotation. Like any other physical activity, I've always believed that the more sex you have, the better you get at it. At least, that's what I'd found in life, and with proper precautions, risks can be kept at an absolute minimum.

Jade was an excellent example of why I followed this outlook. Her kisses on my stomach, her hands precisely dancing along the various spots that made me moan . . . she'd obviously had enough practice to know what she was doing. I gasped as she hit certain spots, ground my teeth and held my breath as her touch grazed, licked and stroked over others.

As I moaned again she suddenly stopped, a look of contemplation in her eyes. Then she pushed me toward the edge of the bed.

"Get a condom. I want you inside me again. Now."

I returned, protected again by a thin layer of latex, and climbed on top hungrily. She was almost feverish in her actions as she hooked her legs through mine.

"You said you were sore," I said as I entered her, relished the tight heat and sensations. Her hands may have been talented, but nothing beat being inside a woman.

"I am, but I just . . . oh, god . . . "

"Feeding off of me, are you?" She nodded. "Does this have something to do with Psychic Vampirism?" She nodded again.

"Just fuck me," she said, and thrust hard against my body.

We continued matching each other's pace for a while, and she felt different this time. Her movement was more demanding, harder, as if she were trying to squeeze my orgasm out of me forcefully. I found myself shaking as another explosion build up inside me, but I was not quite up to the edge of it yet.

I held her face inches from mine with a hand on each cheek, and she opened her eyes.

"Do you want me to come?" I asked.

"God, yes. Please."

"Then look at me," I said. We locked our gaze together, and I was entranced by the malachite color of her eyes. As we thrust and ground our bodies together, I watched a fire slowly build in the light I saw there, and the pressurized knot of heat inside me grew stronger with every movement.

"Oh, god," I murmured.

"Yes," she hissed, and pulled me harder into her. I came hard the second time, cried out and clutched her neck to my teeth, bit down and felt her racing pulse with my tongue. Jade used her legs to grip my waist, to arrest my movement, and flexed her internal muscles to the rhythm of my spasms, crushing down on me. The effect nearly made me lose consciousness, and I lay on her gasping for breath.

"Thank you," she whispered in my ear.

"The pleasure was mine," I murmured back, my face still buried in her fresh-smelling hair.

"What were you doing that last time?"

"Hmm?" I was busy with an attempt to make the room stop its lazy spinning.

"Your eyes. What were you doing?"

"I've never managed to go through an entire orgasm without blinking. It's a game I play, ever since I discovered that there's nothing quite as hot as looking right into each other's eyes when you're inside a lover."

"I'll say," she murmured quietly and snuggled up to my chest. "That was fucking awesome. I liked watching you try to maintain control."

"Although keeping your eyes open all the way through may not be possible, I sure do love to try," I growled, and reached for a cigarette.

We lay beside each other for a few more minutes, melted into each other's skin, flesh and sweat, and then began to slowly get back up. The sun peeked through the bottom of the window shades, and I yanked them completely down to banish the unwelcome glow.

"I can't believe we've been up all night," Jade said as she futilely attempted to straighten the rumpled mass of hair on her head. Naked in front of the mirror, she reminded me of some strange medieval painting. Her hips were gorgeous, and the curve of her waist was the kind that could drive men mad with lust if they thought about it for too long.

"I can." My boots yanked onto my feet and I had managed to find my pants. Although I was no longer drunk, my legs felt like dead, burned-out meat. We got dressed, and I helped her find her stockings.

Grinning and satiated, we walked back down the stairs together as the cool breeze wicked the moisture from our brows.

"Did you want to take the streetcar or what?"

"Oh, I'll probably just catch a cab," she said, and pulled out her cell phone. "Do you have my number?"

"Let me check," I said, and opened my PDA. My twig stylus tapped a few times to display her name in my address book. "Ah . . . nope."

She gave it to me. I entered it and snapped the little display shut, then slipped it back in my pocket. Jade was wearing the dress from the ball, albeit a little crooked in the corset, and I had grabbed my spiked jacket and pants with no shirt beneath. I was sure we made a fine pair.

"Hello?" She plugged her other ear with a finger and spoke into the silver phone in her hand. "Yeah, for New Orleans?" With a smile for me, she turned around to look through the large window of a corner store. "I need . . . well, a cab . . . "

I tapped her on the shoulder, and then walked to the edge of the sidewalk. Traffic was light, with people still using their headlights in the fading gloom of early morning. Jade looked at me quizzically as I stuck my hand up and faced the oncoming vehicles.

Seconds later, a blue and white taxicab swerved to a halt directly in front of us, the driver expectantly smiling.

"Uh . . . never mind," Jade said into the phone, and put it away. "Call me later," she said and wrapped me in a last hug. "I really want to hang with you again while we're here."

"Thank you for the evening," I said as we disengaged.

"No, thank *you*," she said, and with a satiated grin pulled the cab door closed. The car pulled away with the speed of a startled horse, dodging out under the hanging branches along St. Charles, and I waved goodbye as it quickly dwindled away. I stood alone on the corner and listened to the low whisper of the wind in the trees. With my body sore and any sense of lust annihilated, I watched the moss-covered buildings and ever-changing traffic lights. The air was quiet, and lucidity set in momentarily.

Did that just really happen? I thought.

Yes, said the presence in my mind. *You did well, Traveler.*

I walked along the street very slowly, the loudest noise being my boots as they hit the cracked cement. There was a different scent in the air, one I hadn't experienced yet in New Orleans—wet asphalt and sand, and something floral that lingered. Lighting what felt like my thousandth cigarette, I watched a passing streetcar shatter the stillness of the morning, plowing through the median of the road like a hurrying metal cow. Then it was gone, leaving only the placid, empty streets again.

Thank you for the evening, I said to the city, as I had come to recognize the being in my mind. A sparkle of shivers flowed down my back, a chuckle of sorts.

You will need food if you care to continue, it said, and the hunger hit me with such force that it felt like being punched. I mewled aloud, almost spitting my cigarette onto the ground. My gut demanded nourishment so hard it hurt.

Food? I checked my watch. *It's 6:08 in the morning! I could get some donuts, I guess . . .*

Traveler, look across this road. I did, and immediately spotted a Cajun restaurant that, oddly enough, still looked open. *Time means nothing in my streets. Go. Get a meal. Eat.*

I crossed the avenue while trying to ignore the clawing, snarling thing that my stomach had become, and entered the restaurant carefully. I expected only to see a few other bar rats, or maybe nobody at all except a surly bartender. Strangely enough, I had to push through more than a handful of diners in the cramped and dark restaurant. As I sidled up the bar Paul Simon's *Graceland* came on the jukebox and I flagged down the exhausted-looking bartender. He looked about twenty-two, tall, with the same weary face that most beer pullers do at the end of a long night.

"What can I do you for?" His voice was friendly, but the smile didn't reach his eyes.

"A menu, for some take-out." He nodded, slapped a laminated sheet down, and moved to the other side of the bar to fill a mug that an old man was waving like a glass flag. I gazed at the minuscule writing, most of which described foods that I had never tasted.

"Need suggestions?"

I glanced up to see the bartender again, butted my cigarette with a nod and rubbed my chin where stubble was starting to form.

"What's good? I've never been here before."

"Never been in here?"

"Never been to New Orleans."

"Wow. How you like it so far?"

"Do you have Guinness?" I pointed at a keg that seemed to call my name.

"Naw, it's tapped out," he apologized. I sighed, pulled out my cigarettes again, and sat on the barstool.

"Gimme a Rolling Rock, then." He nodded, and retrieved one quickly, uncapping the bottle and plopping it down. "Good man. Putting a Rolling Rock into a pint glass is like buying your girlfriend a corsage to go down to the local gas station."

He smirked at my jest, and waited without a word.

"I'll take the Chicken Fettuccine Alfredo," I said, "And a big bowl of the gumbo . . . ?" I left it as a question.

"The gumbo kicks ass," the bartender said, nodding slightly as he scratched his pencil on a notepad. "That it?"

"Great. Lovely. I'll be here." He wandered off to put in my order, and I laid my forehead on the folded leather arms of my jacket. After a few deep breaths, I sat back up and tried to think about nothing much at all. The only thing that still kept me going, after all the sex, booze, walking, and dancing was my hunger.

The bartender returned, polishing a pint glass as I tapped one fingernail on my beer in rhythm to the music playing.

"You never answered my question," he said as he put the tumbler down and grabbed a second one.

"Hmm?"

"How do you like Norlans so far?" Not *New Orleans*, but "Norlans." I noticed that nobody I'd spoken to so far in this city had even once pronounced it the way I was so used to hearing: Or-Leens. I sipped the beer thoughtfully.

"Well, last night I walked a good ten miles, got stinking drunk and lost, ended up at a Vampire's ball, then went home and spent these last hours having lots of sex with a gorgeous gothic chick," I said in a conversational tone of voice.

He nodded, polishing the pint glass in his hand with a face that said *I've heard that story before*. It may have even said *I've heard that story several times over the course of this evening*.

I rested until the food arrived in a large plastic bag with handles. I paid the ticket amount stapled to it, with a couple dollars tip for the bartender (who was now nowhere to be seen), and left as quietly as I had entered.

Back in the hotel, I cracked open the plastic baggie containing cheap plastic flatware, opened the Styrofoam box of fettuccine, and began to eat like a man possessed. Almost instantly, it was obvious that something foul had been done to the thin slices of chicken that were mixed in with the noodles. The meat was dry, and disturbingly spongy. My mind conjured forth a mental image of some poor, depressed fowl, bereft of half of its feathers, moping about in a coop all its miserable life before being left to die, alone in the cold rain, and let to rot for days before someone offhandedly decided to cook it.

Still, the Alfredo sauce was thick and delicious, the noodles perfectly al dente. Screw it—I ate it anyway, not even slightly worried about food poisoning from zombie chicken flesh. The meal evaporated quickly, and was perfectly filling. Part of my mind realized that the last thing I'd eaten had been a slice of pizza, almost fourteen hours before, and not much else for the last two days. I pried open the large plastic cup of gumbo, and my nose was instantly assailed by a gorgeous mix of spices, a smell as thick and hearty as the mixture that I dipped my spoon into. The steaming, opaque ichor was the color of powdered brick, a soup to contend with, and the first bite burst in my mouth like a tiny hand grenade of heat, rice, sausage, and God knows what. I moaned aloud, and proceeded to take a few more bites, each one retrieving something weird from the murky container. Scallops, crawdads, sausage, beans . . .

My eating utensil smacked into something when I went for a deeper dig, and came back with half of a rock crab.

Half a crab.

On my spoon.

I set it on a napkin while part of my exhausted wits realized that there was no way I could *eat* that with a *spoon*. I chuckled and growled and tore the little crustacean corpse apart with my bare hands, extracted gobbets of savory flesh with my fingertips and felt predatorily mirthful as the sauce ran down my chin. When I was finished mangling the little bastard, the lid went back on the huge cup (which was still three-fourths full) and the remains of my meal went into the tiny refrigerator and the trash can, respectively. At the sink I doused my hands and face with soap, then looked at my reflection. Bloodshot eyes stared back from over exhausted bags.

"That," the man in the mirror said with a demented grin, "was one *hell* of a good time." I had to agree with him as I tottered to the bed, kicked off my pants, and crawled under the covers. *Bone Tired*—I'd heard the term often in life, but until that moment, I'd never realized that the phrase had an almost literal meaning. Even my bones felt exhausted, drained, the marrow sucked out of them. I would not later remember my head even hitting the pillow as I plunged into some of the deepest sleep of my life. The Predator side of me was, for the very first time, completely satiated. I couldn't possibly have taken another bite out of the city, the world, or life itself.

CHAPTER EIGHT

I'm in the hotel room, and the roof is gone. The bed is still rumpled, but when I look around it occurs to me that there should be a ceiling where I now see something else . . .

The front wall is gone too. Where the door to the room stood, there's a gaping wide area, and rolling onto my left side, I can see . . .

It boils and whirls silently, like a violet ocean with swirls of fog mixed in, seen from above. Mixed in the colors are a thousand images, and they're growing and fading at such a fast pace that they're almost like explosions. Houses and buildings, horses, and suddenly I'm standing in my boots again. There's a face I can spy out of the corner of my eye, female, laughing, but as my eyes dart across the roiling images, chasing each one as it fades, I can't get a good look at the face. I'm now walking across the room, black pants, no shirt, and wind is starting to blow. Outside of the wall is a sheer drop. The room is contained in a whirling globe of . . . whatever the hell this is. My toes poke out half an inch over the knife edge that marks the end of the floor, and the violet light is washing across me as I watch a fishing boat, a man in a bowler hat, and a nude hooker in an old bed flash past my eyes. The tingling that has been on the back of my neck is now across my whole body. I reach an arm out, and silvery wisps of this thing, this stuff, reach out like blurred and softer strikes of lightning to play across my fingertips.

"Come away," and there are direct words this time, spoken in a warm and throaty voice. It's a familiar voice, but at the same time, I know I've never heard this person speak to me before. A woman, with low, husky undertones, like a lady who's smoked heavily at some point and then quit. The breeze on tugs harder my skin, and it starts unraveling like spools of thread, the lines tapering into the swirl

of chaos in front of me, like fishing monofilament being fed into a torrid ocean. The ends of the cords aren't pulling me into the mix, but I can feel an urge to go. To topple forward into the maelstrom, let it engulf me and unravel me like an old knit sweater, until I'm utterly consumed and remade into something else.

"Traveler, come away," the voice says again, this time a direct order from a voice so loving and calm . . . I start to take a step forward.

CHAPTER NINE

My eyes snapped open at the sound of someone coming down the spiral staircase from above, only to slam shut again as a million points of pain shot through them. I rubbed my face and tried to remember what in God's green earth I'd done that had armed my hangover with such sharp teeth. Slamming too many drinks? The constant walking? The sex? Probably a combination of all three. All I knew was that an angry swarm of bees had decided to use my cranial cavity as a testing area for their stingers.

Walking will make you feel better, Traveler. Come away.

The footsteps continued down the stairs. I cracked an eyelid, prepared to see either David or his wife walk down to use the bathroom. Rather than either of them, however, a woman who was strangely familiar descended the stairs. Long, brilliantly purple hair hung down to her shoulders, and she wore a cutoff sweatshirt and tight blue jeans. Her body was willowy, thin, and frankly quite attractive, but her face was where my eyes lingered, looking into pale blue eyes and alabaster skin, a face so familiar that I could almost remember a name . . .

Oh, holy shit.

"Hey," she said in a familiar, perky tone as she took the last two stairs and stood next to my bed for a second.

"Tina?"

"Yeppers!" She plopped her petite ass onto my mattress, jostling my prone body.

"Stop that," I snarled, then yanked the sheets over my face. "What the hell are *you* doing here?"

"I came down for Halloween," she said in her usual happy person voice. Tina was the kind of woman that other females wanted dead. She'd been blessed with a perfect figure, the face of a goddess, and never seemed to age a day past nineteen. Even though she was older than me she still got regularly carded for cigarettes, and most people couldn't believe that she already had a fourteen-year-old son. What's more, fate had given her a perfect head of naturally copper-colored hair that had a shimmering luxuriousness one would have been hard pressed to find outside of shampoo commercials. Unsatisfied with the default color, Tina regularly dyed her tresses various strange hues that ranged from purple to green to pink. Although she was cute as hell, I also happened to know that she was just a flirt, nothing more. Sure, she was good at throwing sly winks across a crowded dance floor, or flashing a smile that made your heart skip a beat, but she was also very faithful to her boyfriend, a loving man who didn't mind letting her go off by herself to raise a little hell.

"How's it going?" I murmured from under the covers, while noticing that my legs felt like they'd been broken in nine or ten different places each.

"Pretty good," she said, and did something that made the bed bounce a tiny bit. I tucked the sheet down a few inches and peeked out with one eye. She was swinging her legs off the edge of the mattress. "Want some gum?"

"Uh . . . sure." I rubbed at my face in an attempt to restore some sense of consciousness. A thought struck me, and I flipped the coverlet down fully to squint in the pale light seeping in through the opaque window shades. "Hey, wait a minute. What are you doing *here*?"

"I told you, I'm here for . . . "

"No, I mean *here*," I said, and indicated the hotel room with one hand as she tossed me a cube of bubble gum. "How did you get in the upstairs bed?"

"Oh," she said, then paused to blow a bubble that matched the shade of her hair exactly before sucking it back into her mouth and biting down on it, "I ran into you guys at the ball last night, remember?"

I thought for a moment, then shook my head and popped the gum into my mouth. It was grape flavored.

"No."

"You said hi to me," she chuckled. "You don't remember that?"

"I'm afraid not," I said through a mouthful of artificially flavored goo. "I was kinda drunk."

"Yeah, you were," she snickered, and stretched her arms over her head. The action pulled the cutoff fabric of her sweatshirt over her breasts, letting just the bottom curve of each of them barely peek out from beneath the hem before she relaxed. That tiny slice of flesh hid again. "S'okay. I came back here with Marcus and Soph, and you were already crashed out. We all went to bed up there at about nine or so."

"So you stayed all day, sleeping in the bed?"

"All day?" She pointed at the clock, which read 11:22 am. "I just caught a nap. And before you ask, no, we just *slept* up there."

"One would hope," I said and pulled the covers back over my face as she stood up. I didn't want to imagine my roommate and his wife going at Tina like a pair of starving wolverines.

"When are you guys heading back to Dallas?" she asked.

"Sunday," I grumbled.

"Cool. I'll be back there in two weeks. Staying with some family down here and stuff." From beneath the sheets with my eyes welded firmly shut, I could hear her gathering things from the room. Fuck. I'd been asleep for a whopping four hours.

Come away, Traveler. Come walk down my streets. Come walk and play and sing. You will feel better . . .

I ignored the familiar call as I lifted my face out of the blankets. Tina had just finished the act of lacing up one of her shoes as she sat on the staircase. She grinned at me, adjusted the purse on her shoulder, and patted my leg.

"Catch you later," she said, and headed for the door. I grunted at her as she skipped out and quietly closed the latch. Her light, saccharine perfume stayed behind like a pink miasma of bad candy. Four fucking hours of sleep, oh boy, and here I was awake. What's more, I was kind of miffed. Whenever I seduced a woman, half the payoff was sleeping next to her. If not for Marcus's fucking rule about "nobody sleeps over," I would have attempted to have Jade stay the night. I'd followed that stupid edict, and he hadn't. What the fuck?

Flipping over on my stomach, I wrapped a pillow over the back of my head to blot out the offensive daylight.

Wake, wake up! Come away, Traveler. I am waiting. You are here and you should wake! Come away, come live, be alive and feel it! Come with me!

Fuck off, my soggy brain managed. *I've only slept for four fucking hours. Leave me alone for a bit. Let me sleep.*

I am waiting, the presence said patiently, and then began to croon another unearthly melody. Within minutes I was asleep, this time without dreams.

Awake again, legs still ached madly, hung over, sore. My eyes popped open almost of their own volition, and although the clock only said 12:45, I felt like I'd rested somewhat. I stretched and marveled at the apparent fact that this last nap of an hour and fifteen minutes had actually done some good. Not much, though—my feet were battered, my legs two stalks of extremely tight and frayed guitar strings, and the sclera of my eyes felt as if they were coated in lint and slime.

I toddled around in my underwear, vaguely aware that my roommate was moving about upstairs. Screw that bastard. He'd taken Tina home when I'd tossed Jade out first thing in the morning. I cranked up the hot water in the bathroom, stepped out of my briefs, and made sure there were ample white, fluffy towels at my disposal. After I stepped in and pulled the curtain shut, I leaned against the wall and let the cascade of heat boil my flesh. As I inhaled pure steam and spat out the gum that was still in my mouth, I felt the overworked meat under my skin soften its cries of agony. I stepped away from the water, slathering soap across my hide in copious amounts, when it happened again. The back of my neck began to feel warm, and the city's presence, as I had come to recognize it, slowly increased its intensity.

Come away come play come walk my streets again the sights to see the flavors to taste the music the joy come away . . .

The water sluiced away the previous day's filth, and the ethereal demands grew stronger. After some time spent soaking and sitting on the floor of the shower, I cut off the spray and made sure to use every last towel in the bathroom. Only when I was sure that each one was perfectly damp and on the floor, save the one around my waist, did I open the bathroom door. Fucking roommate. That would teach him to give me double standards.

The moment I stepped out the bastard was right there at the door, waiting to use the toilet. He looked rumpled and not quite awake.

"How's it going, Queenie?" he yawned, and clapped me on the shoulder as we passed each other. It had been his nickname for me ever since I'd done a drag queen impersonation at a party, not long after we'd met. I snarled, he chuckled and shut the door.

"So," I called out loudly enough for him to hear as I retrieved and applied some deodorant, "When did you decide it was okay to have people sleep over in our hotel room?"

"Are you talking about Tina?"

"No, fucker, I'm talking about Cheryl Tiegs. *Yeah*, I'm talking about Tina."

"That's different. She's not a stranger."

I snorted and applied some cologne.

"So it's okay if we know the person?"

"Of course," he said through the door, "I just don't want you picking up some chick and bringing her back here and her stealing everything."

I growled and swore aloud in as many languages as my sodden brain could muster, then stepped into my pants. A few seconds later, David exited the bathroom and looked at me strangely.

"Why do you ask this? Is something missing?"

"Naw," I said, buckling my belt. "Tina's fine with me. I just thought you meant *nobody* was allowed to stay."

"Well, do you know someone you wanted to have stay here?"

"You could say that," I smirked. "I've known Jade for five years online, and I had to kick her ass out of here this morning."

David laughed like a loon, something he'd always done well, and clapped his hands once as his mirth rocked him backwards.

"For the love of Pete! You already got laid?"

"You doubted my abilities to find a piece of ass in this town?" I said, and pulled a loose gray tank top on.

"No, but it's still good to hear," he said with a bemused shake of his head. "Yeah, hey, if you want her to stay the night, that's cool."

"That's what I wanted to know," I said, and pulled on my socks while trying to ignore the rising tide in my mind. The presence was really pushing in an attempt to distract me.

Come away, Traveler. Go out your door and into my arms. Come away and you shall enjoy life and suck pleasure from the fruit of the vines. I have so much for you, come away, walk, play, laugh, and wonder . . .

"What are you doing today?" My roommate sat on the stairs to the loft in exactly the same spot Tina had, and frankly, I'd found her much more attractive in that position.

I very nearly said *Walking, going away, playing, wondering, and living life* as I opened my mouth. *Quiet!* I thought to the city, and the stream of thoughts dimmed, but only a little.

"I'm going back to the Quarter," I growled as I made sure everything in my briefcase was in order for a good day of going out. "I was hoping to . . . hell, I don't know."

He chuckled, and cleaned the lenses of his glasses on the edge of his shorts.

"New Orleans has its claws in you," he said in a singsong voice.

I paused for a second and glanced at him out of the corner of my eye, startled.

"What?"

"This town. You're her bitch now," he said. "It happens a lot really. New Orleans gets in your blood, amigo, and you end up doing whatever she wants."

My arm hairs stood at attention, and I slumped against the bed.

"You mean . . . "

He walked over and clapped me on the shoulder.

"I mean you're having a good time, my dear compatriot. A lot of people end up scrapping plans once they get here, and do whatever comes their way. Don't worry about it," he said, and smiled. I could see it in his eyes—he didn't hear the City, no, he was just talking about the place in his usual form of analogy. I breathed easier and smiled.

"Okay. I'll be back . . . "

"Whenever you return," he finished and began his way back up the counter-clockwise staircase to the loft. "It is all well met, my dear villain. We might even run into you out there. I shall refrain from worrying until I spy your decapitated head in the gutter. Just don't forget you promised to have drinks with the wife and me before we leave."

I quietly closed the door behind me. Out in the strangely dim sunlight, I pulled out my wallet and counted my money. Then I lit a cigarette, and counted it again with a frown. What the hell? Had I been robbed? I rifled through the preceding day's memories, tallied up mentally all the cash I'd spent. With a grimace, I slowly walked down the stairs of the hotel. The day was warm, but not hot, as I very carefully made my way to the evil, satanic coffee area near the front desk. No, I hadn't lost any cash, not that I could tell. I'd merely sliced through my funds like a chainsaw against a tub of margarine, sprayed money all over the place in my carousing. I was down to less than two hundred dollars to last me three days, and I wasn't sure I could manage it.

Hey, I thought to the presence in my mind that still tugged me toward the street, nudged my brain incessantly. *I'm running out of money. How about some help on that end?*

The city merely shrugged through me.

It is of no concern. You have money now, do you not? it asked. *Please stop fretting. Take your money and come away, come and play, come live . . .*

And when I run out of money, what then? I replied, a little bit angry about such a childish response. The city shrugged again, and continued its chant.

The coffee spilled over my taste buds like a horde of Vikings, descended on my mouth to rape and pillage, kicked me further awake, and the presence tugged me along.

Friday
2:35ish
Walking around Prytania St.

That evil bitch, Ms. Nola, wearing a sparkly outfit and the grin of a horny teenaged girl, pulled out a straight razor and sliced my jugular right across the pocket. My bank account has been hemorrhaging cash at an alarming rate, a loss I have filled with stumbling drunkenness and an endless stream of cigarettes.

She tells me not to worry, and strangely enough, I don't.

I wonder if this should alarm me?

The streetcar appeared down the block, and I snapped the PDA shut with a grin. I felt a little bit like a pirate, for no reason I could ascertain. No strange sunglasses for me that day, but the air still had a bizarre ethereal feel to it. The bouncing off my eyes seemed filtered, blocked in some way, even though there were no clouds in the sky. Colors were vibrant, from the red sign of the coffee shop down the block, to the deep, verdant green of the leaves on the weeping willows that tossed their branches in the light breeze. I stomped out my cigarette butt and quietly drowned in the lovely pleasure I'd felt run through me from the moment I'd set out from the hotel lobby, the buttery warmth that spread from the back of my neck and shoulders with each step. It was the city, leading me onward, pulling me down the roads and byways as best she could. The chant in my skull had changed again.

Yes come away yes Traveler yes this is good and this is right follow my paths and come away and come away and come away . . .

No longer pushing or trying to cajole me, the presence had a wonderful note to its thoughts now, sweet and crystalline, that almost mirrored the cries of a lover during good sex. Clean and delightful, and seductive as all hell.

I boarded the huge contraption again, while noting that everyone else on board was quite obviously a tourist. Backpacks and ugly hats everywhere, and each person talked quietly and excitedly to their presumed friends, eyes wide like those of rabbits. I took a seat at the very back and tied a black bandanna around the stubble on my scalp. The sensation that ran through me was a high, not unlike a good dose of ecstasy but without the jitters.

When I got off the hulking beast on Canal in the same spot I had exited not twenty-four hours before, I let out a chortle and immediately headed through the crowds.

We go, we go, traveler, we wander and play!

Damned right, I thought, and chuckled as sparks of excitement and pleasure shot through each muscle in my back.

Once again the warmth on my neck grew, spread a cluster of smooth ribbons through my entire body, warmed me and eased the pain in my legs. I traipsed lightly through the crowds of Canal Street, the wide avenue that had become my beacon, the spine of my travels. Each lane that branched away from it was a rib in the skeleton of the city, and I was ready to let my feet explore every last bone in this place.

I walked. And walked some more. The pain in my legs from miles of pavement had subsided again to a dull throb, and the voice in my head was warm, spoke to me like a whisper into my brain itself, and it was more than just words that the presence slowly fed me. Images began to dance through in my mind's eye, ghostly snapshots of a time long since gone and past.

See here? said the presence at the corner of Chartres and Toulouse. *Many years ago, this entire area burned flat.* I paused at the corner and watched the various others as they continued on down the narrow street, from obvious tourists to placid locals on rusted bicycles. My eyes looked at the stores nearby, the brickwork and wood of the structures on this particular slice of land, and then I closed them while tilting my head back. The wind was sweet, and I felt psychedelic as the entire place thrummed and hummed around me.

Suddenly I saw fire. Fire and flame and houses, not the ones before me but real French houses, engulfed and blazing next to dirt and cobblestone streets. Smoke filled the air, and for a frozen moment in time flames paused in mid-lick as they ate timbers and peaked roofs, windows cracking under the ferocity of the blaze. People froze in mid-panicked-run, some of them on fire as well. I could almost hear a single momentary scream, as if one reverberation, a nanosecond of a terrified human voice had been stopped and let to play out in a longer time span, one that lasted minutes, days, years . . .

Then another image hit me, fast and quick, one of smoke, and mud, and horrible, wretched suffering. People with hunched backs, and dirty holes where their eyes should have been, each mouth lamenting forever, clothing scorched and tattered, moving about like ghouls or zombies, frozen in mid-step, treading with ragged shoes into the filthy ashes.

Then, as quickly as the images had entered my mind, I opened my eyes to a hazy blue sky, the wind continued to pluck at my shirt, and the noise of life resumed. Although each of the two visions had felt like they'd lasted for an unknown, yet *long* amount of time, I also knew that they'd taken less than a second to imprint on my brain.

What happened after that? I thought.

Crowds of the downtrodden rebuilt me, the crying people, and I let them not rest until my splendor glowed again in the night.

I considered the second vision again and shuddered at the thought of the miserable, exhausted crowds.

That was unkind, I thought. *You pushed them hard to rebuild.*

They worshipped me before the fire and after. I am not so easily discarded, as the other gods of man have been. After all, had I not treated their fathers and mothers well? Did I not also give their children the same gifts and lives? I was not to be destroyed by a mere and momentary blaze of fire, Traveler. I do not often need more than worship, but if I do, then those who are mine will do as I command. This is fair and just, that I may prevail. [Here the city chuckled at the cold knot of dread that had formed in my gut from the vision, and the unease melted away almost magically.] *No, Traveler, humans are not my slaves or thralls. They were crying, and I drove them hard, but they also rebuilt me because they loved me, and knew I would continue to treat* [my children/my worshippers/mine] *well.*

I pondered on this as I walked down Chartres and smoked an idle cigarette. As I recalled the first vision, a question formed in my mind.

You showed me a different kind of house burning than I see here. Why did they rebuild different houses? The ones in the vision of the fire had peaked roofs and completely different styles.

Wise you are, Traveler! The city wasn't impressed, but rather used a tone would affect when praising a pet that had done a trick well. Normally, I would have been peeved—I don't take condescension lightly from anyone, but this time I could only feel the pleasure that arced through me spike a little. *Do you know why this is the French Quarter to your people?* I shrugged physically, without the foggiest notion of the answer. *The French settled here first, building many houses in the manner that they brought from over the ocean. The people were lighter in color, and wore fine clothing, even those who were not very wealthy. Those houses were beautiful, and good to look at or live in, but were not the sturdiest that have ever been built in my arms. The fire I showed you destroyed many of those lovely places, but even by then the people living in those houses were no longer predominantly French. Spaniards, their skin darker and eyes lit from within, were now my people. Many of the French families had moved elsewhere, still coming to me to worship but living farther away. The new style of architecture grew under the hands of the different people, and under the others here—the Africans, the Italians, and the Acadians.*

In my head, I visualized a brilliant city full of light laughter and a strange harmony of many peoples, with bright colors and happiness abounding so long ago. Gamblers smiled and brightly colored ladies waved to gentlemen on the street, mirth and music galore . . .

No. Stop.

I paused in mid-stride halfway down a city block, and felt another sudden charge thrum through me. I wondered why, since I hadn't had any drugs or alcohol all day. As I paused another vision hit, this one as hard as a freight train splattering an armadillo across the tracks. My brain was held down, forced open and raped by it.

The picture in my head was of filth. Muddy, sour streets filled with refuse and excreta, as dingy and dirty men, brawny with muscle and scars, trod drunkenly in the mud. Women too thin to look attractive stood on street corners with pustules on their lips, vying for the attention of men riding by in cabs, waiting to spread illness to the fine customers. Dead bodies floated in swamps, and buzzing hordes of vermin and insects devoured them. Ugly men, unwashed, brayed loudly through mouths of rotten teeth as they disembarked from boats, ready to dish out hard-earned cash and abuse in exchange for sinful revelries.

As the hallucination left me, I put my back against a brick wall. My hands scrabbled for a cigarette in my pocket to replace the one I'd just dropped in the gutter. The vision had been too lucid, too much to wrap my puny mind around.

That was what it was like, Traveler, the city said calmly. *You are a child of your times, and people have made films showing very false ideas of what those years were like. Early in the days of this place I was far less bright, and my streets were much more dangerous.*

What changed? I asked, and flicked my lighter to scorch the tip of the trembling cigarette. *Did you decide that you wanted to be nicer to tourists, or something?*

The city laughed again, and the impression of terrible mirth rolled through me like a gigantic fluttering sheet of silk across my soul. I craved her laughter much in the same way that I enjoyed bringing amusement to the lips of flesh and blood women, terrible as her amusement could be.

What changed? People changed. The times you live in, Traveler, have removed most of the dangers that people faced on a daily basis. Your society has, as it is wont to do, defeated many of the hardships that my first people lived in fear of. The illnesses that have killed so many over the years are now a memory to your nation, or can be cured quickly. The laws that govern this city today are sufficient to keep the unsavory quieter, but when I was young my streets teemed with men and women who would have made your blood run cold. Thieves, rapists, killers, and worse used to run like quicksilver under the lamps of these very same avenues on a Saturday night. Yes, your society has created new and original dangers that you face, but there have been times that you would not have lasted half an hour on these roads, Traveler.

I walked again, more than a little bit humbled, trailed smoke and stole glances of the subdued crowds. A trio of bikers crossed the street in front of me, all tattoos and long, unkempt hair, leather and steel galore. Minutes before, I would have automatically thought that these guys were dressed pretty tough. Compared to the kind of men that the vision had shown me, they were merely regular people of my era, just three guys in their late thirties trying to go out and have a beer.

The strains of a lone saxophone slipped around a corner ahead, rough and shiny serpents of melody that wrapped around my neck. In the alley I spied a short man in a black pinstripe suit, his age completely indiscernible, with skin the color of dark chocolate and a head as clean-shaven as mine, his eyes shuttered behind slick sinister Ray-Bans. He leaned heavily against the wall, locked in a slow, lilting tune with the saxophone, played his hands over it the way a masseuse would run their fingers up and down the spinal column of a customer. It was jazz, but the slowest, lowest, most blues-driven jazz I'd ever heard. Each note came forth as if he were weaving it into unnatural shapes, trilling or warbling in a manner that I'd never heard a sax do before, punctuated with a melancholy feeling that slid across my mind like a fingertip through a puddle of oil. I watched him for about a minute, savoring the sound like some bizarre kind of candy, and then began to dig in my left pocket for a dollar. The musician let one note drip and splatter through the air, then took the reed out of his mouth with a blinding, white-blue grin.

"Keep ya money," he said in a baritone voice that had the texture of crushed glass sprinkled across velvet, but never turned his head to look at me. I removed my hand from my slacks and wondered if I'd just made a major mistake. I noted that there was no sax case present and open, nor a hat in which to drop money. This musician, no, this *god* of the brass had been sitting here seducing my ears, and I'd automatically attempted to donate him a paltry dollar bill for his incredible, momentary gift. These thoughts vanished as he leaned back and sighed, tilted the carapace-black lenses of his glasses up to the sky. I noted that he had a growth of short, perfectly groomed ebony hair that sprouted from his chin. This man was quite obviously the Devil, on a momentary break from his responsibilities in Hell, sitting on a quiet street corner and letting his eternal emotions melt out of the bell of a shiny metal tool. It wasn't all that unbelievable a concept to me as I sat there for half a minute and waited for him to play some more. He then paused and gestured at me.

"Get one of those squares off of ya?" he asked, still not facing me as he spoke, and I was certain that behind the sunglasses he had his eyes shut while he basked in the feeling of the Blues he'd unleashed moments before. I was not a raging fan of popular Blues music of modern times—a lot of it was repetitive crap. Stevie Ray Vaughan had been a fucking *god*, this was true, but he'd never quite captured the sounds that I'd enjoyed from B.B. King, Muddy Waters, or even the delicious strains of Gaye Adegbalola. I don't consider myself prejudiced on many things in life. I can't be—my bloodline is a Heinz 57 of various races, and I've never, in all my life, seen that any one race is better or worse than the other. That said, I will state a simple fact that I have *never* been able to find a solid argument for: In order to really play the blues, and capture that thoroughly bittersweet feeling, you have to be black. It's something in the African American vocal chords, mixed with a certain something that I just can't describe that make real Blues sound like they should. Haunting, rough around the edges but smooth like honey.

The man who stood in front of me was so obviously immersed in the Blues that he would never get out alive. I dug a frantic cigarette out of the box for him. His hand languidly plucked the slim stick of tobacco from mine, and he produced a lighter from almost nowhere, a simple red plastic Bic, fired the tip of the cancer stick up, and took in a smooth draw that seemed to make the air around me crackle with energy.

"Thanks," he said, "I'm just pickin' at some old bones." He exhaled the entire cloud, placed the still-lit cigarette on a windowsill, and licked his lips before he returned the reed to his mouth with the kind of delicacy one would use to kiss a lover after a long separation. Offering no further explanation his hands and lungs drove forth a high ululation from the instrument, like a painful crack forming in a perfect block of ice, and then swung it down into a gorgeous slow tune that made my mind picture smoky bars, swollen black eyes three days healed, heartbreak, and the human will to go on in the face of hellish adversity.

I listened for another second or two before I turned and walked away without a word. I wasn't convinced that I'd just truly met Satan on a street in the Quarter, but I couldn't entirely discount the possibility either. His melodies followed me for about fifty or sixty paces on the cement, slowly fading away, but no less breathtaking. As I wandered onward, the city began to speak.

I was the place that Jazz and Blues music melted together, Traveler. My loins created that music, and it has not changed. Listen. Does it not sound sweet, ringing through my alleys and rooftops? The notes of human joy and sorrow, so perfectly mixed together? Pain meets pleasure, happiness and suffering made one. That is what I am, what I give, and what I consist of. Many of those who make this kind of music have spread it to parts and places far from here, and their songs are a subtle preaching of what I am. This is my gift to the world, and you will hear it in me, all through the day and night, without cease if you merely listen.

Walking, walking, pausing at windows to admire art or gifts or various strangeness, but always walking. The cracked concrete squares, each as uniquely shaped as a snowflake in their broken patterns, became familiar to my stride, and as the sun struggled through the haze in the sky to reach me, I realized that I was sober. Extremely sober, for the first time since I'd arrived on Wednesday night. My body was fully awake, with no chemicals in it to blot out my thoughts, and I didn't like it one bit. The only sensation that felt intoxicating was the warmth of the city's tune.

I began to reflect quietly on my predicament as I walked. Until the age of fourteen, I'd been raised in a Christian church. After I'd lost my faith, it had become my hobby to study all the religions of the world; Wicca, Satanism, Catholicism, Buddhism, Mormonism, Hinduism, and a slew of other -isms. Some had revealed interesting aspects of human history. Others had shown themselves to be ridiculous wastes of time. Most had offered no real substance outside of being cults created solely to make the people who created them a fair amount of cash. However, in all my studies I had never found any solid proof of a higher power. All religions were a sham, a creation to help those who were weak believe in something that was higher than themselves, either to praise when life was good or to blame when life was bad. At the same time, I'd also never found any solid proof that the atheists were correct, either. Just because I hadn't found a deity *yet* hadn't meant that one couldn't possibly exist . . . somewhere.

In my travels and studies, I had always written off people who claimed to have had religious experiences as either crazy or fools. I journeyed onward, and felt the most powerful chagrin of my life. Now that I was in the throes of one, I understood fully what people had told me again and again. The peace and tranquility that washes over a person who is feeling and experiencing a higher power, the calm warmth that fills your body, mind, and soul . . . it was almost indescribable. I paused on Decatur and watched the artists ply their trade, listened to the non-stop dialogue the city filled me with, descriptions and concepts that seemed to come from nowhere. The idea that I'd been wrong for so many years was not a nice one. Maybe I'd been hasty to cast all of those people in the past into an automatic Dunce basket. Maybe some people *did* actually talk to Buddha, or Jesus, or the Holy Ghost or whatever the fuck.

Or maybe, I thought as I paused by a shop selling crystal sculptures of beautiful nude women, *just maybe I'm fucking losing it. I'm hearing . . . feeling the presence of some ethereal chick in my head, and assuming that it's the spirit of New Orleans, and in reality this is just a fucking brain tumor or something. Soon I'll be seeing dancing teddy bears and forgetting my own middle name. Yeah, great, what a lovely religious experience, when the various synapses in my fucking head short circuit, and my imagination gives me the thrill ride of a lifetime right before I die from an aneurysm, grinning like an idiot and frothing in a pool of my own fluids, surrounded by strangers who get to watch me die. I can hardly wait. Hallelujah, I'm having a fucking hallucination and thinking it's a spirit. Gods speak to the insane or mentally imbalanced because* the insane people *create them. Praise New Orleans, I'm coming home.*

Without warning or prelude my mind felt an all-encompassing void. For several seconds, everything in my head and body went totally quiet. It was more startling than any sound I could have heard. I almost stumbled off of the sidewalk, stunned as my cigarette flew into the gutter again. I found myself standing in the same position I once did during an unexpected and heavy earthquake in California—legs spread apart, knees bent, hands open wide and held about waist level to steady myself. The sudden stillness was like what you would feel if you were making love to someone comfortably, slowly, pleasantly, and then they suddenly disappeared. For a sickening few heartbeats, all I could hear were the sounds of the crowd, the noise of traffic, and the flutter of brittle leaves in the trees.

Then the presence in my mind came back, the tingling on my neck returned, and I breathed a sigh of quiet, shocked relief.

You are not imagining this, the presence stated flatly as I sat down on the curb, trembling. There was no anger in its pronouncement, but I could sense that it was also not as pleased with me as it had been. No further thoughts came from the city at the moment, just a low hum of that same ghostly melody that I'd heard the whole time I'd been walking for the past days. I eventually stood back up, unable to even apologize, and felt more chastised than I'd ever been.

For the next hour I felt extremely freaked out and refrained from any attempts at direct communication with the presence. I mostly window-shopped. Various quiet corners of the French Quarter were peered into, and what I saw in back alleyways sometimes amazed me. A simple brick and cobblestone pathway that in any other city would have only a rusted dumpster instead could hold a green, lush courtyard, hidden from the public view. I trod in and out of the streets like some strange weaver's shuttle in the loom, and found it amazing that there was still a sense of rebellion to the city, a spirit found on signs and plaques marking the buildings. Large weathered postings that informed anyone who walked by that a street used to be called a different name in French. Whole markers of historic monuments were spelled out in paragraphs of only *La*

Belle Langue Francais, and if a tourist didn't speak it, fuck 'em. New Orleans was not to be trifled with by the outside world, this strange oasis of another time and place and character. The little details began to catch my eyes. One of my favorites, on a street whose names I do not remember, was in a simple brick wall. Someone had stamped a Spanish doubloon into a brick three feet up the barrier. The characters were weathered, but still legible.

I traveled past a filthy alleyway rife with overflowing garbage, and the city nudged me.

Go inside.

Curious, I stepped over the pieces of trash and noticed that the alley took a sharp right turn about ten paces inside or so. Just past the hard right angle, I entered a hidden combination of a courtyard, botanical garden and café. Lush bushes nearly obscured the masonry of the walls, with climbing ivy and thick, twisted tree roots that covered almost everything in sight. An ancient and rusted wagon wheel lay propped against the central tree with a small sparrow sitting on it. He cocked his head at me, chirped his annoyance at my imposition, and fluttered away helter skelter through a hole in the branches.

At the café bar, a tall, lanky man with gray hair and a smooth complexion wiped down the mahogany surface in front of him as more fumes of the thick, New Orleans coffee wafted out of a row of pots behind his hunched body. I also saw a huge, hulking espresso machine that lurked in the gloom, and I grinned as his eyes met mine.

"Yes?" he asked, his face showed a stony blankness of expression that could have been masterfully used in a poker game. He was clad in a cream-colored dress shirt; long sleeves rolled up and spattered with tiny brown dots from the day's orders. He leaned toward me, his palms on the bar, and I noticed an ornate gold ring on his right pinky.

"Un espresso, s'il vous plait, monsieur," I said in my best attempt to make sure that my accent wasn't *too* pronounced.

"Simple ou double?" He switched over to French, matching my change in language without even the bat of an eye.

"Double," I said, pronounced *doo-bla*. He nodded, and turned away quick as a wink to work at the gigantic metal gadget in the corner. I noted that there were no tables or chairs inside the courtyard, which was about fifteen feet wide and thirty long. The tree in the center of the yard, which I could not identify, was taller than the surrounding buildings. The branches formed a perfectly natural canopy over the entire interior. Old wooden doors with padlocks were set at odd intervals into the walls. Ivy and spider webs betrayed them to be long disused, and I wondered what the doors led to. Living quarters? Kitchens? If I'd pried one of them open, would I find myself in an old abandoned speakeasy with an inch of dust on the floor . . . or a broom closet? Would I peer into an alien landscape on another world, right before the café owner approached me silently from behind and beat my head in with a coal shovel, thereby keeping the secret of the hidden coffee shop's dimensional doors a secret, as his father did before him?

I was startled out of my reverie by the owner's return. He unceremoniously plunked down a small Styrofoam cup that was halfway filled with inky black liquid. There were ceramic cups behind the bar, so I realized what he'd told me by serving the drink as he had: Begone.

"How much?" I switched to English at his sudden display of unfriendliness.

"Two fifty," the man said, with a face that was still utterly unreadable.

Without another word I dropped three dollars onto the bar and walked out, a little disappointed about not being able to drink my beverage in such a wonderful and quiet courtyard. But there is an inviolate rule of tourism that I follow: Do not stay where you are not wanted.

The espresso was so bitter that it nearly blew my head apart. I sipped it as I walked, and contemplated the things I had discovered that day.

The afternoon wore on, and my mind stayed abuzz with new and interesting information. Each hour flew by, and my legs grew weary as I explored avenues of cobblestones, brickwork, bright colors and subdued green vines. It was almost five o'clock when I felt the thirst. My mouth craved alcohol like a flower craved water and sunlight. I was on vacation, and dammit, here I'd been trotting around without any beer. What was even more disappointing was that there was only one street left in the Quarter that I had not explored, an avenue that I had intentionally avoided the whole time. The city perked up out of its crooning melody, and nudged me again.

Come down this road, Traveler. It is not as bad as you think.

I finally relented and went down Bourbon Street.

Friday
5:45 pm
Bourbon St.

Well, now.

Here I am in a loud, drunken blues bar on Bourbon St., tasting cold beer and ashes. The band is rocking souls like a hurricane through the bayou, and there's a smile on my face. New Orleans Blues cannot be described or categorized. It has to be heard at full blast and savored like a homebrew beer, it has to immerse you and wash over every square inch of your body, the sweet tongue of this raging harlot as her hands leave no part of your flesh unsullied.

Goddamn. She makes you feel alive. Even if I'm losing my mind, it's an amazing way to go.

Not two minutes after I finished the entry, the band took a break. I was feeling relaxed and warm from the drink. The tavern around me had a strange, eclectic crowd of people in it, and all the tables, chairs, and floor were covered in a fine powder of cigarette ashes. Older cowboys, younger punks, and a wide array of loud tourists sat near me. All seemed to enjoy the experience of life in a breezy bar on a Friday afternoon. I could see it in their eyes, feel it in my own grin– it was a damned fine day. I was tired and my feet felt sore as fuck, but I also had a cold bottle of dark ale in my hand, another full one on the table in front of me gathering condensation from the thick, humid winds, and my mind felt peacefully alert. I watched the crowd quietly for a while, took it all in, held my stylus above my organizer as if to begin writing in it, but never actually did so. Two barmaids darted back and forth behind the bar with the efficiency of sparrows building a nest, filled their customers' hands with drinks and relieved them of cash. An old black man sat next to an electric piano onstage, smoked a long cigarette and played an inaudible tune to himself while he waited for his band mates to rejoin him. Three tables from me a man in his sixties sat with a neat glass of whiskey and stared out at the street. He smiled with his mouth but his eyes seemed on the verge of tears. Normally in this situation I would have been bored and restless, but this time just sitting and drinking ice-cold beer was all I wanted to do.

I thought of Jade out of the blue. She had wanted to meet up again, but I had only her cell number and no idea where to rendezvous with her. My watch showed that the afternoon had grown late, and I realized that I probably needed to get a move on if I was to see her that evening. I didn't get up. The hard wooden chair under my ass was too comfortable, the moment was too right to fuck it all up by leaving. I lit yet another coffin nail and rested my chin on my hands. Smoke rings shot out of my mouth as I reminisced about the preceding night's debauchery. Memories of Jade's ass and legs, her moans and smiles... I took a couple more hits off the cigarette and pleasantly wallowed in recollection.

Would you like to have her again?

I paused. The city spoke to me as it had before I'd questioned it, with a lilting smile in its tone. A few thoughts occurred to me, and I sucked in the warm air of New Orleans through my nose. After a few moments of quiet deliberation, I replied.

Yes, I thought. *I would like that. But I would also like to burn tonight. I would like to prey. Do you understand what I mean? I would have you open yourself to me, New Orleans, and show me how hot a pedestrian wolf can run through your beautiful streets. I am convinced that what I am experiencing is completely real and I now know that you are not a hallucination or a sign of mental defect in myself. However, if this is all true, I ask you to fill me with your wine, give me your women, play me your song, and let a Predator run easy through the dark places you have made. Give me excess beyond compare and the fruit of life ripe on the vine. Give me Jade and give me a night of everything that I could ever imagine.*

One heartbeat passed.

Traveler, do you know what you ask? The tone of the city was mildly surprised, and also held a hint of warning.

No, I thought. *I do not. But I ask it again: Give me everything you can.*

Done, came the immediate answer. The city was pleased with me once more, and I felt the buttery warmth of her smile as I cracked open and drank half of the remaining bottle of beer in one draught. The frigid fluid slid down my throat and froze my tonsils. *Come walk, Traveler, and see what a time I have in store for you.*

I finished my third beer, grabbed my bag, and walked back down Bourbon in a sea of people, wandered to Canal again, placed no phone calls, and made no plans as the sweet and seductive voice of the City murmured in my mind, took me down bright alleys and past gaiety in all of its wondrous forms. My gait may have wandered in anything but a straight line, but my body hummed and my smile felt like it would split my face in half.

The sun was almost down when I finally looped back down St. Charles. I had no idea where I was going anymore. My feet just meandered with no aim or destination. As I crossed Canal St. the traffic light changed, and left me stranded in the raised median as heavy traffic erupted both in front of me and behind. I tapped my foot, whistled and attempted to match the melody of the city's song. The light changed again, and the presence nudged me hard as I took my first step to cross the busy street.

Yours, the City said, and I felt something other than my own volition raise my arm and drape it around the waist of a woman passing me on the right. My grasp swung her around in a semicircle to press up against me. Startled, she nearly dropped the gadget in her hand, and I found myself face-to-face, body-to-body with a grinning woman named Jade.

"Hey! I was trying to call your hotel," she exclaimed. A surprised grin flooded her face as she pocketed her cellular phone. "How did you find me?"

I grinned back.

CHAPTER TEN

That night, I burned indeed. Hot and throwing sparks, I burned.

With my arm around Jade we trod the same beautiful cement walkway, talking and feeling comfortable.

"God, you wouldn't believe the morning I've had," she snarled as we made our way back down St. Charles.

"What happened?"

"Well, I got back to the hotel without problems. I'd been asleep for all of an hour when Matt and a couple other members of the group decided to come in and tickle me awake."

"Oh, good lord," I muttered.

"Yeah. Really fucking funny, a goddamned hoot and a holler."

"So, any bloodshed?"

"Almost," she growled. "I kicked both of them bodily out the door and told them that if they disturbed me again, I'd have their spleens for lunch. Matt got all offended instantly, and insisted on having a fucking 'talk about us' for an hour." She spat on the ground.

"Great," I said quietly as we crossed a street. "He's probably jealous about last night, right?"

"Like you wouldn't believe. Apparently the chick he went home with was a coke fiend, and all she wanted to do was stay up all night talking." She shook her head in a bemused manner. "So yeah, he seemed to hold it against me that I got some last night and he didn't."

"I'll bet he doesn't view me in a flattering light, either," I mumbled.

"Who cares? It's not like he's my boyfriend or anything. He chose to go with someone else last night, I went with you. He can get the fuck over it, or leave me alone."

Jade knocked on the door before entering, then keyed into the electronic lock.

"Hello?" she called out, and flicked on the light.

"Meh," came a feminine voice. On Jade's rather large mattress, her friend Melanie had been napping on her stomach. Shirtless, she looked like someone had forced her to jog fifty miles to get there. She made no move to cover up as we entered, and if she wanted to show off some flesh I wasn't going to stop her.

"Hey," she said, closing her eyes again as I sat on the bed and put my briefcase on the floor. "Good to see you again."

"Same here," I replied, unraveling the wrapper from a fresh pack of cigarettes. "How you doing?"

She groaned and buried her face in her folded arms.

"God, I only got three hours of sleep. I'm gonna die."

"Early morning tickle wakeup?" I ventured.

"They wouldn't dare."

"Too much sex?" I asked. It was always my favorite topic of conversation.

Jade and Melanie giggled in unison.

"No," said Jade, "Melanie can't fuck."

"What?"

"No, really," said the woman in question as she rolled her face over on the pillow. She gave me a resigned shrug. "I can't. I don't have the right equipment."

I gave her a good once-over with my eyes. Tall, slender, and with pale skin that was dotted by an occasional freckle, it occurred to me that if I hadn't already begun to make other plans I'd have wanted to sleep with her. Melanie's hair was a deep natural copper color and cut short in a manner that would have made another woman look like a bull dyke. It just made her look sexy and feral, like a tired female wolf reclining in preparation for the hunt.

At my continued quizzical expression, Melanie sighed and took my left hand in hers.

"Give me your pinky," she said, and then wrapped three of her fingers around it, leaving only the last joint of the digit showing. She held it up in front of her vision the same way someone would if they were looking at the eye of a needle. I noted that her face was not bad to look at, either. A smattering of appealing freckles splashed across the bridge of her nose, and her green eyes had a distinctly impish cast to them.

"That," she said, "is how deep I am."

I wondered for a second if she was merely passing a harsh character judgment on herself, and then got it.

"Really?"

"Yep," she said in the weary tone of voice that people do when they discuss a physical defect for the millionth time in their life. "My pussy is the size of a thimble. I can't fuck."

"Wow," I said, trying not to offend by either being too interested or too sympathetic. "That's gotta be rough."

"Nah," she said. Her eyes dropped shut again as Jade went into the bathroom. "It's no biggy. I still have plenty of other fun, just not the kind that people expect . . . God." She shuffled her shoulders a little with a wince. "My fucking shoulders are killing me."

"Mind if I rub them?"

"Oh *hell* yes. Or no. Uh . . . go ahead." I straddled her slender waist, put a thick curve of her muscles in each hand, and began to knead in a circular motion down her back. Her skin smelled dry and slightly spicy, as if she'd walked through a cloud of cinnamon at some point. She moaned in an uncanny impersonation of a woman being fucked slowly, and dropped her face on the mattress.

"What are you doing to her?" Jade called out from inside the bathroom.

"Shagging her rotten and pissing on your clothes," I answered, and noted that Melanie had really soft skin. Ridiculously soft. Either the gods of complexions had blessed her or she used some kind of fancy lotion after each shower, because nobody's skin was that silken all by itself. It was like running my hands across warm, unblemished rayon. The muscles under her skin were taut at first, but as I rocked my fists up each side of her spine I could feel Melanie's back loosen up. After four minutes of this treatment, she felt almost as languid as if she'd passed out.

"What're the plans for tonight?" Jade stepped back into the room, peeled off her black sweater and unclasped her bra with all the aplomb of a person removing their hat. I let my eyes grace the curves of her breasts, then grinned at her and winked. She smiled back, and moved to her closet to retrieve a black spandex t-shirt.

"I know we have to meet up with Troy," Melanie said with her face half-buried in the mattress. The short rub I'd given her had already unclenched her muscles. "He said that one club was having a thing tonight, and we're all going in a big group after we eat." I propped my feet on the bed and laid parallel to the tranquil woman as Jade wriggled into a lace bra. The mattress felt like heaven to the backs of my legs and the aching space between my shoulder blades.

"I want a Grenade," Jade said as she pulled a brush through her hair.

"Hey, I want a whole box of them," I said, and fought valiantly to not become one with the bed. She giggled and whacked my boot with the brush playfully.

"No, you doof. It's a drink. Supposedly the strongest you can get in New Orleans. They sell them on Bourbon."

"Careful," Melanie cautioned. "Those things are dangerous."

"Pshaw," I mumbled. I sat up to avoid the siren's call of the bed and fumbled for a cigarette. "There's no drink I fear, ma'am. I have a liver made of pure Teflon and granite."

"Whatever," she said with a smile and rolled off the mattress to show me a nice turning profile of her naked breasts. "Just be careful with them."

"So should I come along?" I asked, and dragged an ashtray across the bedspread toward me. Melanie ducked into a black sweatshirt and headed for the door.

"Troy said he could get all of us who worked the party last night in for free, so yeah. See ya!" she said with a wave as she exited.

"We'll be there around eleven or so," Jade called out as the taller redhead retreated. "Anyway," she sighed and dropped the brush on a bedside table, "I don't know if we really all have any plans other than meeting at the club. I think Matt may want to be with me tonight, so . . . " She looked at me with a questioning expression.

"Ah. You want to make sure I'm not jealous," I said, and showed a few teeth in my smile.

"That's not a problem, is it?" she asked as her fingers trailed over my bare scalp.

I interrupted the presence in my mind, which had been crooning the same quiet melody, ever present but comfortably dormant.

Mine? I asked.

No fear, Traveler. You shall have everything you asked for. Something in the way the voice spoke made me wary. It was like having a dangerous conversation with the Devil where you bartered for your soul. I knew that the city could possibly reward me, or use the promise that had been made earlier to . . . well, do harm to me. Perhaps even kill me.

"No," I said to Jade as a different shadow of a feeling settled around my upper arms and shoulders. "Hey, you came down here with him, and if that's what you need to do, go for it. I make no claim to you."

"Cool." She reached for a wallet on the table. "I know, you always told me that you were down with this kind of thing online, but you never know. Thanks for not being a possessive freak. Hey, check these out. Matt got them on Thursday."

I took a strand of plastic red Mardi Gras beads from her hands, and noted the contours of the plastic pellets. Each one was shaped like an extremely reflective fish.

"Now those are unique," I said while they ran through my fingers.

"I want fish too, dammit," she said as she reached for her backpack. "I want some green fish, and I *will* get them, so help me. I just can't find them anywhere."

"Well, you'll have to earn them," I said with an outright evil grin. She winked at me over her shoulder, and then hefted her backpack.

"God, I really don't want to carry all of this crap," she growled.

"What's in it?"

"Some stuff. Actually . . . " she slid the strap back off of her shoulder, and plopped the satchel onto the bed next to me. "Screw that. The only thing Troy really needs is *this* thing . . . "

She produced an ornate and artistic dagger, almost a foot long, and I whistled. It was shaped like a gigantic ankh of hardwood and reflective steel, with the base of the ankh shaped into a blade. I recognized that it was a perfect replica of the Hematarian sigil, a stylized Egyptian symbol. She held it out to me by the wavy blade, and I took it carefully by the handle.

"Jesus. That's a hell of a pig sticker," I muttered and held it up to the light. The grip was embedded into the O of the ankh, and the blade was really very nice to look at. I ran a thumb along the curves, felt the unsharpened edge.

"It's a ceremonial dagger," she said. "Can it fit in your briefcase? I need to get it back to Troy, but I don't have anything to carry it in."

"Uh," I balked for a moment. "I don't know what the laws are around here about carrying a Big Fucking Dagger in one's briefcase, but I'm pretty sure that it's illegal."

Worry not, Traveler. You will not be disturbed by the officials tonight, the voice in my head soothed.

"Never mind," I said before Jade could reply, and packed it up into my briefcase, this time without a second thought. "You need anything else?"

"Nope," she said, and arm in arm we walked out into the thick, velvety air.

It was almost immediately evident that this night was going to be more active than the prior one. We approached Canal on foot, and the lanes of traffic were packed. Cars of screaming people whooped and honked as they flowed back and forth in a stream of revelry, and the crowded sidewalks teemed with people of all ages, most of whom shared my look of wonder and delight. We waited for the light to change at the very edge of the walkway, and an electrical sensation was starting to spark deep in my stomach. I felt like I'd swallowed a small, soft ball of lightning, its trapped energy being digested and filtered into every vein in my body. The sensation slowly but surely ramped upward and set every hair on my arms and legs upright. The haze in the sky obscured all but the brightest stars, and even those couldn't hold a candle to the sparkling lights that lined Canal in various neon, strobe, and incandescent forms.

As the streetlamp changed to WALK and the two of us leaned forward to step into the street, one of the stranger moments of the trip happened. The presence in my mind gave a command so quick and sharp that I couldn't put words to it at the time, as if it had shouted one word with the speed and force of a bullet to my face:

BACK!!!

A mother would bark at her child with the same urgency if she saw her kid playing with a live electrical cord. My body jerked obediently, and I grabbed Jade's shoulder with my right arm, pulling her away from the street. Startled, she turned her face toward mine with a question on her lips a bare instant before a small two-door Japanese car whisked by. It ran the red light and caused no small amount of commotion in the crowd of people behind us. Jade flinched away from the green steel skin of the vehicle, which had grazed so close that I'd heard the rubber of the tires grind against the curb.

Within a second the encounter was over. As my fellow pedestrians shook their fists and raised both middle fingers and voices at the receding car, I steadied the two of our bodies and let out a sigh of relief.

"Damn, that was close," she said with a frown at the car's disappearing taillights. "Drunk fuckers. Good thing you saw them, or we might've been hit."

"Yeah, good thing, huh?" I replied, and something in my voice made her give me a questioning look before we crossed the avenue.

Thank you, I thought.

I take care of my own, Traveler, the city replied in a nonchalant tone. *As I've said: Worry not. You will come to no harm in my arms tonight.*

We walked for a noisy and tumultuous block along the road, and then took a hard right at a narrow asphalt street. To plow through the melee, we had to almost elbow our way through a tide of drunk and reveling people. Once again, a happy peaceful air overtook me as we wandered back into the French Quarter. Jade moved like a hunting fox in front of me, and the muted strains of a lone saxophone played somewhere in the background. I found myself on the verge of cackling like a man gone wonderfully mad.

"Where do we find one of these drinks you described?"

"I know it's somewhere on Bourbon Street," she said and took me by the hand to pull me to the left branch of an intersection. "I'll know the place when I see it."

"Jolly good, then," I giggled, and the electrical sensation tasted like a cocktail of quicksilver and pomegranate, still building incessantly in strength, as slowly as the minute hand moves on a clock. It was a strange feeling, but the best I'd ever felt in my life, as if my nerves were slowly being filled from some odd and hitherto unknown source of energy from a place not on this planet. It made me want to walk fluidly, dance, shout, and grab a random beautiful woman off the street to kiss her stomach.

Not yet, the city cautioned. *If you will but wait, I will give you everything you asked for.*

Bourbon Street was easily found, and as we approached it obliquely I took in the whirling ocean of people. Thousands of tourists and college kids in loud clothing, bright lights as far as the eye could see, and a smattering of nervous, darkly clad police officers who did their best to keep the chaotic circus of drunks in line. I thought about it as we approached the throng, and came to the conclusion that there was no way in *hell* that anyone could have paid me enough money to do the job those cops were stuck with. It would have been like giving a guy a toothpick and a book of matches and telling him that he needed to build a nuclear reactor with them.

We dove into the horde hand in hand and bumped into uncounted legs, arms, backs, and fronts. Everyone made his or her own noises, and the resulting cacophony in this public mosh pit of drinking was so loud that I literally couldn't hear anything else. I accidentally elbowed a young blonde lady's naked left breast—the lower hem of her gray sweatshirt was hiked up around her collarbones, and a swath of multicolored plastic beads formed a giant cheap roll of strands that cavorted on those two bulging globes. I paused, and then wordlessly held my hands out to my sides and bowed a little in apology. She laughed, not two feet from me, but I couldn't hear it at all above the raging din in my ears, and then playfully patted one hand across my cheek in a faked slap before she disappeared back into the crowd.

With a shake of my head, I turned back around and followed Jade deeper into the abyss. Every building had people above and below it, and the air was thick with flying plastic cups, beads, and catcalls. I ducked underneath a wet piece of clothing as it sailed down onto the crowd with no warning or reason, caught glimpses of shirtless and bead-bedecked women, and listened to the howling and screeching melee of sounds in the air. Dante himself could not have possibly heard anything as wild in all the circles of Hell. I bumped along behind Jade and we floated through the miasma of screaming revelers. Suddenly she grabbed my elbow and pointed at a milling crush of bodies at the corner of an intersection. They were clustered around a bar, and their clothing and skin glowed strangely at the edges from the bizarre reflections of several large neon lights. The name of the bar involved something Tropical, and the sign featured an almost cartoon-style section with a big arrow pointing at the front door: **GRENADES SOLD HERE.**

Jade said something, probably "There it is," but I couldn't make her words out at all. The heavy dagger in my bag smacked a rhythm on my hip as we burst into the saloon with all the aplomb of two angry badgers. The guy behind the counter, a gigantic ex-Marine who had softened with age by the looks of him, gave us an emotionless gaze that one would expect from a large chunk of stone.

"Whaddya want?" Somehow his deep and weary voice could be heard above the ruckus.

"Two Grenades!" Jade shouted, her higher voice barely discernible against the mob. The bartender barely nodded and instantaneously produced two long plastic tumblers, both of them an unnatural fluorescent green color that would have been right at home in a cyberpunk robot movie. His beefy, calloused hands jammed ice into each of the containers with no respect for them whatsoever, and then used a spigot to fire a pale green fluid into the tubes until they generously overflowed onto the floor. He plunked the drinks down next to the cash register, each one a full fourteen-inches-tall, inserted two extremely long straws into them, and rang up the cost. I threw some cash on the bar with a dollar's tip. We snatched the drinks, then ducked away from the bar swiftly to let in several intoxicated people. These wild-eyed patrons were already halfway through a crusade that would lead them amok in a sea of inebriation, the shouting of the word "woo" repeatedly, public acts of oral sex, and possibly bountiful amounts of vomit.

Back on the street, Jade's plush lips were already wrapped around the straw, her eyes half-lidded. Her cheeks pulsed as she took a long pull at the drink. She released the sip with a cross between a heavy sigh and a gasp as we left Bourbon Street, a sound that raised the hair on my arm with erotic energy.

"Fuck, that's good," she giggled, and then pushed the one in my hand gently toward my mouth. "Go ahead, it's really tasty."

I gave an experimental suck on the straw, and the ice-cold fluid blasted across my tongue like a rampage of tropical piranhas made of candy. The flavor distinctly lacked the hellacious bite of most hard drinks—that nasty, shivering sensation that came from one's palate clamping down on what it identified as poisonous, even as it was swallowed. Instead I picked up a trashy, fake melon flavor. It wasn't unpleasant but lacked any deeper levels of titillation for my mouth, followed by an aftertaste of something citric. The tang of the liquid reminded me of a Mexican carbonated soft drink for children under the age of ten, cloying sweetness that coated my tonsils with a drastic film of soothing syrup, sticky and wet and delicious.

"God damn," I said after several long gulps. "That's amazing."

"Damn right," she laughed, and together we left the front of the establishment, pushing our way through the stream of never-ending tourists.

We got the hell out of the Bourbon Street bedlam, and we did an increasingly less sober dance around the piles of discarded plastic cups and puddles of anonymous vomit. The strangest part of the departure from the throng was how quickly I found myself away from it—normally with a large crowd of people (for instance, at a concert), the milling assembly petered out slowly, until it was just you and a couple of other folks walking to your cars. Not so with the Bourbon Street mob. One moment, we fought our way past a wall of hooting and screaming drunks of both genders, people splashed each other with alcohol in their frenzy to cajole the onlookers on rooftops of nearby buildings into tossing down cheap plastic adornments. Then, suddenly, Jade and I were alone on a street with nobody else in sight. It reminded me of surfing in the ocean—we'd dived through the wave of bodies, floated around in its warmth for a moment with held breath, and suddenly exploded out of the other side. My shoulders were slightly damp in one spot, and a tentative sniff betrayed the fact that I'd been the recipient of a small amount of vodka from a passing stranger's cup. Jade wiped something wet from her left arm with a puzzled expression, and we both turned to look at the avenue again. Fifteen feet from us the wall of humanity boiled, waved, weaved, screamed, laughed, and partied as if there were literally no tomorrow. My gaze took in the backs of the strangers there, and I realized that there was a strange analogy to be found about the entire human race in this strange and chaotic place.

"Wow," Jade murmured. I nodded as I took her arm that wasn't holding a Grenade. We walked with an unsteady but comfortable gait, sipped our green effervescent poison, and merrily ambled away from the throng while our throats burned and our brains began to loosen up.

And now you see, the presence in my mind stated as I walked, *how I am worshipped by many, Traveler. It is revelry, an orgy, and a celebration of all that is good and pleasurable in life. And for hundreds of years, it has been as you have just witnessed.*

I laughed out loud and Jade looked at me quizzically as she pulled the green fluid up through her straw. I was sorely tempted to inform her about what was going on, spill my guts, but I also realized that there was a good chance that she would have immediately departed my company, fearful of the nutjob she'd taken to bed the previous night. One look into her eyes and I felt the hunger surge. My body was going to reach the boiling point sometime soon, and every blood vessel under my skin felt like it was filled with perfect, hot animal wildness. I wanted to grab her by the hair, and finish our drinks while fucking her hard against the brick wall next to us, here in the dark public places of mayhem and debauchery.

Wait. The time is not yet, Traveler.

Instead I shook my head with a grin and slugged another icy gulp of the Grenade. She giggled and poked me in the ribs.

"What the hell are you thinking about so hard?"

"Nothing," I replied, and restrained an urge to cackle as the bagged weapon smacked against my hip. "Just having a good time."

"Me too," she said. Her face was slightly flushed and the blazing tresses of her hair flickered in the wind like fire. I noticed for the first time that the air in New Orleans didn't seem to change—it was climate that had been taken to extreme levels of enforcement, always between sixty and seventy degrees, always at a humidity level that marinated you in the scents of the city. Even the wind seemed soft and warm, like the arms of a quiet and pleasantly exhausted loved one. When I was seventeen, I'd spent two weeks in Hawaii on vacation, and this was the closest experience I'd ever had to that type of weather.

We passed through a strange pavilion of cement at Decatur Street, and then turned the corner. Jade gulped the last of her drink and almost threw away the plastic, bone-shaped container. I stopped her, dumped the ice out, and dropped it into my briefcase on top of the dagger.

"It's as good a memento as any of the others I've been collecting," I said with a wry grin.

"Hey!"

A voice shouted at us from down the block, female and shrill. Our heads snapped up to find Rachel, Matt, Troy, and a few I didn't recognize as they marched down the street amicably. All of them sported toothy smiles that revealed plastic fangs. Black clad and dressed like characters in a Victorian romance novel, they swarmed around us in a flurry of hand clasping, spoken greetings, and hugs galore. I was reintroduced to several people, including an author by the name of Silvestra whose diminutive height was offset by her striking, pale skin and a face that was classically beautiful, in a quiet and strong way. Her hair was black, straight, and flowed down to her waist evenly, like some strange rivulet of bluish tar that leaked from her head in a thick rope. She walked in high-heeled leather boots and a dark, flattering dress with a plunging, bust-enhancing neckline. She looked like what I'd always thought a modern Witch would dress as; Sleek, black-clad, and sexy as all hell. She grinned as I took her hand and bowed in greeting. Her capped canines glinted while a strange, cold light flickered behind her eyes.

"You're Dave, right?" Her voice had an accent, so light that it was almost unnoticeable, but prevalent enough for me to know that English was not her mother tongue.

"Yes," I said, curious about how she'd known my name. She threw her head back to expose her extremely elegant, milk-white throat and laughed deeply.

"We met at the ball last night," she said, her voice still low and husky, like the purr of a large cat. "We talked for a bit, and you read some of my book."

Memories flittered through my skull; diseased and warped sparks of recognition that fought through the haze of alcohol and chemicals that I'd immersed myself in at the function. She'd had a table, books for sale, some kind of Vampire thing, and I suddenly remembered that I'd read several of the opening pages before I'd closed them, and made tactful noises while thinking the words "abysmal," "tripe," and "utter filth."

"Well, my apologies for having such an addled memory," I said smoothly, and released her cool, dry grip from mine. So far, with the exception of Jade, the members of the Hematarium that I'd met had been paper tigers at best—overgrown children who had never learned to stop playing Make Believe with one another. Silvestra, however . . . there was something to her movement, her eyes, her entire demeanor that screamed "Predator." That she was a mediocre writer had no bearing at all on the fact that I would never lock horns with this one—she would have fought as passionately as any other of my kind.

All of the twelve or so people we'd run into began to move down the sidewalk, headed for a destination that some conversation had decided upon while I'd greeted Silvestra. Jade grabbed my arm gently as she passed, guided me along wordlessly. As she did so, I felt a different sensation on the back of my neck, one that I was already extremely familiar with from everyday life. A glance over my shoulder confirmed my suspicion—Matt had been glaring daggers at me in an attempt to make my head explode with his gaze. As soon as I spied his glower, he looked away and feigned nonchalance. I snickered, and turned with the rest of the group to enter a staircase that I'd walked up before.

More than a little surprised, I found myself back in the red room that I'd started my debauchery in, two days prior. The crowd was larger, slightly noisier, and there was no room for a live gypsy band this time, but it was definitely the same bar. I slipped into the milling weirdoes and freaks more easily than the first time—the place no longer shocked me with every step. Jade and her friends had taken up residence throughout the packed area. Their conversation and laughter added to the cacophonous din. I grinned as ripples of excitement rushed over my arms and my feet took me to the bar. My elbows nudged between a morbid looking young woman whose eyes betrayed greater years than her body indicated and a rotund gentleman wearing chain mail and a beard of the kind worn by fat, greasy motorcycle enthusiasts. After my hand was wrapped around a Rolling Rock I wandered through the crowd, eavesdropped on snippets of conversations and listened to bizarre utterances.

" . . . And I just learned how to make an energy ball, so it was kind of like 'wow, this is cool,' and my mentor said . . . "

"What? That's bullshit. Everyone knows that you can't go thicker than a ten-gauge needle for a hood piercing . . . "

" . . . that? Oh, honey, you can't go there dressed like some mall refugee. Come by my hotel room and we'll find you some . . . "

The chatter was strange, as if I had found a radio that only picked up broadcasts from another dimension and I was slowly twisting the tuner. My wanderings led me to a tiny window, and I wondered if the full conversations would have made more sense. The breeze played over my scalp as I peered down onto Decatur while I eavesdropped on two young ladies who were hitting on a man in a white suit and derby hat. The girls were dressed like faeries, in gauzy and translucent black dresses and cellophane butterfly wings, and had the kinds of bodies that would keep people guessing about their ages until they were well into their thirties. The man looked to be about my age, a little bit taller, and sported the physique of a weight lifter. Their conversation seemed to be centered on the concept of summoning demons, and in the state I was in (namely plowed to the gills), I found myself less skeptical while listening to such a topic. The man spoke in a tone that indicated his supposed experience in such matters—as if calling forth ethereal and malicious spirits from Hell was something he did when he was bored, a mere act of fancy that he could perform at any time. The girls tittered as they sipped pale, iced drinks that showed pastel colors through the plastic cups, and asked questions every so often as if they knew better ways to bring forth demons than the pompous suit did. I wiped a sheen of sweat from my brow and enjoyed the flowery and polluted scents of the draft from the open window.

After the man in the suit had finished touting the uses of sea salt in the casting of a magic circle (which, from what I could gather, was meant to either keep the summoned demon confined or to protect the summoner *from* the demon), the two faeries giggled, and mentioned that they were about to go to a different bar. The suit didn't take the hint easily, but after several iterations of the implied invite he caught on and mentioned that he had to close out his bar tab before he could join them at the pub in question. Off the pair of winged vixens fled, fleet of foot and with evil smiles.

The man in white reached into his lapel to retrieve a wallet, and I nudged him in the ribs with my elbow. His air of propriety and pompousness evaporated like a puddle of spilled grain alcohol that had been set on fire, and was replaced with a frantic and wary facial expression and posture. Immediately I could tell this man was afraid that I might rob him, or do something evil.

"Beware the Fair Folk," I said in a relaxed manner, and turned back to the window to watch as a gaggle of female college students bumbled across a sidewalk in a manner that made their bodies jiggle.

"What do you mean?" he asked suspiciously.

"Ask Bottom and heed his warning," I said, continuing to admire more than a couple of denim-clad derrieres from afar. He snorted, and left in a hurry. The man probably thought I was mad—in his reality, demons existed, but those two girls were just *dressed* like faeries.

We're all mad here, I thought as I gulped my beer and leaned against the wall. The city laughed inside me, and my skin felt it with the same lovely pleasure that one would feel when a newfound lover breathed hotly against the back of their neck. A surge of passion flowed suddenly, hard, urgent. I looked around the room and drank deep breaths as I realized that all of the females here were well above my standards for a lover. Each one was extremely attractive, and it made me clench my fingers around the cold glass of my drink. The beast in me was still rising, still slowly gained on my ability to control it, and I wanted to run wild, cry havoc and let slip the dogs of debauchery . . .

Wait, the city said again. *You would loose your bonds of manners and fly into the fray so rashly. The time is not yet, and you must wait if this is to be right. You know this, Traveler. Soon enough it will happen.*

Moments later, Jade struggled through the crowd and grabbed my shoulder.

"Hey," she casually greeted me and stole my beer to take a sip. "We're going across the street to get some grub. You're invited."

"Cool." I followed her and put my arm around her waist as we stepped toward the exit. She quickly ducked to the side and fired me a not altogether friendly warning look.

"Hey, cool it on that," she said and distanced herself a little farther away from me. "Matt's been giving me shit since I got here . . . "

"Ah," I said as I placed my empty beer bottle on a nearby table. We left behind the red room and its cargo of bizarre creatures. "He's getting jealous?"

"Yeah," she said, suddenly less stern. I couldn't read her expression, and didn't trust my addled senses to discern between different emotions that I could have seen there. "He was under the impression that I was going to be *his* for this trip, or something."

"Well, did you two have an agreement before . . . "

"*No*. God, you know I'm not looking for a boyfriend. He's totally out of line on this, but I don't want more drama on this trip than is necessary."

"So you're going home with him tonight?" I asked, my voice as neutral as a referee's call.

"I don't know . . . maybe. Is that a problem?" she asked as we walked back down the stairwell. Each footfall squeezed creaks out of the worn wooden walkway.

Mine?

Yours, the city said soothingly. *You asked, and I shall give you all I can tonight.*

"No, not a problem. You know me," I replied, and managed to keep the combination of mirth and hunger out of my voice. She grabbed my hand in that dark hallway and squeezed it for just a moment.

"Thanks," she said gratefully, and then we were both on the street, under the lights, heading after the black-clad others who were already disappearing into a nondescript and basic single-story, brick restaurant.

CHAPTER ELEVEN

Friday
?:?? late at night
Wasted, French Quarter

A hand grenade is a dangerous thing. A redhead with an ass that just won't quit is doubly so. Only a suicidal fool or a fearless cretin would mix the two. It appears that I am such a man.

I snapped the case of my PDA shut and surveyed the table around me, then hefted my beer and waited patiently for the onion rings I'd ordered. There were eight of us seated around two small tables that had been pushed together to form one *big* rectangular eating space. The room was fairly unpopulated for a restaurant on a Friday night, with only an elder couple eating a quiet dinner in the corner, emanating the same aura one would expect from a pair of archetypical Russian peasants—stoic, silent, and enjoying their solitude. By comparison our table had the low hum of youthful conversation that one grows accustomed to hearing in various low-priced eateries, discussions of music and other such aspects of the lives of Twenty-somethings. At the same time, the dialogues I heard had some very odd twists indeed.

Rachel was explaining to Jade the different methods of using magical energy to protect one from the spells of others. Troy was describing the different kinds of "safe houses" a modern vampire could find in New York City, places where a person who thinks drinking human blood from a willing partner is a normal part of a healthy life could go to safely enjoy their fetish. Silvestra was bemoaning the various different annoyances that a modern day author had to go through, sitting next to me and delivering the account of her publishing nightmare in that delicious and unidentifiable accent.

As I sat quietly at the end of one of the tables closest to Silvestra, sipping on a beer I'd purchased elsewhere, one thought kept occurring to me:

What a bunch of loons.

Jade may have noticed the sardonic gleam in my eye, and from two seats away gave me a half-lidded warning glance, her mouth twitching ever so slightly in a wry grin. I silently raised the bottle of beer in my hand in a mock toast, and nodded in a manner to reassure her that no, I wasn't about to start a ruckus. Listening again to the author, a strange thought came to me like a creeping burglar in my head: I wasn't as drunk as I should be. A quick mental tally told me that I'd already imbibed more than enough alcohol to normally leave me in a state of incoherent stupor for the evening, yet here I was, tingling and burning, and although I felt a strong buzz that was wrapped around my brain, the dizziness and disorientation that should have accompanied it were completely absent. It was an entirely unfamiliar state of intoxication.

The food arrived without any fanfare, aside from the comments of "Yum" and "That looks good" one would expect. I'd ordered a plate of Onion Rings, which were served in a mangled heap of sliced ovals crusted with a beer batter, accompanied by a small white bowl of a strange, spicy mayonnaise dressing. Although I wasn't terribly hungry, I joined the happy throng of suddenly busy "Vampyres" (who were frantically removing fake fangs so that they could eat) as I slipped a sliver of fried onion through the sauce and bit down on it.

My tongue exploded with flavor, and my salivary glands gushed with a literally painful shock. The batter was paper-thin and crisp, with absolutely no subtlety in the amount of different spices that the cook had filled it with.

"Oh, my god," Jade said while cutting into a steak that looked like it had been ripped from a living, breathing cow not minutes before and then cooked mercilessly over an open flame. "You have to try this." She speared a slice of beef and delivered it with her regular grace onto my plate.

"Only if you have one of these," I said, handing her a bread plate with several onion rings heaped upon it. This seemed to have a chain reaction around the table, and the next few minutes were filled with flying hands and dishes, each person foisting pieces and chunks of their meals onto one another's plates, and before the maelstrom of food trading had finished I believe we had each sampled a bite of every platter. I grinned when the switching and swapping had ended, marveling that everything I'd nibbled had exhibited the strong, overpowering style of New Orleans. Any proper gourmet would have been horrified by the lack of delicacy that the chef had shown in creating this food, using heaps of pepper in various colors, mustard powder by the handful, paprika, and a hundred other ingredients to create a monstrous army of flavor that raped and pillaged your taste buds like an invading horde of wild Cossacks. My stomach opened wide inside me, and I found myself gobbling down the onions as fast as I could dunk them in the sauce, trying desperately not to look like a starving mongrel as I did so. Nobody seemed to notice—they were all brain-deep in their own meals and conversations.

My flavors may be severe, the presence suddenly spoke, nearly causing me to jostle my beer into Silvestra's lap, *but they also reflect my spirit, non?*

Mais oui, I replied, grinning as I finished the rings and sat back in the chair. *Never let it be said that your wares are anything less than intense, be they your wine, women, song, or food.*

The city seemed to laugh again, a sensation that obliterated any of the normal lull I experience after a good meal. My skin was on fire, and I had to fight an urge to jump upon the table, sing bawdy lyrics and smash the dishes with my boots before running away into the night.

No, not yet, the spirit said, like a mother scolding an impatient child. *You will burn, I assure you. But not yet.*

I glanced at my watch, stunned to find that it was already ten at night. When, then? I asked, feeling a touch frantic.

The night is truly young, Traveler, and the time to burn is not yet. A fire started too early will die if the wood is not ready.

We paid the checks in a flurry of denominations and ambled out the door. Some of the "Vampyres" were obviously logy from their meals, their strides languid. I waited until we got to the corner, following the group without question. Troy was in the lead, telling some private joke to several listeners, and their laughter infused the air with meaningless music as we approached a large white van. He fumbled a key into the lock, then cracked open the doors. The giggling mass entered single file, and the doors clanged shut with a melodramatic sound of finality behind us. The briefcase was uncomfortably nestled into my back, and I found my legs resting against a woman whose name I would never learn. Behind a steel grating, Troy entered the driver's seat to rousing cries.

"Let's go! C'mon, Father Troy!" "I'm fucking thirsty!" "Are we there yet?"

"Hold your goddamned horses, people," he said, and cranked the ignition. As the ride lurched into motion, I felt a prickling sensation interrupt the delicious warmth of both alcohol and the presence in my mind. I caught Matt looking away with a sudden twist of his neck, turning to stare at the back doors. He had obviously been watching me angrily.

And if looks could kill, I thought, *my skull would be splattered all over the inside of this van.* The city chuckled in my head, and I sighed, laying my intact head against the steel interior.

You [speak/think] in a musical tongue, Traveler. Many others have done so while in my arms.

I pondered a concept that occurred to me almost out of nowhere. It was suddenly lucid, like a moment of perfect clarity after being surrounded by a roiling ocean of fog. I paused, wishing dearly for a drink to banish the unsettling moment of sobriety, and then made up my mind.

May I write about you?

The city laughed in my head. It was a dismissive chuckle, like that of a woman being asked by a man whether skirts were drafty.

Do what you will. Many others have sung, written, and spoken my praises. When you go back, create what you will, how you will. It does not matter.

And then the city began to hum again, a song that coursed through me as the touch of a sleeping lover, a melody as soothing as the sound of rain and twice as hard to plot, while at the same time it goaded me, led me onward into the hazy mindset I'd grown accustomed to.

The van hit a pothole, eliciting shrieks and laughter from the party. Limbs were strewn helter-skelter throughout the interior, then jerked back and rearranged clumsily into positions that were less awkward or embarrassing. I found my left leg suddenly resting between both of Jade's and our eyes met across the darkness, an electric zap from her gaze to mine, palpable and fierce. I hooded my lids slightly and gave her a smile to convey the fullness of my hunger. Her own orbs registered surprise, and then the moment was gone. I snatched my leg back, and she shuffled herself to sit cross-legged, the two of us both guiltily glancing at Matt. We relaxed when it was evident that he'd been busy staring at the back of the van like some poor lost waif. I chuckled. *Fuck him.*

The ride screeched to a halt, and Troy slammed the little metal arm of the transmission into park with a flourish that was visible through the metal screen. "All out that's getting out," he spoke loudly.

Out we poured, a black-clad congregation of active and fluttering freaks. As I rearranged my clothing and satchel, we swarmed toward another anonymous brick building. I felt the thrumming of my heartbeat so strongly that it was like being pressed up against a 400-watt speaker cranked to full blast, invigorating and empowering. My skin was a piece of paper held inches above an open flame, heating, turning brown and brittle but not quite burning. So close, so very close . . .

I made my way toward the group, shaking and vibrating with expectant tension. At the door I noted that this was a prestigious nightclub, one that regularly booked popular live bands. The posted schedule flyer made me more than a little frustrated—two of my favorite musical acts would be playing at this very venue a week after I would be leaving. I finally moved to the door as the haphazard line of Goths in front of me entered the establishment.

The doorwoman was a chunky bitch, with hair the color of cold lead and a butch manner that told everyone *don't fuck with me*. Her face was made of chewed leather, and her mighty bosoms would have looked attractive, clad in a corset on a less massive maiden. As it was, she gave off an aura of squat aggression, as if she'd seen the worst life had to offer and stoically smashed her way through it.

She took my proffered identification with a practiced ease, handed it back after a cursory glance, and then studied a sheet of paper that was filthy with scrawled names and dates—apparently a list of people who would be allowed in free of charge.

"You want the bar, or the dance floor?" Her voice had the texture of asphalt, as if she smoked cigars chest-deep.

"Dance floor," I said quickly.

"Twenty dollars," she said, chewing a wad of gum with jaws that could likely bite through an inch-thick chain. The light glinted off of her earrings, grim hoops of steel as thick as a pencil.

"I was told my admission would be comped," I stuttered, suddenly nervous.

She snorted derisively, and slid a finger slowly down the list.

"What's your last name, again?"

"Livingstone," I said. A cold vine of doubt crept through my ribcage.

"Nope," she said, raising her frigid eyes to mine like a pair of loaded shotgun barrels. "Twenty dollars, or the bar is free."

Troy was directly behind me, looking awfully unsure of himself.

"Hey," I snapped while stepping back out and grabbing him by the arm. "I thought you said I'd get in for free."

"Yeah, well..." He stared at the ground and shifted his weight from one foot to the other, like a child being scolded in a classroom. "There was a misunderstanding. I can only get a couple folks in, and I already used that on three other people." He looked at me then, searched for any sign that I was going to happily brush away any hard feelings, but I left my countenance in a state of Fuck You. "Dude, I'm sorry. I'd pay your way in, but I don't have enough cash." He was as petulant as a toddler.

A tally of my pockets discovered only seventeen dollars.

"I was told my admission would be free," I repeated stonily. "If I'd known otherwise, I would have brought enough money to get in."

Troy glanced down the block at nothing, avoiding my gaze.

"Sorry, man," he said quietly. "I mean, the people I got in were folks who I owed it to...."

"Well," I interrupted, hoisting my briefcase, "I was told that I would be doing you a *favor* by trucking this god damned deadly weapon around." The zipper parted for my angry hand, and I pulled out just enough of the dagger for him to recognize it. "I don't normally cotton to bringing such things to establishments like this. Now what the fuck?"

His face blanched at the sight of the blade, and he pressed closer, one hand meeting mine to shove the implement back into seclusion.

"Holy shit," he whispered. "Why didn't you leave that in the van?"

Oof. I hadn't thought of that.

"I was told that I was to only turn this over to *you*," I hissed at him.

"Give me your bag," he said, and he backed away clutching the attaché to his chest. "I'm gonna go put this away. Uh... I'll be right back," he said, and darted toward the vehicle.

What the fuck ever, I thought before I turned back to the golem guarding the door. She raised her scraggly eyebrows at me, and I knew that if I gave her further grief, she would slam a meaty forearm through my skull like a piston, splattering my brains all over the street, and nobody in this town would even cough dismissively.

"Bar," I said lamely, then looked inside just in time to watch Jade enter the hallway to the dance floor. Fuck. I'd have to catch up with her later.

The joint was hopping. About fifty Goths and freaks populated the staggered and chaotically strewn tables, and I could hear more carousing from an upstairs lobby. I sidled to the bar, and dumped my forearms on the heavily lacquered wood.

"Hey, fucker."

I glanced to my right at the sound of a familiar voice, and was astonished by a familiar face. Lars was an old-school friend of mine from Dallas, about my height and lanky, with a profile that reflected his Nordic heritage—all angles and godly good looks. Even the onset of male pattern baldness had taken nothing from his natural advantages with women. Some guys are just too good looking, and a hairless scalp makes them sexually enticing. I'd often argued that it was because the profile of their skull evoked subliminal phallic images in the female brain. Lars usually counteracted his aura of perfection by growing his beard out and wearing biker clothing. He was older than me, but only by half a decade, and although I'd never discussed my theories with him, the guy was a Predator to the core. We'd partied many a night in Dallas together.

He was leaning against a bar in his leather jacket and black jeans, a dark bandanna covering his hairline and a cold beer in his hand. The lights of the bar reflected off of his ridiculously blonde beard, and I took his proffered handshake.

"What's up, Nordic Boy?"

Raising his eyebrows above a half-lidded, friendly gaze, he shook his head slowly and took a pull off of his beer.

"Not a lot, man." His voice was low and smooth. He always spoke with a languid tone, even when pissed off. It gave him a catlike air. "Just taking it easy in the Big Sleazy, that's all. What brings you to town?"

"Halloween, good times, women and sin." I plumped my ass down on the barstool and my overworked legs curled up in relief, every nerve whimpering pain. Lars signaled the bartender with one upraised finger and pointed at his beer, then held up two fingers. The bartender was a willowy and attractive brunette in her mid-twenties. She nodded, her eyes sparkling. It was obvious that she would love to take Lars into a back storeroom and ride his face like a unicycle seat. He seemed oblivious to her stare, and lit one of his tiny imported cigars.

"This your first time here?" he asked, puffing a cloud of sweetly fragrant smoke.

"Yeah." I lit one of my own cigarettes and surveyed the crowd. "Decided to check it out."

"What do you think, man?" he asked as our beers arrived, and gave the girl one of his blinding grins as he paid. She took his cash with a lingering brush of her hand on his, but if Lars ever knew his effect on women he'd never shown it. We clinked bottles.

"Thanks," I said after taking a gulp. "Uh, well, so far, I'm . . . Jesus, I'm overwhelmed in ways I haven't been in years."

Lars nodded, swallowed his drink and smiled faintly.

"Yeah, man, she does that to you."

It took a second for his statement to register, and when it did I choked on a mouthful of brew.

"What did you just say?" I asked, wiping my mouth hastily with a bar napkin.

"This city, man. She likes to overwhelm you every time. It's like, wow, here's everything you wanna do, everything you like, and it's all good, man. She's a big ol' bitch with perfect titties and an ass that could go all night." He pondered for a moment, reflecting on what, I could only guess. "I been coming back to Her for years. Came down here for the first time when I was seventeen, and I make it a point to return at least once a year and let it all hang out, man. She takes care of me, and the human soul needs a place to go where fear is a stranger."

I nodded, a little awestruck and on the cusp of confessing everything. Here was someone else I knew and trusted, and he seemed to have shared the same bizarre experience that I was having.

Lars slugged some more beer, then leaned over a puddle of condensation on the bar, playing a fingertip idly through it. When he spoke again, his voice was relaxed, but the most passionate I'd ever heard from him:

"She is a goddess of pain and pleasure
and the swampy sand in her belt measures
the theft of time.

The streets fill with baubles and beads,
the living and dead have needs
in her streets.

So I run a stick on the staves
Of iron and wander past graves
and rusted fences.

Mama New Orleans, please bless
This sinner with your spicy breath
And kisses.

I am drunk on your voodoo tonight
And my tears shine under gaslights
With no secrets.

I'll return when the time is right
And you call me to play through the night
But I'll miss you."

My face was frozen and my brain felt cudgeled as he finished. My voice was completely gone, and I had no words to use anyway. I had spent many a drunken night alongside Lars, but had never in all our time together even guessed that such deep currents could lie beneath his surface.

One of mine, the city murmured within me. *As are you.*

Lars looked up, smiling and shaking the moisture from his finger. "I wrote that the last time I was down here, about six months ago. That's what She's like, man," he said, and finished his beer. "When the world gets too sharp, too hard, too cold or too gray, I come back, man. I come back to this place, and she makes me alright again." Lars glanced at his watch, and then did a double take. "Fuck. Hey, good seeing you, but I have to meet some folks." He stood up and slapped me another handshake, this time a hard one. "Peace out. Just be careful with Her." He winked at me, and then he was out the door and gone, leaving me with an abrupt sense of *weird*. A mental image flashed through me, that Lars was *right now* getting on a giant black bird and flying back to Dallas . . . a place that I would also have to return . . .

A warm ribbon of pleasure wrapped around my neck and melted into my bloodstream, dissolving any thoughts I'd been creeping up on.

You are here, and that is all that matters. Revel and play, walk and be ready, for tonight you will be set alight, Traveler.

I drank some more of my beer and looked for any other familiar faces. Finding none, I noticed that many people were going up a stairway in the back of the bar, and decided to check it out. The steps led to a second floor with its own separate bar, and I noted at the top that people were traveling in and out of an open window. I ducked through the opening, and discovered myself on a rather large second story patio, whose only entrance and egress was a regular open pane, like in a living room of a house.

As is my usual intoxicated wont, I was sucked into conversations already in progress between people I'd never met. It usually helped if those people were good-looking women, and the deck had no shortage. I met some inebriated young lassies from Boston on a getaway trip, far from their boyfriends and husbands. I felt my grin grow. The burn was fast approaching. I could feel it, like a freight train slaughtering miles of track, still distant but discernible in the darkness. My senses began registering little things, delightful stimuli that made my teeth feel sharp or my skin ripple with lovely heat. Maybe now I would start letting the others see it in my eyes. Show my canines. Get slowly, smolderingly wild. Let the excitement bleed into my laugh as I finally ran a fingernail down the arm of a gorgeous stranger, lightly, and she giggled and cooed like a wild animal in rut. The music grew louder, I grew more inebriated.

"Want a shot?" A query from one of the dazzling blondes, with eyes the color of ice. She held a lime and a tiny glass of amber liquid.

"Without a doubt," I growled, but she tucked the drink away when I reached for it.

"Patience!" She tipped her head back, dropped the lime past succulent lips, and then poured the shot into her mouth. Her lips twisted into a tight, evil smile, and she grabbed the back of my head.

Our mouths met, and she gushed tequila over my tongue. When our lips parted, I was the sole owner of the lime. Her friends laughed, the balcony roiled, my heart raced and my mind reeled. We told jokes, the blonde and her friends slithered against me, and I eventually memorized their names.

After half an hour and a few more beers, I felt a sudden touch on my shoulder. Turning, I found Jade standing behind me with a stony expression as she held out both my briefcase and a shot of golden alcohol.

"Here," she said, thrusting both at me. "Troy wanted to buy you a drink, and he says he's sorry for earlier." I shouldered the familiar strap of my attaché and gently plucked the shot glass from her hand.

"No worries. Care to sip the top layer off?" I asked, smirking. Jade turned her head, crossing her arms.

"I'll be back later. You're hanging out, right?" Her voice conveyed a tiny sliver of anxiety, and I touched her shoulder carefully.

"What's wrong?"

"Nothing. Matt just wants to talk about 'us,' whatever the hell that is. Look, I'll be back, okay?"

"Let me know if you need anything," I called after her as she ducked back inside. I found that one of the Boston Blondes was raising her glass in a toast, and everyone slammed their beverage to seal whatever pact they'd made. I followed suit, and more tequila splashed across my taste buds like a gush of liquid wasps. Gasping, I wiped my mouth and leaned against the blonde named Eileen. "What did I just toast?"

"To a life without men!" the three busty and inebriated beauties yelled, laughing.

"I'll drink to that," I said. "Or, I, uh, did. Drink to that. Seeing as I'm only after *gorgeous women* tonight!" Nothing I said felt corny.

A war whoop from a passing gaggle of sorority girls answered my exclamation, and I leaned over the railing (noting the steel in question had been new around the time of President Roosevelt and therefore should *not* be leaned on quite so hard) to leer. Over the past two days a few strands of cheap purple beads had ended up inside my satchel, and I held these for the girls on the street to see.

"Behold!" I yelled, shaking the plastic baubles about. "These need a new home!" The lovelies in the avenue screamed and giggled, and two of them raced each other to see which could pull up her shirt first. The taller brunette won, not only baring her medium-sized, well-formed tits proudly but also grabbing the left one and squeezing it. I tossed two of the strands down.

"Hey, I already have these ones!" exclaimed the second girl.

"And I've already seen other tits tonight! What's your point?" This elicited boos from the females on the road as they turned away, and laughter from the fifteen or so people around me.

Thusly did the night progress. Surrounded by merriment I spoke to strangers, bought drinks for some, had drinks bought for me by others. On my way to the bathroom downstairs, I still did not feel as intoxicated as I should have. I'd had far too much alcohol, and not nearly enough food, yet all I felt was the equivalent of a four-beer buzz. My steps didn't wobble or sway, and there was no nausea.

After relieving myself, I happened upon Jade and Matt next to the top of the staircase. They hadn't noticed me, and I immediately walked the other way. I didn't like what I'd glimpsed in her eyes. They were very obviously having an argument, and I didn't need a hand puppet to spell out that my presence was unnecessary. Although I *was* involved, I wanted no part of the drama. I had faith in the promises of the city. I was in the clutches of a greater being, and an exhilarating feeling of hunger coursed through me with every heartbeat. Jade would be mine.

I drank. I cavorted. And the city began to speak one thought to me, through me, whispering it into my pores and bones, quietly, but faster and faster, like a lover teasing my thighs with light fingernails:

Wait.

My skin was on fire. The glow of the streetlights held a hazy attraction as I wrapped my fists around the guardrail of the upper porch. I knew that if I gripped any harder, my fingers would tear right through the aged metal. The air was a heady autumn wine, spicy and delicious, and each drag on my cigarette fired pure molten glass into my veins. Beautiful women surrounded me, wonderful beverages abounded, my cock a turgid weapon in my pants, seeking a target. God help any man who challenged me, as I would tear his spine out of his body and floss the crack of my ass with it before I dropkicked his liver against a brick wall. The pressure was unbearable, as if I were a plugged fire hose.

A tap on my shoulder spun me on my heel, hackles raised, with a grin of absolute hellraising lust. Jade stood with tears in her eyes and a flustered look that bespoke anger, though not at me. She'd obviously had harsh words with Matt, and as much as she had tried to portray herself both online and now in real life as an ice queen, I could tell that something he'd said had cut to the bone.

Her mouth opened, and then two things happened simultaneously.

"I want to go back to the hotel," she said, fighting to sound like a tough, impermeable bitch and failing just ever so slightly. A thread of pain filtered into her voice, and an undertone of anger.

At that moment, the city charged through me like a live wire suddenly switched from a trickle of voltage to full capacity. It was a command and a release at the same time, one thought, one word emphasized to an unshakable degree. It could not be argued, fought, or debated:

NOW. BURN.

My hands flew out and cupped Jade's cheeks in my palms. She started to duck away, but my arms locked fiercely, and I planted a kiss directly between her eyes, tasting the skin there ever so slightly.

"Yes, lovely," I growled, and flashed my teeth at point blank. "Burn with me. Let's tear this shit apart."

She pulled away from me, a reflex from having my nose too close to hers, but I could see curiosity steal over her features. She opened her mouth as if to ask a question, and then closed it. In return, I put her hand to my heart, which was pounding not rapidly, but strong enough for her to feel it.

"Your energy," she chuckled. "Wow. What have you been doing?"

"Come on," I said, licking my teeth. "Let's get this party started."

Leading her by the hand, we ducked back through the open window, down the stairs, just enough time to give fleeting goodbyes to her fellows. The front door was in sight when I felt a sudden tug from her end of our joined hands.

"Wait, I need a shot of tequila," she said, and I followed her. After the bartender took her order, Jade looked at me quizzically, and leaned closer. "What's gotten into you?" she asked.

"I'll explain later," I said as the tequila arrived. "Let's just say I'm feeling fucking great. It's time to go out and dance in the ashes, and rip this world up."

"Uh . . . are you okay?"

"Never better," I cackled, as my hand lifted the amber fluid. I used my free arm to pull her close. "A toast. Here's to two Pedestrian Wolves out in the jungles," I said, and we touched our glasses together before slamming the alcohol down. She immediately stuck a lemon into her mouth, sucking hard, and offered me one as well. I shook my head, enjoying the acidic and torturous afterburn of the liquor in an entirely new way. I swallowed once, twice . . . I was still riding that buzz, but not to the point of pain.

"Let's go," I said, a new thought on my mind. "Your hotel or mine?"

"Mine," she said, looking at the top of the bar. "Matt's being a dick. I . . ." She shook her head. "God, why does every guy I fuck want me to be his 'girlfriend'? What happened to good sex between friends?"

I chuckled, grabbed her hand, and motioned toward the door with my head. The air outside was cool and humid, a comfortable temperature that wicked away sweat and replaced it with a fine mist of condensation. We walked across the street and lit up a cigarette each.

"First off," I said, leaning back against a wall, flooded by the firework explosions of need, "I think you know fair and well that I'm *not* out to make you my girlfriend."

"I know that," she said, and hugged me. I had to fight for control as a wide variety of urges struggled against me. "I wasn't talking about you. It's just . . . Jesus, I've had this happen so many times recently . . . "

"So what's Matt's damage?"

"He thought he was coming down here *with* me. I still don't know where he got this shit. He knows I *don't* want a relationship with *anyone!* Gah!" She kicked the wall viciously.

"Okay, fuck it," I said, straightening up and trying to figure out which direction I was facing. "Let's see how trashy we can get. I'm burning like a bonfire here, and this is too good a feeling to waste."

"Okay," she said. "Shall we get another Grenade?"

"I'm game if you are."

"Which way to Bourbon Street, I wonder?" She turned to look down the avenue in the same disoriented manner as I had been.

This way.

Feeling a shove, I took Jade's hand and urgently led her down the street.

My breath came in deep draughts. Each step felt incredible as we made our way back to Bourbon. Colors were lucid and bright in this blackest time of the night, as if I had taken several hits of pure LSD. Laughing aloud, walking with a grin to kill by, my hands fleetingly touched her body—my arm about her shoulder and pulling her close to tell a joke, or running my fingertips along the back of her neck. Although she was unsettled at first, eventually my touches and utterances brought a smile, then a hungry grin back to her succulent lips.

We rounded a corner, and there it was again—the cacophonous crowd of the world famous Bourbon Street. At the corner we took it all in: A storm of confetti, beads and detritus flew through the air above a multitude of multicolored strangers, a whirling din of inebriated tourists whipped into frenzy.

I heard Jade take a deep breath of awe.

"This," she said, "Is what Hell must look like."

The presence burned a hearty laugh at her words.

"So let's go," I said with an evil leer, and away we went.

Down through the milling, screaming, howling throng! Drowning in a swirling torrent of people clutching, rocking, dancing, puking, and drinking! Immersed! Baptized in bumping, swaying bodies, the odor of vomit, and sin as far as the eye could see! From dark of night to ridiculously well illuminated streets we ran, and the instant my boots hit the avenue, that tripping high blasted me again! Naked tits and smashed glass, beads descending on crowds below, thrown by lecherous throngs from the rooftops! Everywhere, policemen desperately trying to look like they weren't seeing any of this, the only cops on earth who actively avoided my gaze!

All the while, my feet met the earth like the rolling, unstoppable wheels of a juggernaut, crushing the cups and trash beneath me like hapless worshippers. In less than a minute I was misted in strange fluids flying from the crowd. Hands locked together, Jade and I first hit a tiny bar, little more than a one-room. All of the patrons were over-aged frat boys and sorority sisters, and the bartender looked like his head might blow up from dealing with the torrent of fucked up assholes who came in. He was a swarthy older gent, around fifty or so, with a scraggly red beard on a head as bald naturally as my shaved one.

"What?" he screamed above the raucous clamor, without bothering to affect politeness.

"Two shots of vodka!" I screamed back, also eschewing any pretense.

"Here!" he yelled with the same inflection he might have used while stabbing someone in the neck, and slammed two dirty shot glasses down. After wiping one hand on his stained jeans, he grabbed a bottle of Stolichnaya and deftly pour two overly full helpings, his grip as steady as the tides. Once the glasses were slopping over, he smacked his other hand on the bar, palm up, and gave me a *Fuck you, buddy* stare from across the bar. "Eight!"

I reached into my pocket and grabbed what turned out to be a ten-dollar bill, and threw it at his face. He snatched it out of the air with the speed of a striking snake and pocketed it, then spun away without even a backward hint of a glance. I slid one of the glasses to Jade, and the vodka drooled over the rim. Raising our shots, I decided it was a perfect time to use my regular toast.

"May we get what we want, may we get what we need, but *God fucking help us* if we get what we deserve!"

"Amen!" she shouted back, and we slammed the shots, grinning and shuddering. After wiping her mouth with the back of her hand, she pulled me close and bit down hard on the lobe of my ear.

"Hmm, this is a 'burn,' you said? I like it," she crooned through her teeth, then released and kissed my neck. "Let's go get a fucking Grenade and light this shit up."

"Rock on," I snarled, and we dived back into the flowing, screaming and whooping Damned.

As we elbowed and shouldered our way through, we burst into a crowd cheering expectantly up at a rooftop, where patrons waved fists full of beads, tossing them down to those who earned them. I spied several women in their late thirties doling out strands, and released Jade's hand to pause and unzip my slacks. I locked my gaze with a brunette fifteen feet above. With semi-rigid cock in hand, I shook my jewels at her and swiveled my hips.

"Give me some fucking beads!" I hollered loudly enough to be heard above the din. She war whooped and flung a purple strand down. As I watched the loop of plastic baubles wend its way through the air, I followed the trajectory almost by instinct and ducked a few inches expertly to catch them on my cock.

As I zipped back up, the crowd applauded and cheered wildly. Jade turned around, having missed the spectacle, just in time to see me zip back up and tuck the beads into my pocket.

"What the hell did you just do?" she asked as two cackling college boys patted me on the shoulder and uttered incoherent congratulations.

"Nothing," I said smugly, and we aimed our steps toward the neon sign a block away. It advertised the strongest drink in New Orleans.

Friday
?:?? Later still
No fucking idea.
I have officially written off my soul as damned.

Jade returned from the crowded stand, holding two Grenades in their fluorescent yard-long containers. She handed me one as I snapped shut the case of my PDA.

"To good times with good friends!" she toasted.

"I'll drink to that!" I roared, and guzzled half the beverage without mercy.

We edged our way away out of the whirling masses, and eventually found ourselves walking alone through the blackness of night. I was charging like a power generator, and the alcohol finally took its toll on my brain. I still didn't feel dizzy, didn't feel like puking, but invisible fire crackled across my skin.

Your worship is excellent, The city spoke. *You worship me well, Traveler.*

Thank you, I thought back. *You are a goddess unlike any I have read about. Thank you for showing me life.*

"Free!" I cackled and tossed my now-empty container into the briefcase. "Fearless! I am fucking alive!"

"Alive!" Jade chimed in. "Fuck everything! We're on fire!" Her voice was now as throaty and jubilant as my own.

"Yes! Fuck the world!"

"Fuck the haters!"

"Fuck the critics!"

"Fuck the sheep!"

"Fuck the possessive lovers!"

"Yes!" she said with emphasis, and tossed her Grenade container into an already overflowing trash bin as we approached two drunk college boys walking in the other direction. "*Fuck* them! I'm tired of sleeping with guys that want to be my boyfriend!"

The frat boys looked at us funny as they approached, and I bared my teeth at them. One was a little taller than I, but considerably less stocky. The other was a shorter Hispanic lad, with a goatee and all of nineteen years under his belt. The taller one looked like he was about to comment on Jade's proclamation, and that his words were going to be crass. His mouth opened, and he jerked a thumb in our direction.

"Quiet, cretin," I snarled, pushing my face toward his. "Keep on walking."

"The fuck?" he said, backing away to safety, and all the flame went out of his eyes. "What's your problem?"

"Ah, ah, ah!" I said, and wagged a warning finger while I matched his backwards walk, chasing him slowly away. "No problem! You and your buddy just keep fuckin' walking, and have a good night!"

"Jesus Christ, dude, chill out," the guy said, and the two of them continued away.

Jade's face showed shock as I walked back, put an arm around her waist, and led her down St. Charles.

"Wow," she said.

"Hmm?"

"I just . . . do you do that a lot?"

"Do what?"

"What you just did," she said gesturing behind us. "Do you regularly pick fights with strangers?"

I chuckled, and then let out a war whoop, throwing my fists in the air.

"Let them come! Let the bastards wash over me, and try to erode me! Man born of woman cannot kill me! Damn you! I sang on the mountaintop and my scream held back the tides! The stars answer my command, and my cock is pure dy-no-mite! I am . . . "

Jade put her arms around my neck and slammed me up against a concrete wall, bit my chin and growled.

"Look, you're going to get us arrested, godly cock or no," she cautioned, pressing her lovely curves against me.

No, you're not.

"No, I'm not," I said, with my hands on her ass and nibbling an earlobe. "But I'll tell you one thing—I *am* about to abduct you and spend the rest of the night fucking your brains out."

Her breath hitched, and I could feel the tension of indecision for an instant in her muscles. Then she pulled back to look me directly in the eye.

"I'm yours tonight."

Yours, as promised . . .

"Done deal," I whispered. "Still going back to your hotel?"

"Only long enough to get some stuff. I'd rather not be around anyone but you right now."

I could see trepidation in her eyes as we turned to cross Canal, two drunken wanderers cavorting through the darkness, a pair of midnight wolves playing and biting.

In the hotel elevator, my hands found purchase on the firm curve of her ass, and the sweet plush heat of her neck tasted of salt and lust. Jade went into her hotel room. A few seconds later, she emerged looking unshaken and as inebriated as I felt, with an overstuffed knapsack. A sense of urgency was upon us—every touch we gave each other was a promise of more to come. At the front of the hotel, I hailed a cab immediately, and we departed posthaste for my own room. Inside the lightless interior of the cab, our hands and mouths lit each other's nerves up like neon circuits of reckless abandon. When the taxi stopped at my hotel, I tipped the driver generously and hefted her backpack as though it were filled with crumpled newspaper. Hand in hand we nearly ran up the stairs, flirting and burning the entire way. I fumbled at the door with the passkey, my actions slightly hampered by the delicious caresses and gropes of the purring vixen behind me, and then opened the portal, ready to bodily evict my roomie and his wife if they were present. My mental processes were disjointed, but I knew that the night still held plenty of hours before dawn.

The room was blessedly, wonderfully vacant.

This was the last truly coherent, linear memory that the night would give: My brain slowly succumbed to the alcohol as the door clicked shut behind me. A moment later her hands were upon my hips.

"Let's get started," she said, reaching around to the front of my pants and deftly undoing my belt.

She stood naked before me, the most incredibly feral expression on her face, blazing red hair cascading across her collarbones, eggshell-white skin faintly luminescent in the glow of the lamp. The smattering of haphazard freckles across her shoulders made her look like something wild from the South American continent. She took two steps backwards and folded her legs into a coiled position to kneel on my mattress. Every nuance of her posture invited me to join her.

"What's your safety word?"
    She wiggled against me as her hands stroked my cock none too gently.
    "I don't have one that I usually use . . . "
    "How about 'feather'?"
    "That'll work."

Yes, let it flow, tumble and clench, feel it flow through you, Traveler. Your worship is [absolutely untranslatable concept]. *Alive, you are sublime and I will always treat my own as my own and this is as it has been and as it shall be let it be forever, and my arms will always open to you . . .*

"Oh yeah?" Her grin was as wicked as wicked gets, and her feet planted firmly in my stomach in an attempt to shove me off the bed, onto the floor. Before she could push, my hands grabbed her ankles and I pulled her legs apart hard, my waist sliding down between her clenching thighs.

"Yeah," I retorted, but it came out as a half-snarl.

With a strength I would not have guessed, she twisted her waist, effectively using her thighs to fling me sideways. My right leg shot out, but too late! One flailing hand caught the edge of the lamp, and it followed me down to the carpet.

I rolled into the impact and somersaulted backwards, ending on my hands and one knee, feeling hot and outrageously excited as she darted to the opposite edge of the bed.

"Come on. Come and get me," she said, licking her lips.

Pinned beneath me on the floor, face down, she fought with an incredibly strong resolve. My right hand had her by the hair, my left clamping her wrists together in front of her face. She was breathing deeply, hard, as was I, both of us dripping with sweat and sporting bruises.

With my knees firmly holding her legs apart and her ass pushing against my stomach, I pulled back on her hair and shoved into her hard. Part of me was worried that I might hurt her, but she still hadn't said the safety word.

She was so wet that I slid into her feeling nothing but heat and taut muscles. We both gasped, and as I pulled back and shoved into her again, she let out a low moan, bucking back against me, engulfing me.

Now against the wall, her legs locked into mine, facing me, with green eyes blazing and a perfect rhythm between us, her feet completely off the floor, our hips rocking in tandem, stroking, clutching, gasping, biting, scratching, wild . . .

Cold beer, both of us slick with perspiration, lying back on my mattress. Not a denouement, but a sweaty, gasping break.

Where the fuck did I get this beer?

Buried in her, wrapped in her again. All thought slowly melting together, tripping on overload, our limbs and skin joining, melting together as one entity pleasing itself. I can feel her dripping down my thighs, mingling with the slick sweat there, her internal muscles crushing me with each stroke, her teeth gripping the muscles of my neck, and the orgasm tears me the fuck apart, suddenly, mercilessly, my skull fracturing and blowing apart under the relentless flood of animal delight, spiraling into oblivion . . .

On top of her again, relentlessly continuing like gluttons for this sensation.

We twist and flip, muscles straining, and now she rides me, her breasts in my hands, rocking, thrusting, gasping . . .

Losing my mind in an orgasm that is cruelly dry, as I have no further reserves left to squeeze from my overworked loins . . .

Falling.

Releasing . . .

Into darkness.

CHAPTER TWELVE

I stood under a sky the color of dead steel as it whirled in a furious, flashing storm. On all sides, the bayou stretched, the water even murkier than the scene above, and far off in the distance I could make out groves of trees. I was naked in the swamp, my feet finding purchase on an unidentifiable kind of sandbar, so narrow that I could not take a step in any direction without submerging my feet to the ankle in that brackish, silvery fluid.

A crash of lightning punctuated the creation of a waterspout to my right, thicker than a sequoia, roaring and swirling angrily. I used my elbow to keep the fluid out of my eyes, and fell to my knees in this malicious wind, praying that I would be safe. With the same soul-battering noise, another tornado of water sprang up to my left, and then another in front of me. They twisted and gnarled into serpentine, destructive columns that changed shape, sucked up fluid and dead tree branches and filth and channeled it all into the clouds above them. The terminus of each column became a section of unclean black sky, roiling and putrescent, like an infected boil that would not drain.

She rose from the water, her giant head dwarfing my puny body. Not silvery, her hair was mottled black and grey, filthy and decrepit, wild and flying in the wind. The sandbar shook as she emerged, floating out of the bayou like a terrible embodiment of Lilith. Her torso was naked but a waterspout clung to her like clothing, and her face was hidden behind a fog of impermeable shadow. Only her eyes were visible, which glowed with a rotten and malevolent incandescence.

That gaze met mine, and although I could not see her mouth, I could sense that she was grinning. Not smiling, but twisting her mouth upward and baring her teeth. She held her arms out to her sides with *moss and*

filth and

trash *dripping from them, slowly rotting off and splashing back down into the water by where her feet should have been, but her legs simply terminated into stalks plunging down into the depths.*

"Traveler," she roared with the wind as her voice, and I could not defend myself against her power when she called my true name. The mere utterance yanked me forward like a marionette, and I was stricken with an icy bolt of panic. "You are mine," she leered, her voice raging through the air without competition. "Mine and you would do well to give yourself over with no argument."

Although my soul was composed of pure terror, deep within my chest
I felt a fluttering,
a fighting tiny furred animal in my ribcage, snarling and snapping.
No.

I would rebel, I would not be purchased, nor would I be owned. Submission was not in my soul. It was something that I fought against as a rule and even in the face of a goddess. I would not kneel.

She stopped for a moment, and the tableau froze—the clouds ceased their tumult, the water went as flat as glass, and the dancing waterspouts collapsed back into the swamp without leaving ripples to mark their passage. Her gaze was white, hot light, and I could feel her muscles coiling, gathering, angrily bunching together in preparation . . .

CHAPTER THIRTEEN

I woke into a world of pain.

My eyes were crusted firmly shut; the headache began stabbing me even before I opened my lids, two thick rusty railroad spikes that hammered into my eye sockets from merciless mallets. I lifted my palms to the source of the pain, but that turned out to be a hideous mistake—each of my shoulders voiced a chorus of agonies with the movement. Bruised, strained, abused muscles and joints all screamed in twelve-part harmony. I felt as though I'd been hit with acute arthritis overnight. Hands over my eyes, I clenched my teeth and rolled over, pulling my legs into a fetal position to stave off the pain, but that proved to be yet another error on my part—my legs were worst of all. Each one reported to me that through the prior evening's revelry I had done serious damage to them. Of course, clenching up in such a manner smashed my bladder with pressure, and with no small amount of horror I realized I would have to *get up and use the toilet* if I didn't want to piss all over the bed. After a few seconds of debating the pros and cons, I experimentally pried open one eyelid. This resulted in ultimate proof that my headache *could* get substantially worse. Eyes shut again; I tried not to rouse the sleeping redhead as I tenderly managed to get my feet to the floor, and then stood up. The fanfare of Hell sung by demons in my skull climaxed as I did so, throwing long strands of razor wire down my spine, through my nerves, and into my every pore. I was left breathless and trembling like a man teetering on the edge of death.

In my self-imposed darkness I slowly groped to the bathroom, feeling with my bare feet and outstretched hands. I refused to relax my eyelids even one iota, fearful of another bout of blinding torture. It was like walking up the beach in the opening scene of a movie about World War II, being mercilessly riddled with hot lead. My fingers found the door, half-open, and it clicked shut behind me with the deafening sound of a huge, rusty portcullis. Only when I was sure that the light switch was in the "off" position did I open my eyes fully to blessed darkness. Groping around, I located the toilet bowl and carefully aimed for the center of the target. The stream of caustic fluid that burst from me smelled like something from the bladder of a dog or cat.

After the torrent subsided, the pain I felt was still horrific. My skin felt absolutely filthy from head to toe, as if I were coated with dried grease. Fumbling about, I managed to turn on the shower and adjust the temperature in a ham-fisted way. When the spray was almost hot enough to boil off my skin, I tenderly hoisted myself into the tub. My hands yanked the curtain shut, and I curled up on the floor of the shower, shuddering from the mixture of heat, nausea, and ever-present pain. After a minute or two, I felt some of the filth and putrescence that saturated my body begin to melt away. While I remained prone, my hands located a bar of cheap hotel soap, and with a quivering grip I began to rub it across my skin aimlessly. Everything felt tainted, burned, crushed, and hideously mangled in some way, and I could not blame anyone but myself for the state that I was in.

True, Traveler, the city noted in a manner that made my fucking skull feel like it was about to burst like a rotten melon. *You asked. I gave. You are wise for recognizing your folly.*

With all due respect, I replied, digging my fingertips into my head with almost enough force to crack bone, *will you kindly pipe the fuck down?*

The presence retreated, leaving only its familiar melody barely discernible in my mind, and my head slumped to the fiberglass, breathing through my mouth to avoid snorting water up my nose. Droplets formed on my tongue, and I reflexively swallowed.

Yes, said the presence in a much more subdued manner than before. *Drink water. Your body is in dire need of it.*

I spent the next half hour on the floor of the shower, alternately dozing dreamlessly and waking to gulp a mouthful of water from the streams pouring down. My body was floating in a void, without light or sound aside from my own labored breathing and the streams of water as they splashed across my skin. In tiny increments, the pain began to subside to a more muted ache, the combination of heat and moisture leaching the toxins and damage from the cells I'd spoiled. It wasn't until the water finally began to lose temperature that I carefully clambered to my feet, still wincing but feeling slightly better.

Rather than turning on the light, I cracked the door open and let the morning sun filter in as I used up all the towels. Part of my brain noted that my roommate would soon be awake, and I'd once again left him nothing to dry off with. That section of my mind was swiftly beaten into submission with belts and lead pipes by the rest of my brain, none of which gave a rat's ass. I stumbled, squinty-eyed, back to the bed and flopped down next to Jade, who mumbled and spooned up to me without waking.

With the glow of the rising sun oozing through the closed curtains of the room and no reason to stay conscious, my head met the pillow with outrageous force, and the darkness that took me was blessedly without dreams.

Sleep was extremely difficult to maintain. Sweating, shivering, and praying for death is no way to spend a day beside a lover, but we rested our bones until the sun had meandered its way past noon.

At about two I woke to Jade moving against me in a manner that intimated possible interest in more than mere snuggling. Her skin was soft and warm, and she wiggled again, eliciting a response from my own body. I kissed the skin behind her ears.

"Awake?"

"Mm hmm," she purred, and reached a hand back to fondle me gently. Her fingers were deft, and soon I was fully aroused, letting my hands wander in her deliciously supple curves. Our foreplay was the wordless, comfortable kind that happens the morning after. We both moved slowly, so as not to jar one another and create any bursts of pain in our wracked bodies.

After a few more minutes, I turned over and retrieved a condom, marveling internally that more than half of the box was gone. As I rolled it on, she also leaned over the side of the bed and retrieved a tiny black plastic bottle.

"Here," she said, pressing it into my palm and laying back down. "Use some of this." I inspected the tiny white writing on the bottle: **Silicone lubricant**. I undid the cap and smoothed a couple of drops across the head of my cock, more than enough to make up for any dryness she might be experiencing. As I climbed back into bed, careful to not get any of the lube on the sheets, she spooned up to me again, this time a little more aggressively. Her hand found my erection and deftly maneuvered me in a manner that I was not expecting, pressing my tip first against, then into her ass.

"*Fuck*," I gasped, wrapping my arms around her from behind, my eyes slamming shut from the overwhelming sensation of crushing pressure.

"Hold on a sec," she whispered, halting the motion of her hips as the muscles inside her tightened to a point where I could not have moved if I'd wanted to. "Just be still for a moment." She took a deep breath and then turned her head to kiss my neck.

"Is this hurting you?" I whispered, quivering from the new sensations. In reply, she made a noise that was a half sigh, half moan, and then rocked her hips, shoved back on me, sliding and taking me fully in one slow, smooth plunge. I gasped and shuddered, kept my body motionless as she pulled away from me, running over me like a clenched fist, then driving backward toward me again as slowly as the first time.

"God, that feels good," she gasped, reaching behind her to grab my hip and guide me to match her motion. I found myself utterly speechless, aside from gasping under the onslaught of stimulation, and my hand found her throat. I pressed my thumb and forefinger to either side of her windpipe in a move I'd done with prior lovers several times, pushing down hard enough to restrict the blood flow in the two major blood vessels there without impeding her breath. She shivered without pausing her slow, tight strokes, and made a noise in my ear that was soft and scorching.

After a few minutes of this, I was literally fighting to keep myself from losing all control. She enveloped me again, the curves of her ass pressing deliciously against my groin. I shuddered hard, biting my tongue to hold myself back.

"Are you alright?" she murmured.

"God, yes," I said quietly, my throat barely allowing the words out. "I just . . . this is so good . . . "

As she pulled away from me again, she reached behind my head and pulled my mouth against the side of her neck. As I bit down, she gasped and started moving faster.

"Come with me," she ordered, and I felt that last bit of restraint dissolving. "God, please, yes . . . "

Our orgasms hit hard, like being smashed in the back of the head with a baseball bat—but not painful, only shockingly intense. I couldn't breathe.

I couldn't think. My eyelids were welded shut, and it felt like my soul was flowing out of me, into her, as we shuddered and gasped and shook.

A few minutes later we carefully disengaged, and I washed up with only a modicum of consciousness before stumbling back to bed and spiraling into sleep the second my head hit the pillow, my arms draped across the softly dozing redhead.

The light was different when I next cracked my eyes open. Jade was on her back, stretching like a cat, and turned to look at me.

"Ah, Jesus," she said, running a hand down my arm. "Good morning, I guess."

"Nungh," I announced, and wiped thick grit from my eyelashes before looking at the clock. "More like 'Good Afternoon'. Is it really almost four?"

"Yeah," she said, standing up and pulling on some pants. I could hear my roommate and his wife snoring away upstairs, a harmonious tandem of buzz saws. "God, where are my socks? I need to find out when I'm meeting with the others. We're supposed to go on a ghost tour after a meeting of the Houses."

"Houses?"

"Each area we're in has a 'Court'," she explained while stepping into her underwear. "I'm in the Court of Sandalphon, for instance. A court is basically a group of people who all share the same belief system, and you can have members spread out all over the place. On the other hand, a House is geographically centered, and has members from a mix of Courts. I'm of House Atasha, of the Court of Sandalphon."

"More vampiric shenanigans," I said as we gathered clothing from the floor. "So what's this House Meeting about?"

"Uh, well, we discuss various ongoings in the community, and, er . . . " She was looking a little flustered as she pulled bra on and fumbled with the snaps in the back.

"Is this the kind of thing that you're not supposed to talk about with non members?" I asked with a wry grin.

"Kinda," she nodded, and then stepped into her jeans.

"That's fine," I said evenly, and then picked up a tank top I hadn't worn yet.

Why do you need so much?

I paused, the shirt limp in my hand like a dead weasel.

Say what?

You take so much. That [briefcase and all the various accoutrements inside of it] *slung over your shoulder. Your clothing. Everything in that wallet in your pocket, and your electric writing tablet. You encumber yourself with so many things. Why not walk free?*

Jade went over to the bathroom to straighten her clothing as I stared at the satchel. Inside were so many tools of my daily life. For years I had stuffed it full of various implements or removed them as necessary: toiletries, papers that I might need at work, and so forth. Going anywhere without it was unthinkable.

Leave it, the presence said, and it seemed a command. *Take only your money and something to cover your skin. Walk in me as I am meant to be walked in.*

After mulling it over for a moment, I dropped the shirt and reached for my leather jacket. By the time Jade had hastily stuffed a few things into her backpack, I was wearing some fresh slacks, my boots, my leather jacket, and my fedora. Shirtless and with my bare torso showing, I felt somewhat silly. Still, it was a comfortable getup, and when I checked the mirror the ensemble seemed to work well. At the same time, my face reflected the exhaustion and bone-weary aches of my body. Somewhere during the revelries of the night, I had burned something inside me down to a cold cinder.

You shall walk in me, Traveler, and you shall be rekindled.

"So, back to your hotel first?"

"Yeah," Jade said, hefting her pack, having surrendered the idea of brushing her hair, which was wild and uncontrollable in the humidity. "You want to take a cab, or what?"

"Have you ridden the railcar yet?"

"No, but I'd like to."

"Cool. Let's hit it. You got everything?"

"Yep," she said, wiggling her oversized backpack. "You?"

My PDA was in my jacket. I gave my briefcase one last look where it lay, at the foot of my bed.

Not needed. I shall take care of you, my own.

"Yeah, let's go," I said, and we wandered out into the dying daylight.

After we'd waited a few minutes on the hotel's grassy median, the railcar loaded us on with many other travelers. We stood, laced our wrists into the worn leather straps bolted to the car, and rocked against other passengers as its wheels carried us through the city. The car disgorged us back onto Canal Street, which was now so familiar to me that I considered it my true north. We painfully hiked back down between the towering, cracked buildings.

Saturday
2:30 pm
Hotel Parc St. Charles

Everything in my entire body is screaming. Every breath and shaking movement brings painful reminders of recent debauchery. This trip has degenerated into a gruesome game of stamina. I cannot give in, and Nola will not stop gleefully beating and hammering at my kidneys, brain, tongue, heart. I can only hope to maintain my mettle, to continue this journey for one last day. May the gods prop me upright one final night.

"Hey," she called as she walked out of the bathroom, freshly scrubbed and sporting a stylish pair of towels around her waist and her hair. Her breasts, naked and pink, sported a rash of darker spots where our carousing had marked her skin. I would have ogled her hungrily, naked from the waist up, but I couldn't even muster a single twinge of sexual need. I felt ridiculously exhausted on all fronts.

"Feeling better?"

"Ugh," she said, bending at the waist to shake her hair out of the towel. "God, you wore me out last night."

"I'm not feeling like a spring chicken either." I flopped backwards onto the bed and stared at the ceiling. Jade turned on the television and a quietly babbling weatherman told of blah blah thunderstorm blah blah. The gentle vibration in my mind was calming, but I still felt beaten and wrung out.

I dozed at this point, at least partially. My brain completely shut down and my eyelids drooped.

She sat next to me, and my eyes instinctively snapped open from the motion of the mattress. Smiling demurely, she again attempted to pull a brush through the tangles of her hair.

"You okay?" she asked. I sat up, rubbing my eyes and stifling a yawn.

"Yeah. How long was I asleep?"

"Only a couple of minutes." She winced as the brush snarled into her tresses, still wet from the shower. "Can you get me some of that hair tonic in the bathroom?" I stood, stretching my arms, and felt the tendons within them pop like strings breaking on a guitar. After retrieving a clear plastic bottle of detangler from the bathroom, I walked back and took the brush from Jade's hand.

"Hey," she said, and snatched at the bottle as I tucked it out of her reach. "I need that."

"I know. Lie down on your back, and I'll take care of it."

She did so, looking at me funny as I made the quick semicircle to the other side of the bed. Once there, I kneeled next to her head and spread the wild mass of her mane across the covers before uncapping the tonic. I applied a liberal sheen of it to my palms, oily and smelling of floral essences.

"You're only supposed to use a little of that," she giggled, peering up at me and clasping her hands over her stomach.

"Quiet, you." I began using my fingers to knead the fluid into her tresses, and carefully avoided any motion that would worsen the situation. Further tangling would have given her dreadlocks. After I could feel the slick liquid throughout the mass, I grabbed the brush and began at the tips of her locks, forcing the hairs apart as cautiously as I could.

"Are you alright?" she asked quietly.

"Hmm?"

"You've been awfully quiet today."

"Just really tired. This trip has been amazing so far, but I think I may have overdone it a bit." *And I'm in the thrall of the strangest experience of my life*, I silently added. "I think I can go another night, but part of me wants to lay down on the floor and sleep for a week."

"Yeah, I'm pretty sore too," she said. "God, I can't wait to tell the people back home about all this." She shut her eyes and took a couple of deep breaths. "Mmm. That feels good."

"Well, it'll take me a few more minutes to make this wreck you call a head of hair go away, but what do you want to do after this?"

She slapped my arm playfully.

"Shut up, dick. You helped my hair get that way, remember?"

"I plead the fifth, ma'am."

"Well, I'm really hungry. Wanna go get a bite to eat before we meet the rest of the group?"

My stomach sank claws of red-hot hunger into my spine at the thought of any kind of food at all.

"God, yes. I could eat a whole bull moose right now."

"Me too. And I really need a Bloody Mary."

"A whole moose and a ten-gallon drum of Bloody Marys. Where can we get that?"

She snickered, rubbing her eyes.

"Well, I wanted to see the river while I was here," she said. "It's down at the end of Canal, they have this bunch of shops called the Riverwalk. Wanna see if we can find something there?"

"Sure," I said. "Did you want me to come along with you when you hook up with the rest of the group?"

"Yeah," she said with an enthusiastic inflection that told me she wasn't just being polite. "Most of them seem to like you."

"Cool," I said, and patted her shoulders. "You really made this vacation for me so far, babe. I hope you don't mind if I tag along with you for the night?"

Jade sat up and gave me a soft, curvaceous hug.

"This is the best time I've had in a while," she breathed in my ear. "I'm glad we finally got to know one another in person."

"In the biblical sense as well," I chuckled.

"Yeah. Don't worry about the others. I have to fly out tomorrow morning at six, so let's go have a last night of this party." She disengaged the embrace, swinging her legs over the edge of the bed and getting to her feet. I did the same, lighting yet another cigarette and noting that my last pack was halfway empty. I wasn't sure I had enough cash to get another. For once, the hunger in my gut outweighed my nicotine addiction.

You will be provided for.

"You ready?" She tossed her freshly brushed mane out of her face, and I nodded in answer to her question and wordless acknowledgement to the presence as we exited the hotel room.

The sun had set and the air was thicker than chowder with threats of rain. I donned my fedora and held the door open for Jade. A doorman in front of the hotel saw us and smiled, his teeth impossibly white in contrast to his pitch-black skin.

"Can I get you folks a cab?" His voice penetrated the noise of the traffic like a clear note from an oboe. Before I could say anything, Jade hooked her arm through mine, guiding me away.

"No, thanks, we were just going to walk," she explained cheerfully.

We were? I thought as sharp jabs of ache shot through my legs. *Oh, Jesus.* My knees already felt like they were filled with shards of glass, and my feet were still throbbing from the night's escapades.

"Looks like it might rain," I said instead, peering upwards. Roiling clouds the color of old lead stuck to the sky like breath from a dying dragon. I decided to suck up the pain and venture onward without complaint.

"Yeah," she said as she eyed the churning clots overhead. "Well, if it does we can duck into the first place we see. God, it's probably snowing in Ohio."

We wandered through the streets, our feet eating up sidewalk and spitting it out behind us. We made idle chatter about one another's lives. Neither of us wanted to face what we were skirting carefully in the conversation: That for both of us, the vacation was almost over, and soon things would go back to the way they usually were, with her and me halfway across the country from one another, conversing via phone calls and sporadic emails. I wasn't in love with her, and I knew she wasn't with me, but a strange new level of friendship had blossomed and strengthened in the preceding days, and I did not look forward to leaving Jade behind.

Soon we crossed a heavily populated street, wending our way between the bumpers of cars blocking the crosswalk. I pointed out the glowing sign of the New Orleans World Trade Center, which looked nothing like its now defunct counterparts had in another city far away. It was a large hi-rise building with a huge artistic disc for a roof, as if some alien had landed a saucer on the top to find out what the current exchange rate was for Galactic Credits.

A few minutes later we crossed a fairly expansive, yet deserted wooden platform that had slices of railcar track slammed through it. Above our heads a sign swooped with faintly lit neon letters: **RIVERWALK**. We passed beneath these, climbed a short amount of wide concrete steps, and found ourselves looking toward the great Mississippi River just beyond a cement promenade. Between the water and our slowly marching feet lay a dimly lit establishment that had walls made of wide windows. One of these panes sported a glowing sign that said **FOOD** in steady, pale white letters, and behind that we spied a small eatery/bar, with black wooden tables and chairs and a bartender polishing glasses in the gloom. All around the establishment, a semi-circle of pale yellow light was thrown through the windows and onto the smooth concrete like a flat, electrical snowdrift. Several people sat and ate inside, and I was reminded of one of my favorite paintings, *Night Hawks* by Edward Hopper—the scene had the same pervasive feel of comfortable loneliness.

"Still hungry?" I asked, slightly spellbound.

"Yes!" she said in a way that let me know how much, and we hurried to the doors as the first drops of water plummeted from the sky. The air had coagulated around our bodies, so thick with humidity that you could have wrung out a handful of it like a wet dishrag, and I knew from having lived in the south that the sky was about to pour down a raging torrent.

As we entered, a blonde woman in her fifties emerged from behind the bar, carrying two laminated white sheets. Her hair was curly and thick, having been obviously styled with a gallon of products.

"How y'all doin'?" she asked in a friendly drawl, her smile never quite reaching her eyes. "Y'all eatin' or drinkin'?"

"Both," Jade and I said in perfect unison, then glanced at each other and chuckled.

"Alright then," the waitress said, "Smoking alright with you?"

We nodded, and she led us to a quiet corner of the eatery that was devoid of other patrons. We sat at adjoining sides of the table, our backs to the other patrons, facing the inky shimmer of boat lights on the river. My legs let out a whimper of relief as my knees popped, and my ass came down on the hard wooden seat. The waitress passed us each a single placard of a menu, in black and white.

"What can I getcha to drink?"

"Bloody Mary," we replied simultaneously.

"Make mine hot," I added, and with a swish of her coiffed tresses the waitress bustled away.

"Wow," Jade said as she scrutinized the various offerings on the menu. My eyes wandered down the uneven text, and my stomach suddenly dropped down through my feet to become an aching, empty cavern. The list offered pretty much everything that could be pulled out of the river, beaten to death, yanked out of its shell, and tossed in a vat of hot oil while coated in batter. My mouth flooded with anticipation and saliva. I was acutely aware of the scents emanating from the kitchen, as if someone had abruptly turned on my olfactory nerves. Taking care not to visibly drool, I noted from glances out the window that the storm was beginning to dump rain down hard.

With a thick red drink in each hand, the waitress returned as we chattered anxiously about what we would order. I went with a fried oyster sandwich, while Jade cast her lot on a shrimp platter. We took swigs off of our drinks (which were not the best I'd had in New Orleans, but still ranked well above any Bloody Mary I'd had elsewhere—thick, spicy, and with a perfect helping of vodka) and watched the torrent gush out of the sky.

"Jesus," Jade said, unable to look away, "is this a hurricane or something?" The rain splattered against the windows like waves from a violent ocean, completely obscuring the twinkling lights of the boats.

"Nah. Welcome to your first southern thunderstorm," I grinned, enjoying the thrumming bass vibration from gallons of water that forcefully slapped the windows. "We usually get these in the spring in Dallas, but there's always an odd storm or two in the summer or fall. It'll stop in a bit."

We spent the next quarter of an hour making idle conversation and watching the rain, laughing and letting the drinks take the fangs out of our hangovers. The city hummed a tune at the edge of my perception, one that ebbed and flowed chaotically to match the intensity of the storm. It was a soft song, one that promised further sights to be seen, and I found my eyes alternating between Jade and the flowing streams of water on the window. The storm sluiced away the dirt and filth, and I found a strange urge to go dance in it, let it clean me the same way, to be baptized in its drenching caresses.

The food arrived on huge white platters, and we fell to it with the hunger of ravenous wolves. I'd ordered my meal out of blatant curiosity, and was surprised to find that a fried oyster sandwich is an incredible dish. Topped with shredded iceberg lettuce, and each oyster flash-fried to a perfect crisp texture, my palate was given a blitzkrieg of flavor that made me moan audibly with the first bite. Jade's meal was no less enticing, and the two of us gorged on fries dipped in a spicy mayonnaise, talking amicably between wolfing bites and watching the storm slowly ease up. The hunger was drowned beneath delicious hunks of food, and once we would not, *could* not eat even one more horseradish-dipped French fry, the two of us fell back against our chairs like lions lazing next to a kill.

"Okay," she said while lighting a cigarette and dragging the ashtray between us, "We're supposed to meet the others at a clothing shop called Demonix. I have a funny feeling it's closed, but they'll be somewhere nearby."

The rain pattered down, left splashes and ripples in the wide, shallow puddles that the storm had left behind. All around the restaurant, the cement had been turned into a miniature rainwater bayou, and I could tell that the drops had yet to really quit. Although I wore something that could stand some drenching, I wasn't too sure about how my companion felt about getting her black spandex top soaking wet. Just as I was about to bring up the topic of possibly calling a cab, the presence spoke up in the back of my mind.

Walk in my streets. The rain will fall, but you will not feel it.

I might have felt more incredulous if the city had said such the day before. As I got to my feet the acrid smoke of my cigarette scraped against the sandpaper tissues of my lungs. I felt no sense of rebellion or distrust—only curiosity.

As the waitress gathered our money to pay the check, I started walking out the door.

"Hey, hold up a second! It's still raining!"

My hand pushed the door open. I steadily watched the ripples on the surface of the puddles as they splashed, proving that yes, although it had eased up, the rain was still heavier than a drizzle.

"One second," I called back to Jade over my shoulder, and took three wet steps onto the concrete. The water came up to the leather of my boots, but not much farther than that. I stood with my head bare, and held my breath for a moment.

The only sensation I felt was that of the hairs on my arms as they slowly stood on end.

Wild-eyed, I spun on my heel to look back at Jade. Between us sat a wide stretch of shallow water, and I could see ripples dancing across it from the toes of my boots back to the door I'd just exited. All around me the reflected streetlights on the ground gave proof that water was still falling from the sky, still dripping off of signs and lampposts, but my scalp felt nary a drop.

Jade said something else, but I would never be able to recall her words. I was too busy holding my arms out to my sides, palms up, slowly turning in place and trying to catch even one raindrop. A smile crept up on me, and I chuckled softly, stared up at the spinning clouds as momentary glints of water fell down to the ground, yet not one of them landed on my face. It was a moment when my mind finally let go of something intangible that had been holding me back. I suddenly realized that there truly were more things 'twixt heaven and earth than had been dreamt of in my prior philosophies. Even though the sky was still storming, I felt like I was standing under the most brilliant noon sunlight during an orgasm.

"Hey," she said, and I found Jade standing beside me with an expression that indicated just how far off of the deep end I seemed to have gone. "Are you crazy? Let's get a cab before we get drenched!" She held my fedora over her head as a makeshift umbrella.

Several different answers challenged one another for the rights to my voice, so I silently grinned and took the hat away from her.

"You jerk," she said playfully, and reached for the felt headgear. "C'mon, I don't want . . . "

"Hey," I said softly, and dropped the hat into a puddle before wrapping my arms around her waist and hugging her to me.

"Hey what?"

I ran the fingers on my left hand down the lapel of my jacket, and then touched them to her cheek. Her eyebrows came together, puzzled, and she looked into my eyes as if I had a riddle typed into the center of my pupils. Then she got it.

"Oh my god," she said, and pushed me away as all the blood drained from her face and the wind played with her tresses. With an almost frantic air, she was glancing around madly through eyes as painfully wide as they could get—first at the puddles around us, then at my jacket, then straight up into the sky. "We're, uh . . . we're not getting wet."

I nodded.

"It's still raining." She held out a hand, fingers spread as she tried to catch a single drop on her palm. "It isn't . . . touching me."

"No," I said, and gently took her hand in mine before placing it against the dry skin on the side of my head, which by all rights should have at least been damp. "We will walk and not feel the rain." Once again I teetered on the edge of confessing all to her, every detail of what had been happening to me in the previous days. At that moment, I was sure that she would have believed me.

She snapped her hand back, and that was when her eyes went a little bit glassy.

"Weird," she said in a noncommittal manner, and then hitched her shoulders and looked back down the streets. "It must not be raining as hard as it looks. You ready to go back?"

My mouth snapped shut, and I felt a little touch of sadness. As if tiny cartoon signs had appeared in her eyes reading "NO SALE," it was obvious that Jade was doing what many people did when faced with an utterly weird situation that they could not resolve—they quarantined their thoughts, jailed their memories of the strange happenings in life. The data their eyes, ears, and other sensory organs gave them in a bizarre situation was wrapped in a tight little bundle and tossed into the darker recesses of the person's brain, never to be handled or visited again.

For the first time in my life, I was experiencing something that by all rights my mind should have isolated and ignored, but instead I wallowed in all of it. The end result was a constant, life shivering sense of wonder that submerged me. I had an exhilarating and terrifying sensation that some core part of my value system had been false for all of my life, and I was finding something wonderful, terrible, and new. As the rain fell all around us, soaked into every bit of concrete and each separate leaf on the trees, I knew that this was the kind of proof that one could hold onto, the kind that would affirm my memories of this trip.

But I watched Jade's eyes gloss over and her mind scurry away from this disturbing phenomenon, and a little piece of my chest dropped through my feet. It saddened me to know that this Predatory sister to my own soul would not allow herself the sensations that I was feeling. Maybe she just didn't want to question the universe. Perhaps she felt what I did, for just a moment, and shied away from it as fast as possible because the feeling was not one she enjoyed.

She walked. I followed, and soon we were stomping back to the hotel together. At the same time, a rift had occurred, and I no longer felt that I was in the company of another I could easily share this time with. We strode not two feet from each other, talking idly, but I was alone again.

My legs truly protested, and it occurred to me in passing that I had lost some weight. The leather belt I'd purchased just before the trip felt loose on my hips, and some "regular" or "sane" part of my mind, the part that normally ran my life noted that I should feel more alarmed about this fact. Instead I ducked into the bathroom and tightened my belt a notch.

When I emerged, she was nude, her ivory back to me as she lifted a silvery-blue cocktail dress over her head. It fell down over her body like a splash from a waterfall. I admired the way the fabric flowed down the small of her back and slithered over the curve of her ass. Turning around, she winked at me, and then retrieved a pair of stockings from her backpack.

"You ready to go have some fun?"

"You bet," I said, lighting a cigarette and feeling the smoke tear through me like a cloud of caustic chemicals. I exhaled and sat on the edge of the bed as she tugged on the pair of black thigh-highs, then debated aloud on which color of plastic beads would look best with the dress. I pointed out that the blue ones were too dark to truly match what she was wearing, so she instead put a strand of tiny, silver dice around her neck before striking a come-hither pose in front of the mirror.

"Yeah, baby," she said, and her reflection licked its lips.

"Looking tasty," I said in return, and stood up. We walked out of the room, and I never went back there again.

I am so very tired.

What of it, Traveler? I shall carry you on . . .

No.

We'd caught a cab to the bar where the other Hematarians waited for us, the very same Red Room that I'd started at days before. Jade had immediately joined a lively conversation with her friends, but I stayed to the shadows, pausing only to order a beer at the bar and then returning to my thoughts.

An idea had been growing stronger as I had entered the pub, and my body was joining in the debate. I'd once walked thirty miles in a day, after a car breakdown when I was younger, and the aches I'd felt so long ago had been but a pittance compared to what I felt now. Pain conquered every muscle from the soles of my feet to the back of my neck. The voice of the city seemed to soothe the discomfort every so often, but the pain only returned stronger.

I cannot go on. I am spent. I am a husk.

But you must, she said. You will spend this last night in my arms, and then I will release you.

I cannot. I have a limit. You may be immortal and great, but I am merely a man. Although I like to think I'm strong, you have exhausted everything in me.

The city laughed, and I suddenly knew what I had to do. A quick check of my funds showed that I had ten paltry dollars left to my name. That was it. Ten more bucks.

It was more than enough for what I planned.

Without alerting anyone in Jade's group of black-clad Dracula clones, I ducked back out the door of the pub and down the rickety stairs. The steps creaked beneath me, a sound that I had already grown accustomed to. Back on the street, I wandered for a block before finding what I needed at a tourist shop. I purchased a small package for four dollars, and thanked the man behind the register as he sneered back.

Walking back to the pub, I ripped the package open to remove a wad of multicolored plastic beads of a very distinct shape. I felt as if I were working some strange spell, some bit of urban magic as my fingertips untangled the strands from one another, stuffing first the red ones into the pocket of my leather jacket, then the blue, then the silver, carefully prying the confused bulge of beads away from one another. Not until only the green were left did I wind them around my right hand, and then go back up the stairs.

Jade noticed me as I reentered, and I beckoned to her with a stern look on my face. She excused herself from the group, and approached my solitary corner with a worried, curious look.

"Where'd you get off to?" she asked. "We were thinking of taking off and hitting another bar."

My left hand reached forward and pointed at the dice around her neck.

"Those will not do," I commanded as gravely as I could, and kept my voice disdainful. "The silver does not go well with your dress. It looks bad. Take them off."

She did so, her face a mixture of bewilderment and a touch of rebellious annoyance at my suddenly overbearing attitude. Before she could become angrier with me, I brought my other hand up, and swiftly placed two strands around her neck. Each bead was a green, shiny fish, and her eyes lit up like a kid at Christmas when she saw them.

"Hey! You remembered!"

"You said you wanted some, ma petite," I said, and kissed her cheek. Squaring my shoulders, I prepared myself for a short speech I'd been writing in my head. My mouth opened . . .

And a hand came down on my right shoulder. Looking up, I found Troy behind me and to the right, smiling through a set of immaculately crafted false vampire fangs. He tipped a tall top hat, and chuckled.

"Greetings! How is your evening, sir?"

"Actually," I said, glancing at my watch, "I was . . . "

"I do so apologize for the mix-up at the bar last night!" he interrupted, and guided me towards the door just as the rest of his ridiculous group of spookies began to exit with us. "Really, I cannot apologize enough! Allow me to make amends by taking you elsewhere and plying you with alcohol!"

My protests were drowned out by the laughter and music, and I was carried away like a paper boat bobbing helplessly in a raging river.

You will spend another night in my arms, she stated in a manner that would have, on a woman's face, amounted to a mischievous grin.

We were at yet another bar, this one much smaller and packed to the gills with Jade's crowd. I'd had several more bottles of beer and shots of hard alcohol, but was dismayed when I discovered that although I had a buzz, I couldn't quite overcome an invisible barrier that blocked me from becoming truly *drunk*. The alcohol merely vanished down my throat, but attempts to numb the sizzling and sharp pains in my legs turned out to be futile—my liver was now in overdrive, capable of keeping up with a few pitiful gulps of beer and vodka.

An hour previously, Jade had offered to spend the rest of the night beside me, cavorting and partying, and I'd agreed to see her off the next morning. As I put another empty bottle of Rolling Rock on the bar, a new thought gained momentum:

I cannot do this.

The city continued to mock me, laugh at me, and cajole.

You can and you will. You will worship me one last night, drink my air and my wine and kiss (me on the lips of) my women and sing and then I shall set you free.

So I am a pet, to be allowed out when you so desire? My mouth tasted sour, and my eyelids were leaden shutters.

Not so, dear one. You are here to worship, and I shall have my pound of flesh.

Although debate was my forte, I was locked in a disagreement with a different kind of woman altogether. The tattered pack in my pocket yielded one misshapen cigarette, and I lit it from the flame in the waiting bartender's hand. The smoke hurt. Everything hurt. I was *not* enjoying this. For the first time since I'd arrived, I was utterly without pleasure, without excitement, without life. I flicked an ash, and watched the tiny flakes slowly fall apart in descent before looking up again. As I raised my eyes, Jade's perfect ass, clad in that blue silk dress, disappeared into the Ladies' room.

For some reason that I still cannot comprehend, that sight sparked my decision. A tiny, sputtering flare of energy melted through me. I hopped off the barstool, squared my shoulders, and walked across the floor to Troy.

"Nice party," I said, and gave him a firm handshake, "but I have to get out of here."

"What?" He looked honestly surprised, and took me aside to stand beside the jukebox. "Dude, I thought Jade said you were going to party with us tonight!"

"I was, but I am thoroughly exhausted." My foot came down on the cigarette I'd dropped, squished it into a cold smudge. "Really. I've been doing this for three solid days, and I'm totally bent."

"Aw, hell. Well, you said goodbye to Jade, right?"

"Not yet. Tell her I'm out front when she gets out of the Ladies room, yeah?"

He smiled, and clapped me on the shoulder.

"I'll tell everyone else you bade them adieu," he said jovially, and winked. "I hope to see you again. Maybe next year?"

"Perhaps," I said, and began walking for the front door. As the music dimmed slightly, I noticed that the city had stopped its tune. Instead, it was making a strange note, one that was too low for human ears. It wasn't a tune of enticement, or a melody of any kind. Instead, I felt the quiet, subaural sound of the city becoming very, very angry.

My hands moved by reflex, and the pack of smokes spat forth yet another horribly deformed cancer stick. As I lit it, Jade stuck her head around the doorjamb, smiled, and then stepped down onto the street. My eyes followed the curve of her leg, the fishnets and pale skin forming a sinewy, animal pattern.

"Hey," she said as we embraced, hugging cheek-to-cheek. "Troy said you're splitting. What's up?"

I looked in her eyes. They were shining with the gaze of a wild thing, something that comfortably waits just outside of the firelight for the right time to pounce.

She's yours if you want her, came the presence, more coldly than it ever had. It wasn't dangling Jade under my nose—no, this time the city was bargaining with me. *You can roll in her soft warmth and tumble together with all bites and heat and sweat and wonderful*

No, I thought, and quietly touched Jade's cheek.

"Thanks for the time together," I said. "I'm just . . . I'm utterly out of energy or ability to continue."

"I understand," she said, and hugged me hard. "It was great meeting you. Don't be a stranger, okay? We should get together again sometime."

"Yes," I said, and took a final draught of her skin's feral perfume. "Meet me here again in a year?"

She smiled and looked me in the eyes.

"You got it. Have a safe journey." She let our hands linger as we took a slow step away from one another. Then as she released, I spun on my heel and set my right foot down on the concrete.

Traveler, go back. The presence demanded immediately. *Do not end it yet. Stay, and worship me for another night.*

I decided not to answer, and stuffed my hands in my pockets as my boots thudded steadily. The night was cool and my watch's face showed the time of one thirty fast approaching. The quarter seemed sparsely populated for so early on a Saturday night. Far behind me I heard the uproar and cacophony of Bourbon Street, and somewhere nearby the sounds of someone playing a guitar spilled across the bricks and stones.

Just before the intersection, I stopped and looked back at the bar. Sure enough, Jade was leaning against the doorjamb, smoking a cigarette and watching me. I grinned and waved, and she blew me a kiss quickly before she ducked back into the establishment.

Looking up at the sky, I took a deep breath, then another, drinking deep the mélange of smells strewn through the night air. A last burst of energy ran through me, and I finally replied to the presence in my mind.

I am finished.

She did not make it easy to walk away. Almost immediately the presence surged like an unexpected, giant wave crushing down the body of a beachgoer, flooding angrily through me. I felt an intense thirst for beer, followed by an urge to go back to the bar and run my fingers through the hair of a gorgeous woman, sing, dance, and play. Startled to find my hands forming hungry claws, I jammed them back into my pockets and shook my head.

Traveler, the night . . .

NO. I am finished, I replied.

I continued back down through the Quarter toward Canal Street, and hooked a hard right on a road whose name I did not make note of. My voice was hoarse with carousing, my singing ability shot to fucking hell, so I whistled as I walked, a blues tune I had written a long time before in Dallas. The avenue was mostly deserted, with only a few other anonymous dark figures walking both toward and with me. The tune sounded ethereal as it echoed off the bare concrete and large glass windows of the shops, and more full than I'd ever sung or played it.

I walked past an alley without looking inside, and two men ejected drunkenly from it, arms around each other's shoulders. One of them carried a plastic bag from a grocery store. They crashed into me like a bowling ball picking up a spare, and I was knocked on my ass with no warning.

As the adrenaline surged in me, and I began to stand up as quickly as I could, they regained their unsteady position of mutual support with brays of laughter and looked at me with surprise.

"Aw, holy shit, bro!" said the one not carrying the bag, and helped me up with a sheepish grin. I took his proffered assistance, and he dusted away some imaginary dirt from my jacket.

"Christ man," his neighbor said, giggling. "You should watch that shit!" They both cracked up and staggered against the nearest wall, laughing like best friends sharing a private running gag. I noted the underlying scent coming from the pair—the acrid, earthy tinge of marijuana, and lots of it. As their giggles subsided they regarded me through ridiculously swollen eyelids and retinas that showed more vein than white.

"Sorry 'bout that, dude," the first one said, and reached into the bag. I was no longer worried, although the adrenal rush I'd felt still made my heart thud. If these two wanted to fight, I could have taken them out easily, in the state they were in—it was obvious that if one of them had been knocked over, the two of them would have gone down like dropped stones. "Here," he said, and thrust a black bottle of beer into my hand before I could protest. "This is on us!"

"Enjoy!" his partner replied as they wobbled away, bursting into another fit of giggles. "Be alive, mothafucka!"

Drink! Do not go!

I smiled down at the Guinness in my hand. Beads of crystalline sweat ran down the outside of the bottle, seeping between my fingers. Before I could yield to temptation, I turned and dropped the beer into a waiting trashcan. The presence ebbed, and then conveyed:

You are a fool.

With a slight spring in my step, I continued. Striding and whistling, my feet ate up city blocks and spit out concrete in what I wanted to be my final foray through the cracked, chaotic pathways. The air smelled divine, carrying all the good and bad smells of the human race mixed with lovely, rich humidity.

I craved nicotine, so I paused at a dark street corner, leaning against a red brick building that was warm to the touch. A thorough bout of searching my pockets revealed that I was completely out of both smokes and money with which to buy them. I had exactly enough to pay the streetcar fare, and then that would be that. Game over. Of course, once I got back to the hotel, I could always bum some cigs off of my roommate's wife. Even if they *were* the filthy, oily clove cigarettes she swore by, I could...

As I rounded the next corner, something pale caught my eye. I stopped cold as my eyes centered on a pack of cigarettes that lay propped against a windowsill, unopened. Looking around at the empty streets, I was left with no explanation on how a pack left so obviously in plain sight had survived for more than a minute in the Quarter. I scowled at the white cardboard box. The fable of Persephone filtered through my mind. I started to reach for it, and then stopped. On the one hand, I realized that if I didn't immediately grab the pack, someone else was liable to. But on the other hand, I was aware that something strange was going on here, and I might do best to . . . leave a perfectly *free pack of cigarettes out for some homeless fucker to grab while I'm jonesing for a smoke?*

I smirked, and snatched it up.

See? The night is far from over, Traveler. I can give you more. Your money means nothing. You are mine now. I can give you a final night of pleasure before you go.

The cigarette crackled to life as I shook my head, and with the cotton in my teeth I soon made it to the glittering lights of Canal Street. No sooner had I crossed to St. Charles than a rust-colored streetcar pulled up, its carriage lit from within by pale amber bulbs. I gave it my last buck and a quarter, nodding to the old and dilapidated driver, and sat at the back. Nobody else was in the car. With a hiss and a creak, it rumbled down the rails. The presence settled on a quiet, humming tune as I peeked one last time at the receding streetlights out the rear window.

How many others? I wondered. *How many people on the street do you talk to? How many alive today have heard your siren's call? I cannot be the only one.* Facing forward, my greatest urge was to rest my forehead on the seat and doze, but I knew that doing so could possibly make me miss my stop. I gazed out the glass at the passing blackness, which was broken only by the passing glow of cars and electric signs. *Can anyone else talk to you, and hear you?*

Some, she said in reply. *One must be able to hear me for me to speak.*

And why? Why do you speak to them? I watched a man drive a pair of horses in an old-fashioned cab across a quiet intersection. *Is there anything special about those who can hear you?*

Silence. Then the slow, soft hum resumed. The streetcar continued down the black streets, and I never received an answer.

The doors folded open at the same grassy median I'd grown accustomed to, like the wings of a steam-driven, mechanical bat. I stepped out, almost stumbling, and then waved in thanks to the driver. He didn't notice, merely staring dead ahead and letting the doors shut before the machine took off into the night. I watched it go, and pushed yet another cigarette into my mouth. The first drag scraped away the filth in my throat with steel wool—I had definitely smoked too much on this trip. A quick glance in both directions of Prytania showed me the street was remarkably empty. I could hear nothing but the rustle of leaves and the humming lullaby the city was singing. One exhausted foot in front of the other, I painfully made my way along the cracked concrete, glad to finally begin the long, homeward journey. I'd go to the room, stuff all my clothes into my bag, hit the sheets like a sack of lead, and then head back to Dallas sometime around noon with my roommate and his wife.

Back at my hotel, I paused at my room's door long enough to pull out the faithful electronic organizer and type my attempt at a final entry. It felt right, putting down words to seal my trip.

Sunday
12:48 am
Hotel

Done.

I snapped the shiny cover to the PDA shut, fumbled my keycard, and ducked into the room.

CHAPTER FOURTEEN

Sunday
1:02 am
Prytania Place Hotel

Oh, god. Not done.

With the click of a sword deposited back into its sheath, the green light on the doorknob blinked. I pushed, and the door creaked open, giving me a perfect view of my roommate and his wife in mid-packing, one half-full suitcase lying on my bed. Sophia was folding a pair of slacks to drop into it. They looked up with a pair of grins at the sound of my arrival.

"The prodigal son returneth!" Marcus set a stack of dress shirts on the foot of the mattress before walking over to give me a hearty embrace. "I take it you have been enjoying yourself well?"

"I am fucking done," I stated blankly, and flopped facedown on the half of the bed that was still empty. "Done. Finished. This town has destroyed me."

"Are you going to survive?" His question was wrapped in a leer, and Sophia giggled.

"Sure," I said, rolling over on my side and tossing my fedora toward the basic vicinity of my duffel bag. "I just need about a week of sleep, an extra paycheck to undo the damage to my bank account, and my blood filtered of all the poisons I've dumped into it. Barring that, I'll accept just some sleep tonight and a drive back home tomorrow."

"Uh . . . " Sophia glanced at Marcus and bit her lip. They exchanged a moment of psychic married communication while obviously holding back sniggers.

"What?"

"Well," Marcus said, and punctuated his words by dropping a pair of shirts into a briefcase on the floor, "We've been waiting for you to come back so we could finish packing and then go out."

I shook my head and smiled like a man being hit up for a dollar immediately after he'd filed bankruptcy.

"Not happening, chum. I'm utterly wiped. All I want to do now is go to..."

He snapped the suitcase shut, and kicked it under the coffee table before turning around with his hands on his hips. The look on his face was one of stern amusement.

"I am *not* accepting your excuses. Suck it up, soldier," he explained in the tone one would expect from a drill sergeant. "We haven't seen you for longer than a few minutes each day unless you were crashed out. I understand that you wanted to do your own thing on this vacation, but I refuse to let you ditch us entirely. You're going to stand back up, get your party shoes on, and go have a drink or two with us." He crossed his arms as I opened my mouth to object. "And that's final."

"But I'm out of money!"

"I'm not," he smirked. "Your drinks are on me."

"But... but you're diabetic," I spluttered lamely. "You can't drink!"

His laugh was merciless at that one.

"I can have some coffee while you and my wife have something more alcoholic. Oh, and we have to take you to *Café Du Monde*. You can *not* miss their beignets."

"But..." I sat up wearily, and knew full well that any further protest was now hopeless. I'd heard that tone of voice in my roommate before, and he was a stubborn son of a bitch when he wanted to be. Furthermore, he had some leverage on me; we *had* driven down here in his car, and I seemed to remember promising him that the three of us would have cocktails together at some point.

"C'mon," he said, pulling me to my feet by the shoulders. "Let us away. We've been looking forward to this."

"Yeah," Sophia said, and gleefully hooked her arm through my half-limp one. "Let's go party!"

We headed out the door and the city began to laugh at me in my head, gloating with an ancient, yet almost childish cackle.

As my ankles screamed and my knees finally scorched their last pain nerve into a crisped cinder, I hobbled to the car with my sickeningly energetic compatriots.

So near had been my escape . . . and yet so *far*.

We drove to *Café Du Monde*, a world-famous location where the coffee was slightly less sludgy than the water of the nearby river and critics had described the beignets as the food of the gods. An alarming amount of people were there, and I had to check my watch several times to assure myself that it really was almost two in the morning on a Monday.

We each ordered coffee and beignets from a hurried waiter as my brains puddled in my skull, and I tried to stifle the horror I felt over the concept of continuing to walk on legs made of dead flesh. The muddy ichor in my cup did little to revive my energy, and I drank it mostly out of reflex. When the beignets arrived, however, the little pillows of sugar-smothered dough hit my tongue like a sweet bomb. Stifling a few whimpers, I pulled out my PDA again.

Sunday
1:22 am

Cafe du Monde, c'est magnifique. Beignets and cafe au lait—this city suddenly smothers me in kisses and motherly, warm hugs.
   My terror and trepidation from such an about-face are immeasurable.

After I'd downed several beignets and a cup of the best Café Au Lait on earth, Marcus uttered a death sentence for my last shred of sanity.

"Let's go get some drinks. Dave, you have *got* to try a Jet Fuel." He stood on legs that showed no signs of shaking as mine did, and I hated his fucking guts for it.

"Yeah, it's really cool," his wife chimed in. "It just evaporates off your tongue."

"What is it?" I asked, trying desperately to let the desperation and fatigue I felt bleed into my voice in case the two of them might reconsider and show mercy.

"It's a drink," his wife tittered, "and it's a taste sensation you won't soon forget."

And so, minutes later at a pitch-black bar across the street, I was handed a plastic cup with a shot of blue fluid shimmering at the bottom. Sophia held a matching cup with a sweet smile, and Marcus held a demitasse of espresso in the same manner.

"All right," he said in the tone of a commanding Roman emperor, "let's see who can fully quaff theirs first. You two have the advantage, as your drinks are cold, and mine is hotter than the fires of Vesuvius."

"One," said Sophia.

"Two," I groaned, my arm cocked and ready to toss the cocktail down my gullet.

"Three!" Marcus immediately threw his cup up to his mouth in unison with us. I opened my throat and swallowed desperately. Tired though I was, I was still unwilling to let a challenge like this go by without at least trying.

I slammed my cup down a hair of a second after his wife did, and said, "Damn, girl, you beat meeeeaaaaaaaaggggghhhhh!"

The room spun like a centrifuge around me. My esophagus was in flames. White-hot gasoline tore through my mouth and tonsils, and I reflexively clutched at my throat. As my roommate and his wife cackled at my expense, I struggled valiantly against my rising gorge. Hornswoggled! I'd been duped into drinking what tasted like a mixture of grain alcohol, paint thinner, and hot, steaming death!

I only managed to keep my upright position by holding onto the bar with both hands. As I won out against my nausea, I gave them both the best Predatory grin that I could muster, a sad weak show of teeth at that point, and said, "You guys can go fucking die." This sent my cohorts into further paroxysms of laughter. We ordered another couple of drinks and tottered out into the Quarter like a trio of slightly disoriented apes.

Once again my memories of the night's exploits became blurred. This time, however, I went over the edge, too far into the city's embrace to retain anything close to sanity. The alcohol tore through my already tortured mind like a rampaging pit bull through a room of anaesthetized kittens. My wandering feet began to stumble, but I managed to continue my grinning, demented gait. The city herself was almost unable to communicate with my mind in its ridiculous state.

"How are your legs?" Marcus quizzically observed my unsteady steps as if I were a three-armed homeless panhandler.

I grabbed the steel signpost next to me (*NO PARKING AT ANY TIME*) and swung around it dramatically, my other hand extended joyously into the air.

"*I'm siiiiiinging in the pain, just singing in the pain,*" I warbled in a cracked voice. He thought this was quite humorous, especially when I caught the toe of my boot on a snag in the walkway and fell into the gutter. Thankfully, as gutters in the French Quarter went, it was relatively clean.

The concrete was shattered. Every last tile of it on every sidewalk was cracked, splintered, shivered by the relentless pounding of waves upon waves of human feet. The city laughed.

They replace them every so often, you know. Chunks and plates of old cement are tossed into a truck, and a new section of walkway is levered in. Pristine for all of five minutes, and then the new tiles are swallowed in my crowds, all those feet walking and laughing and wandering. The power of these crowds is such that the tiles do not last very long.

How long do new members of the crowd last before they *crack?* I asked.

Look to yourself, the city laughed.

We got another (motherfucking, goddamned, evil, satanic) Grenade. Sophia had been making noises about getting something else to drink, and I'd hit the level of inebriation that a layman would have referred to as "trashed." I was barely able to keep my steps within the confines of the sidewalk. As I remembered that Marcus had made the offer to purchase my booze, I'd snapped my fingers and led them to the now-familiar stand on Bourbon St.

Wild, whirling was the throng through which I shouldered none too gently this time. At the brightly lit bar, I showed all of my teeth and asked for two of the tall, plastic tumblers.

Burn, Traveler?

Hell no, I replied. *I'm out of fuel for the fire.*

I sipped, and below the saccharine tropical tang that coated as thickly as latex paint, there lay a harsh, almost ugly flavor. It was like biting into an apple that was about five days too ripe, or sipping lemonade that had gone bad yesterday. I still drank, letting the swirling cacophony of the city drown out Sophia's exclamations of delight when she had a taste. The flavor of the cocktail became apparent.

This is what the pussy of a dead seventeen-year-old hooker would taste like.

Faeries again!

As Sophia and I wobbled back and forth through a thin fog, I was brought to a screeching halt by the sight of two petite women, each with long, wild hair held down by a wreath of flowers, and pairs of large butterfly wings sprouting from their backs.

"Auberon, call in your trollops! I've nary a glint of patience for their kind this eve!" I called out at the two as they vanished around a corner. "Take your little harlots into your realm, and spank them soundly for their trespass! Is it not enough that this city already drives men mad?"

"What in God's green Earth are you on about?" Marcus asked as he passed me on the right, a bit wary behind his smile. Sobriety intruded for just a moment, and I realized that I'd been shaking my fist at the empty street in front of me.

"Uh. Nothing."

I remember seeing Jade again, but the memory is so blurred that I hardly recall what she was wearing. She and a group of people were walking along, taking a guided tour, and there she was, striding toward me. Her hair and eyes were wild, and I kissed her hand.

"In a year."

"Yes."

"I will find you, and we will burn again."

"Yes."

And then without warning or segue, I was in another bar. Black walls, smaller, filled with Goths and tired-out Blues lovers and a gaggle of drunk, scantily clad women with red eyes alternately playing pool and doing body shots off of one another. A quick, panicked scan of the room revealed my roommate and his wife over by the pool table, and I was actually quite startled to find that I had a cold beer in my hand.

How the fuck did I get here?

The beer tasted smooth and frigid, trickling over my tongue like an Alaskan stream. I struggled to retain any memory of what had happened between seeing Jade and entering the bar, and failed.

You are mine, the voice inside me said, although this time it seemed to be coming from a person. I stared at the beer, throwing all of my concentration into listening. Clearly, I was so drunk now that I was beginning to hallucinate. On any other night, this level of intoxication would have resulted in my stomach puking itself inside out, but I'd achieved a Zen-like state of self-destruction, no longer able to react as a normal human would.

"You are mine."

I nodded, staring at my right hand and the way its fingers bowed around the beer. A lone, slithering bead of condensation rolled from the neck of the bottle onto my knuckle, like a damned soul falling down an ash-coated cliff, plummeting toward hell. My left hand started to reach for a cigarette, but someone put a filter into my mouth, and I took a pull. It was already lit.

"I will give to you, Traveler, for you are one of mine. You will not deny me, nor will you follow any request but mine while in my arms." Spoken aloud, the voice was soft, slightly husky for a woman's. My eyes stayed riveted on the bar top. She was standing to my right, even if I didn't see her. I took a hit and blew the smoke at the ceiling, a cautious grin showing on my lips. "You will ask anything you wish of me, but worship well when you can. My power is such that you can use it, but never forget to worship." The tone of the voice was tender, exhilarating, and also deeply intimate.

A woman's hand, the skin pale as milk, fingers as slender as tapered candles, intruded into the edge of my sight and stroked the back of my hand. The touch was gentle, silken and cool. I could see no scars on the skin, and the nails were unpainted. The wrist faded into my peripheral vision, and I almost let my eyes follow it.

Almost. The fingertips continued stroking my hand, and part of me wanted to see, to gaze upon that which I had been wrapped in for the majority of this trip, this grand spirit, this goddess made flesh... but I didn't dare. Maybe I'd read too many Greek myths when I was a child, or too much Shakespeare in my teens, but I had the firm conviction that associating with a powerful entity on such a personal scale would be fatal.

"I am yours," I croaked, and the hand vanished. It did not fade away like smoke, or slowly disappear like a ghost in a movie. It was there one moment, gone the next. I hazarded a glance to my right, and found nobody sitting at the empty barstool.

"Let us dance, Traveler," the voice said from somewhere behind me, and I stood up, turning toward the doorway. "First, drink to your limit. This is yours."

A shot of Grand Marnier lay at the table next to me, pristine, and a survey of the room showed that it had been abandoned. My eyes detected no lipstick on the edge, or even a sign that it had been picked at all. I snatched it and hurried toward the door, tossing the drink into my mouth.

Citric flame flashed through my palate, and I swallowed, choking, gasping, and stumbled outside. The shot glass tumbled from my hand toward the concrete, but no tell-tale ring of slivered crystal ever reported its impact. The glass simply vanished.

My eyes, trying to watch the sidewalk and help keep my feet under me, glimpsed a woman's bare foot walking backwards before my own strides. The hem of her dress appeared, made of ratty and frayed white cloth. The other foot came into view as she laughed, a tiny anklet of brass bells jingling. I looked up, but there was no woman before me, and the laughter continued. Behind me I heard a group of people, walking, laughing, anonymous strangers parroting my own obedience to the path she'd blazed for us to follow.

I stayed ahead, following that laughter, listening to the wild melody of her voice whenever she chose to sing that strange melody. The cackling of many people around me was strong, and we stomped in a herd through the quarter. Nobody asked me my name, nor did anyone try to walk in front of me. The terrain ranged from cobblestones to bricks to crushed cement slabs, and at times raw earth. I kept my gaze pasted to the ground, the better with which to navigate in my well-sauced condition. Every so often, my drunken missteps would start to take me off-course. The third time it happened, two cool pale hands came forward and clasped my own, pulling me back onto the sidewalk, and that wonderful voice sparkled with joy and laughter, like a mother would while watching her toddler take bumbling steps in the world, or a lover watching a partner make an inconsequential faux pas. Glints of light, like fireflies in myriad colors, flew about us as if someone had kicked a log in a bonfire.

The ground underfoot at times was weird and wild, and I'm pretty sure I saw some things that night that do not exist on Earth. It crossed my mind that I had no idea where I was being led in this happy crowd, a thought that normally would have inspired alarm. Instead I trusted that she would take me only where I would be happy to go, like one of the children led by the Pied Piper. At other times I knew that if I'd glanced up at the moon it would not have been the satellite that I was so accustomed to, but some alien rock, glowing bigger and more brightly than anything in the skies of earth, and the stars would have been in new and demented configurations.

And in that strange crowd of people I caught a flash every so often of a alabaster hand or foot, at other times barely glimpsed her wild and steel-gray eye, or a pair of lips without makeup, enticing and delicious. I was devoid of fear, of hatred, or any other disturbing emotion. She led me, just barely out of reach, dragged me through her streets as blackness edged in on all sides. The wild chase went on and on, taking a right turn at this crossroad, and then a left at that one. I was lost, lost in her, and wouldn't have stopped for any reason on earth. Lost in the arms of that which made me complete, I spiraled away into the night, with feet that hurt and teeth that grinned, every step an agony and a comfort, so alive that my feet surely left boot prints of blood and charred concrete behind.

CHAPTER FIFTEEN

An alarm in the darkness went off, scoring my brain like a hot soldering iron. I was coming out of a void, swimming in it, wishing only to stay immersed in an absence of light, sound and thought. I struggled valiantly to stay in my little place of non-being, but consciousness came slowly, like a cancer.

The pain was now a part of my very existence. Hot bolts of it stabbed through my eyes and my first waking breath seemed inhaled from directly over a flaming campfire. Even relaxed in the bed, my legs could no longer be termed merely "painful." Groaning and throwing a forearm across my eyelids to block the sunlight, I remembered dimly a time when I wasn't in agony, days before . . . it seemed like years.

It occurred to me that I had no memory of how I'd returned to my hotel room, nor even the most vague recollection of what had happened after I'd gone out to dance with the city. I cracked an eyelid (bravely facing the headache that doing so gave me) just long enough to confirm my whereabouts before slamming that eye shut again. Yes, this was definitely my hotel room, and I could hear the commotion of my roommate and his wife preparing their bags. Clenching my teeth, I glanced at my watch to discover that it was now 10:10 in the morning. Checkout time was eleven.

I rolled from the bed, still slightly intoxicated, limped to the shower, and let the water try to flush away the sins and damage I had done unto myself. The city's melody was now so much part of my thoughts that I found myself humming along to it, voice cracking on the higher notes, from too many cigarettes and shots of hard alcohol. The water was roasting, and sluiced away a little bit of the remaining alcohol in my system, but being clear-headed was even worse in my physical state. I could barely stand up, and rather than being soothing and cool, the fiberglass wall of the shower felt uncomfortably hard and unforgiving when I leaned on it. Even the towel I dried off with seemed to be a source of pain, rough and dry on my skin like the tongue of some sadistic demon cat.

One gray t-shirt and a pair of black basketball shorts had survived the weekend unscathed. They were hardly stylish or even sharp looking, but they were the only clothes in my wardrobe that weren't marinated in the stench of old booze, ashes, and the stink of the streets. I threw them on without really noticing. With fingers as responsive as dead flesh, I haphazardly tossed my various filthy garments into my duffle bag, wordlessly smashing the clothing into a congealed wad. I made a mental note that once back home, I would do well to just toss the whole damned bag into the washing machine without opening it, and run the load with the most powerful detergent I could find.

As I zipped it shut, my roommate walked past carrying a suitcase. He chuckled, and clapped me on the shoulder.

"Well, it's good to see that Lazarus can walk again. Are you alright?"

"Fuck you," I mumbled conversationally, scanning the room for anything I might have missed. His wife was wrestling with a rather large suitcase upstairs.

"I thought you might have overdone it last night," he said, shaking his head. "You were pretty wild."

"Yeah, I'll bet," I grunted, hefting my bag, and carelessly crushed my now utterly deformed fedora onto my head. Something had happened to it during the night that had rendered the brim into something resembling a week-old sun-dried pancake. Marcus flung wide the door of the room for me, and we both went to throw our stuff in the car. Each time I descended one step on the stairwell, I felt as if my knees were about to let out an ear-splitting crack, tumbling me to the bottom of the steps like a rag doll.

No such disasters occurred. We loaded the rear of his green hatchback with our bags, and I ran into Sophia on my way back up to the room. She was struggling with a suitcase the size of a steamer trunk, so I helped her. The pain in my shoulders was easier to deal with than it should have been, mostly because my brain was still numb.

While the husband and wife secured the car for the trip home I scanned the room a final time, finding only trash and cigarette butts throughout.

The final glance at any hotel room usually saddens me a little, and this time was a worse. Here were the walls that had witnessed an amazing vacation, comfortable now and even somewhat welcoming. I stared at the bed, in which I had both slept and cavorted. The shower, bathroom, carpet . . . . They had all borne witness to a piece of my life, and I'd probably never set foot in this particular space again. I'd left many rooms like this, feeling like I was leaving someone behind that I had just become acquainted with, and that I would never have another chance to see in this lifetime.

I walked out the door, checking my watch. Eleven on the nose—Jade had left the city a good five hours previously, and I winced at my dim and foggy recollections of the final time I'd seen her. Although I hoped that I hadn't been too obnoxious, I knew also that the reality was probably quite grim. I snatched a look at the sky, and smiled.

Hey, I thought to the city. *Keep her safe, would you?*

Indeed, the city spoke before lapsing back into its song.

The door snapped shut with the sound of a cracking pane of glass, final and cold. I was halfway down the stairs, when Sophia appeared, flushed and looking uneasy.

"Hey, was my purse in there?" She was panting, dressed in a low-cut spandex top and gauzy skirt, and my roommate's wife would have normally been enticing in such a position. The sight, however, failed to inspire even the slightest carnal inklings in me. I was spent.

"I didn't see it. Did you pack it, maybe?"

"God," she said, hurrying up the stairs. "We just tore the car apart looking for it, and I don't remember if I had it when we came back last night."

"What's in it?"

"Everything. My ID cards, my credit cards, and all of Marcus's cash. Without it, we're fucked."

A little help, please? I thought to the city. *Did she lose her purse out there?*

In the very back of my head, I felt the presence do something, a movement of sorts. We arrived at the door of the room, and through the wall we could hear the phone ringing.

As you wish, the city spoke softly.

My keycard snapped the lock open one final time, and Sophia rushed inside to pick the phone up on the fifth ring. I stayed outside, lighting a cigarette and enjoying the feel of the breeze on my skin, windy caresses that smelled of honey and hot cement. As I leaned against the guardrail, blowing plumes of smoke, the urge to curl up on the doorstep and go back to sleep was overwhelming. I shook it off—It was time to have one final meal and go back to Dallas.

Right after I butted the smoke, Sophia snatched the door open and tackled me with an exuberant hug.

"Holy crap!" she squealed, releasing me and bouncing on her heels.

"Who was on the phone?"

"This guy, he was at the bar last night and found my purse! And he was calling to give it back!" She began skipping back toward the car, and I followed in the wake of her giggles. "Oh my God, he just gave me his address and everything and all we have to do is pick it up!"

"Cool," I said, trying to sound shocked.

Thank you.

The city smiled through me and continued its melody.

Half an hour later, I sat down at a table under a canopy of interwoven tree branches, listening to live Jazz in the courtyard and facing a plate piled high with Cajun food.

We'd intercepted the purse (Sophia had been stunned to discover that all of her money was still in it, as well as the rest of her valuables) from a fat and kindly Goth at the edge of the Quarter. Marcus had then dropped us off at the restaurant, and left to check out from the Hotel. We got to our reservation almost an hour late, but nobody there seemed to mind. Sophia and I had walked into the courtyard and taken our seats at a large, square table with a linen tablecloth and fine crystal water glasses. I'd ordered coffee, and then stumbled over to decide what I wanted to eat.

The buffet was nothing short of amazing. An obscene pile of food stretched across two gigantic tables, from breakfast items such as made-to-order Eggs Benedict and fresh sausage, to barbecued pork ribs and curried chicken salad. From one end of the second table to the other, every ocean creature could be found slaughtered in tremendous quantities, from prawns to trout, calamari to crab, and every river creature I could have imagined. Had the god Neptune wandered by, he surely would have wept over the sheer horror of seeing so many of his children deliciously spiced and served for the humans to devour.

Although I was tremendously hung over, something about the feast clicked a switch, activating part of my mind that hadn't been working correctly for days. My stomach didn't just growl as I wandered the tables—it lunged and snarled, a wild, slavering beast in my ribcage, screaming to be fed. Before I knew it, I had piled up enough chow to feed a family of four for a week. I carefully made my way back to the table, taking it slow to balance the wobbling heap.

The first bite was supposed to be a mouthful of egg, English muffin, and hollandaise sauce. Instead it was the closest thing to an orgasm for my tongue that I will ever experience. I moaned audibly, and Sophia raised her eyebrow at me while tearing into an omelet that looked like you could sleep on it.

"This is fucking amazing," I managed to say very softly after swallowing the bite. "I've never had Eggs Benedict with white pepper in it, and I just realized what a tragedy that is."

"Yeah," she said, sprinkling salt over her plate. "This place rocks. We always eat here right before we leave."

We plowed through our food with the ruthless hunger normally reserved for the homeless, and decided to wait for her husband before refilling. I sensed something in Sophia's demeanor, a strange standoffishness, and hoped I hadn't done something unforgivable the night before. Marcus showed up about five minutes later, looking fairly pleased to see both of us chatting quietly about nothing in particular.

"Hey," he said, clapping my shoulder, "Let's get some grub." We adjourned to make another run at the buffet, and soon returned to the table with a second plethora of food. Marcus unfolded his napkin with a whipping snap before laying it across his lap.

"So," he said, brandishing his knife in a gentlemanly manner at a cold potato salad. "It appears that this city has its hooks in you, eh, old chum?"

I nodded through a mouthful of chicken and dark red spices while every pore in my forehead opened up to vent the heat.

"I have to say, this is the best damned vacation I've ever been on."

"You certainly seemed to enjoy yourself last night," he chuckled.

"Ah. About that . . . I, ah, have very little recollection of what happened."

Marcus and Sophia exchanged a shocked glance.

"You don't remember?" His mouth was twisted into a strange smirk.

"Last thing I really recall is doing the Jet Fuel with you two." I didn't like the way they were both leering, and I put down my fork. "Why?"

"Oh, you know," Marcus said, digging back into his plate. "You came onto my wife, got trashed, and disappeared for an hour."

"I did *what?*"

Sophia nodded, grinning and giggling.

"Oh, yeah. You tried to kiss me on the street a couple of times." She reached over and patted my hand in a most condescending manner. "Thank you, though."

"Ah, Jesus, I'm sorry . . . "

"No harm done, sir." Marcus winked at me. "She valiantly fought off your advances each time."

"Oh, my god . . . "

"In the state you were in, *compadre*, it took her all of one half-hearted, womanly shove to rebuff you. No worries about forcing yourself on her. I let it happen because you were funny to watch."

"Dude, you were *thrashed*," Sophia said before taking a sip of her water. "I don't think I've ever seen you so wasted."

"Ugh. My apologies to both of you." I sat back, silently belched into my fist, and then resumed my feeding. In our happy group, once an apology had been offered and accepted, that was that.

"That's good. I take it you'll be coming back to this city?" Marcus was eating as he always did, with the manners of a highborn noble. For once, the environment suited him.

"Damned right," I mumbled. "I have to say, Dave, you were correct. This place . . . "

We both fell silent. I was trying to find words to describe anything close to the experience I'd had and coming up short. After a long pause, Dave nodded with a large, friendly smile showing.

"It's unique," he said. "I told you on the way down here—there's no place on Earth quite like New Orleans. This city brings out the best and worst in everyone." He took a swift bite of beef from his fork, and resumed eating.

It was only then that I noticed that the presence in my head was being very quiet. Not utterly silent, but humming on a very low end of the spectrum, as if half-asleep. Since the experience had begun, I'd not felt the spirit in such a subdued fashion. As if sensing that I had finally spent all that I had financially, emotionally and physically, the city was now content to lull me and remain docile. A final crumb of food passed my lips and the napkin covered the corpse of my plate as curiosity got the better of me.

Why? I asked with my eyes closed. I could be no more precise than that. After a moment, the city replied.

Traveler, do not ask such a thing. There is no why. There is no balance, nor reason to this, that I can tell you. You are not a [untranslatable as a thought—"necessity," but with a definite meaning towards a thread in a weave or fabric], *but a mere traveler. I have treated you no differently than I have treated others, even those who will not listen. You are strong, and we have danced together well.*

I thought about this in silence. Millions of questions clambered over one another in my head, but each one was half-formed or poorly worded. A devout agnostic for all of my adult life, I found myself speechless when presented with a chance to ask a real higher power a question. The presence seemed to sense this.

I am enduring. You will leave, and we shall be done . . . for now. You have not, I think, felt what it is you have become part of. Come with me . . .

"Hey, I'll be right back, guys." I stood up suddenly, but my fellow vacationers didn't seem to notice. "I have to go do something really quick."

"We'll be here," Dave noted cheerfully.

A quick scan of the courtyard showed me that beyond the multitude of other diners, a back entrance was visibly marked. The sensation in my head and chest was one of being led again, but this time without the cajoling call to walk and play. Behind the restaurant I found myself on one of the smaller side streets of the Quarter, and let my stride be led to the left. The concrete, ever shattered, ended at an intersection, and the feeling of being led did as well. At the corner I looked around carefully, thinking that maybe the city would show me a sign of sorts, or maybe I'd see something new, a last memento of the trip to take home. The streets had only a meager trickle of tourists lining the sidewalks, however, and I found nothing special to see. I lit a cigarette and slumped against the brick wall, wondering what it was I was supposed to see.

It washed over me like a wave.

I nearly screamed aloud as my vision blurred, then refocused in a manner that was almost indescribable. The street before me shimmered on multiple levels, and I found myself facing a dirt road, cobblestones, concrete, and asphalt all simultaneously. Not translucent—I did not see them as a character in a movie sees a ghost, but rather all at once in the same strange textures, mixed together the way five handfuls of differently colored uncooked rice could be combined, each one identifiable. All of the buildings around me did the same, fluctuating in size, shape, and style, ebbing and flowing like a non-stop collage, brick surfaces melting into stucco and windows shifting style and shape as though made of water.

All around me people flowed in every kind of description and dress, crowds of them, of every race and age imaginable. I noted that they were all walking through one another, although which were ghosts and which ones were actually there I could not discern. An instant after the vision began, an olive-skinned man in a pair of high, tan moccasins, grey pants made of a rough material, and white, open-collared shirt walked through my legs, his calves intersecting mine as I fell against the wall. His seemingly real flesh passed all the way through mine without causing the slightest sensation, and then he was gone, walking among and through the swirling horde of people, hundreds on hundreds of human beings milling about this one demented, shifting and rippling street corner.

The combination of visuals hurt for a moment. I felt something in my head bend, twist, and try to wrap around what I was seeing. In retrospect, it's probable that I came within a hair's breadth of plunging into a permanent psychotic episode. If such had happened, the city would not have felt remorse. For the rest of my days I might have become another strange person on the street, walking aimlessly, begging for money and talking to myself.

When the presence within me spoke again, it was with the all-encompassing power that I'd dreamed of in the preceding nights. The voice was of such intensity that I would not have been shocked if all the people around me had stopped and stared, turning to look at the shaking man from whom originated the deep, bone-rattling sound of a goddess speaking.

Mankind has created much. Man created me, but I have outlasted my creators, their children, and their grandchildren's grandchildren. My bones were laid down before America was born; my blood pumped through these streets ere your ancestors lived. Through toil and hardship and happiness and misery was I formed, and through the power of human pain and sweat was life breathed into me. I have seen wars. I have seen prosperity. And death, destruction, plague, sorrow, happiness, weeping and laughing have all occurred here in amounts you cannot fathom, Traveler. Every story in my streets I see and remember, from that which forms the course of lives halfway around the world to the mere chronicles of those who only affect themselves. Through these memories and the love of my [dwellers/children/people] *I have become strong, capable, and enduring. I have treated many cruelly, but I have also been kind. I cannot be destroyed, as so many other cities, men, and gods have been, Traveler. Even when the last human within my streets disappears, I will stand strong and continue until I am worshipped again. I will endure, but arrogance does not befit me, so I enjoy giving to those who worship and ask of me. The tales continue, the threads are woven further, and the love some feel for me adds to the weave in a manner, which pleases me greatly. My arms open to all, and what they find inside my embrace is my own affair.*

The voice was filling me, from the top of my head to the soles of my feet. I felt electricity throughout my body, a burning fire that healed and hurt at the same time. I was sure that any second now, my brain would either die or be driven mad from the exposure to such a focused power, like a gnat burning under a magnifying glass. The throng around me milled, walked, chaos incarnate, not running but moving faster, and I wanted to jump into their midst, wander, walk forever . . .

With no warning, the vision stopped. It did not fade, or breeze away like the half-remembered dreams on a Monday morning, but just ended. I was standing on the street corner again, a few people passing by, and the feeling of energy flowing through me had disappeared without a trace. The silence was deafening as I struggled to find thoughts or words. I'd dropped my cigarette, and I slid down the wall into a crouch.

You are so terribly beautiful, I finally told the city, humble and shaking. The presence had resumed its melody, which I listened to carefully. My mind felt like an elastic band that had been mercilessly and forcefully stretched, yanked to the point that a few threads had begun to snap, and then released. Even though the air around me was warm and pleasant, I was uncontrollably shivering. My vision blurred again, and I wept openly, the tears cascading down my cheeks, liquid tracks of salt squeezed from my eyes by overwhelming wonder. Stifling my sobs, I withdrew a cigarette from my pocket and banished the tears with the back of my hand. The lighter licked the tip of the tobacco into a glowing coal, and I breathed the smoke in deeply, trying to expel the tremors in my hands. After a few minutes I gazed at the hazy sky, still overcome.

I would stay in your arms forever . . .

You would die, came an instant reply, as if the city had expected such an offer. The voice answered without malice. *Do you wish for that?*

With a sorrow I had not felt since I was a child, I shook my head and wiped more tears away. The city was right. I could not live in this Garden of Eden for hedonists, not without dooming myself. This was a place of too few restraints, too much encouragement toward self-destructive behavior for me to last very long—I could imagine the rest of my days spent in an alcoholic haze, wandering the streets while amped to the gills on street drugs, haphazardly seducing women until my internal organs failed or I poisoned myself by accident. At the same time, it hurt to know I could not live here.

The voice remained silent for another moment, and then seemed to smile in my soul.

You may return as often as you like, Traveler. My arms will always open to you, as it is open to all of my children. I will be watching and waiting, and you will always be welcome. I will be your shelter, your refuge when the outside world is too much to bear. You can hear me, and that is good—although very few wander my streets without feeling my influence, it is always good to have more that can hear my voice. I am here, I will never leave, and you can always come back to me.

I love you, I thought.

I know this, she replied.

And then I had nothing left to say. Blotting my eyes with my shirt, I stood up on legs that still trembled and tossed my spent cigarette in the street before walking back to the courtyard restaurant.

Before going back to the table, I plodded to the bathroom and looked in the mirror. My eyes were as bloodshot as those of an allergy sufferer, and my hair was attempting to grow some stubble out. I looked like fried hell. After washing my face in the bathroom sink, I dried off with some paper towels and pulled out my PDA to write a final note on the trip.

My roommate parked the car next to the D-Day museum. He and his wife adjourned to go look at World War II artifacts, and I laid the passenger seat down flat before throwing a forearm over my eyes. Although the day was quickly becoming overcast, the air was still too hot inside the hatchback. I rolled down the windows, no longer fearful of being robbed in this city. The hum of the presence inside me lulled me to sleep after a few minutes, and I dozed lightly, dreaming of never-ending midnight alleyways, perfumed air, warm, scarlet wine and laughing, beautiful women. It was probably the most restful sleep I'd had on the entire trip, with the lullaby of the city humming in my ears and her light breezes caressing my flesh through the open windows. I was at peace.

After a couple of hours, Marcus and Sophia came back, rousting me from my snooze at three. The two of them looked almost as haggard as I felt as I clambered into the backseat.

"Well, time to go back to Dallas," Marcus said, sounding as enthusiastic as a man being led to the gallows. He started the car and grunted. "God, I hate this drive every time I do it."

And with no further fanfare, we left.

We passed the city limits, and I rubbed my face hard enough to wipe away the groggy wisps of sleep. My eyes turned one last time toward the skyline of downtown New Orleans. The presence in my head was growing less palpable with each second, a sensation that alarmed me. I could feel it fading, like the sight of a lover standing at the station, waving good-bye as the train departs. I pressed my forehead against the rear window, taking in a final look, trying to hold on to the warmth and feel of it all.

Au revoir. Je vais rentrer, I thought.

Au revoir, mon petit, she said dimly as we passed over a rise in the freeway, and then a ghastly silence filled my skull for the first time in five days. Where this strange being had filled a part of my soul I now felt a void, an emptiness that I had unknowingly possessed all of my life, but never noticed. In the days to come, I would never find an adequate substitute to fill that hole in my being.

It still brings tears as I type this right now, my fingertips slick on the keyboard.

CHAPTER SIXTEEN

Of the drive back there is not much to tell beyond exhaustion, depression, and boredom. Rather than sleeping, I stared at the ceiling of the car and listened to the sound of the storm as I tried to digest everything that was running around in my head.

I'd been raised as a strict Christian for more than half of my life. At the age of fifteen my faith had evaporated, and I'd broken away from the church—especially after I'd realized that if there was a God or powerful being controlling the universe, then nobody on earth really seemed to have a good grasp of that. My personal spiritual path had turned me into a walking freelance skeptic, researching religions of the world and dismissing them one by one. Although I'd learned a great deal about human history in these studies, I'd decided by my early twenties that if there *was* any kind of higher power, it was either hiding from us, or else humans were completely incapable of perceiving it.

Flat on my back in the cramped seat of the hatchback, I realized that I'd just had my first really religious experience. No priest or church leader would recognize my story as such, and the being I'd encountered hadn't been as omniscient or omnipotent as anything described in the Bible. Hell, any Old Testament characters that had gone against God's directions had paid dearly, and I'd only walked away with a hangover from Hell. At the same time, I'd definitely had an encounter that could have been called spiritual.

The rain hammered at us, and the car rocked as my roommate swerved to avoid something I couldn't see. I thought about all of the people who'd had religious experiences in the past and chosen to share them with me. I usually had classified these kinds of people as "assholes," and avoided the subject of their fervor as much as I'd been able to. I'd taken it as a moot point that "devout" people were merely delusional morons with very little imagination.

Now I wasn't so sure. Considering what I'd just experienced, who was I to say that a guy in the airport *hadn't* had lunch with Jesus one day? Maybe the homeless guy walking around the bus station really *was* talking to the creator of the universe. If it had happened to me, then it was possible that other people had also had communications with higher beings, and I would do well to change my attitude toward those I had previously spurned.

The thought gave me a headache. Life had been so much easier when I'd been able to write off the zealous nutballs of the world. After a bit of riding and trying to wrap my mind around this revelation, I decided to test it.

"Marcus," I said, sitting up. Startled, he nearly wrecked the car before regaining his composure.

"What's up, dude?" he asked. The night fled past us, as black as the tongue of a drowning victim, and the rain had eased up enough for my roommate to push the accelerator to eighty.

"Sorry 'bout that. Didn't mean to startle you."

"It's fine," he said, taking a swig from a bottle of water. "What's on your mind?"

"Do you believe that a city can talk to you?" I blurted out, and attempted to keep my voice from sounding *too* crazy. Marcus merely laughed, and nodded.

"I see that New Orleans has its hooks in you. Yes, that city talks to me as well," he said in a conversational tone. The tiny, stubbly hairs on the back of my neck stood at attention, and I felt a chill slither up my spinal column.

"It does?"

"Surely! That city speaks constantly, in volumes! From the art, to the music, to the sights of the town, New Orleans is very much alive!" His wife mumbled in her sleep, and Marcus lowered his voice. "I love that city, and you know what?"

He turned and looked me square in the eye for a moment before planting his attention back on the road.

"I think you're going to go back as often as I do," he said, "Because you love that city on the same level."

"Thanks," I said, and lay back down on the seat. *Brother, you have no idea.* My eyelids began to finally droop, and I came to a realization:

The people who shoved religious experiences down the throats of others, with little to no encouragement, *were* assholes. If you had a brush with the powers that be, no matter how real it was, nobody else would fucking believe you. If you continued to insist that people *should* believe you, you were an asshole.

Part of me prayed that our car would hit a tree on the way back, and I wouldn't have to live with my newfound knowledge. It would have been so much easier to just die in a horrible, twisted accident out in the bayou than to deal with the Gordian knot that the vacation had put into my personal philosophies.

But we survived, even if the rainstorm did slow us down considerably. The distance that we'd covered in nine hours before stretched out interminably. I was behind the wheel when I saw the familiar skyline of Dallas and pulled over to a gas station to stretch my legs and let Sophia take over the wheel. As I paid for gas, I forked over a couple of quarters and received a cup of coffee. It tasted like the regular crap that I'd been drinking my whole life, without the thick, bitter, scorched flavor that my taste buds had grown to crave during the vacation.

I wanted to dump the weak, filthy brew onto the ground, but I needed the caffeine.

We arrived back at the house at about three am, all three of us sore and tired from the drive.

"C'mon, Queenie. Let's get this a-here covered wagon unloaded so's we can go ta bed."

"Your normal diction may be impeccable, Marcus, but your southern accent sucks."

"Well, aren't we in a foul mood? Heave to, chum. Between the two of us, this task can be finished in minutes."

"Two? What about Sophia?"

"She's gone inside to sleep. It is a woman's prerogative to leave such physical tasks to strapping lads such as thee and me."

"Marcus, you haven't been a strapping lad in over a decade."

"Bite your tongue, boy, or I'll cut it off."

The November wind was cold, but my skin felt dead to its harsh chill.

Once the car was emptied, I tossed my bag on the floor near my bed, set my alarm to wake me for work the next day, and collapsed into my covers like a dead body.

My dreams were uneasy, full of laughter and sorrow. When my alarm woke me the next day with the sound of an alien chainsaw tearing into a live cat it took me almost four minutes to get out of my bed and turn it off.

By rote, I grabbed a cup of watery coffee out of the kitchen and tottered back to my room. On the Internet, I found headlines on my favorite sites. The words screamed out that we were going to war with Iraq. Politicians had promised to support laws that would make life easier for everyone. Some parent had done something horrible to their child and was facing a court of law.

I didn't give a damn. It occurred to me that I hadn't even read a single headline when I was in New Orleans, not a single scrap of newspaper. I normally spent a lot of time online, yet while in New Orleans I hadn't touched a computer at all. I hadn't felt like I'd been missing anything, either.

After four cups of coffee failed to wake me up, I tottered into the bathroom and took a lukewarm shower, listening, ever listening for any remnant of that melody I had heard during my trip, and heard nothing at all. My bathroom scale told me I'd lost six pounds in four days. I didn't doubt this one bit—my legs were still screaming from all the walking I'd done.

The badge reader in my office building chirped, and the door opened freely on its blued steel hinges. The rows of cubicles were an ergonomic sorting system for human beings, lit by cold fluorescent bulbs and flanked by plastic trashcans. As my feet found their way to my cubicle, my ears detected the low, unintelligible hum of my coworkers on the phone, talking to other technicians on the phone and keeping the mechanical blood packets of electricity flowing through the network. We were good little drones, mindlessly maintaining a pointless system so that we could afford to party at home.

I dropped heavily into my chair, and looked into the black square of my computer screen. The eyes of my reflection were bloodshot and haggard, the gaze of a walking dead man.

My finger stabbed the power button on the CPU and another workday began to plod by. I managed to hold it together, taking calls and acting like everything was all right, but a depression was slowly setting in that made me want to go home early. Everything around me felt fake, and I was a bad actor trying to put realism into a part I didn't want to play.

During my first break a few hours later, I sat on a bench outside of the office and stared into the late autumn sky. A cloud cover kept the day grey, and the wind had grown teeth that chewed the warmth from my body. All leaves had rotted from the trees, and I realized that my soul felt like those bare branches—lifeless and bleak. Normally my breaks from work were spent planning my week's Predatory excursions. Which parties to hit or throw, which nightclubs to frequent on which days, and so on and so forth.

I stared at the glowing tip of my cigarette. Everything that came to mind was weak and dull now. Sure, I could probably hit a couple bars, but why bother? I'd be bored. Parties had normally offered fun and crazy excitement, but now they held all the allure of a bowl of cold, plain pasta. No, I wanted to be in a town where the streets shimmered in warmth, and the air was a thick, creamy breeze that licked my skin. I wanted to hear jazz and blues in its natural habitat. I wanted to wander around long after midnight, drunk and excited.

The only sounds around me were those of a few tinny songbirds.

The wind smelled like nothing.

The only places I could walk to held no interest whatsoever.

My fingers dropped the cigarette butt onto the gritty concrete, and I hobbled back to my job like a good little corporate bitch.

At lunch I sat at my computer and thought, not really reading the screen. I wasn't hungry for food, not the flavorless crap that the cafeteria would serve me.

On a whim, I fired up my word processing software and began writing down the tale of my trip. Before I knew it, I'd finished two pages, and each sentence seemed to lead to another as naturally as one shattered sidewalk tile would take you to the next.

I spent the rest of my free time that day writing between calls. Typing was my salvation, for my tongue still burned from her coffee, my hands still ached to be filled with her alcohol, and as I left work for the day my eyes searched often for another gorgeous street or woman to pursue.

Marcus was home when I came through the door, reclining on the couch.

"Dave! What does your schedule look like tonight?" he asked amicably.

"Why?"

"Sophia and I found a new Goth nightclub that's opening in Arlington!"

"Have fun," I mumbled, and went to my bedroom before he could utter another word.

My briefcase flopped on the floor and I fell into the mattress. A few minutes later, a rap at the doorway made me stick my head up.

"What?"

Marcus peeked into the room with a worried expression on his face.

"Is everything okay?"

"I'm fine," I lied through gritted teeth. "I just need some downtime."

"Anything I can get you?"

"A plane ticket," I growled into the pillow.

"What?"

"Nothing." I sat up and yawned. "You two have fun tonight. I have something to work on."

"Well," he said with a touch of disappointment, "Alright, then. Talk at you later." He clicked the door shut, and my world contracted in size instantly. All it contained was my bed, my computer desk, and the empty feeling of nothingness inside me. My fingers reached out and flicked a switch. The monitor screen jumped to life.

The pages stacked up next to me on the desk, and I started to feel more human. It's the life experience that makes us all want to share our stories, and this one was an event that I needed to get out.

I opened a beer to nurse while writing. Then I had another. Two empties on my desk quickly became four, and then six.

I glared at the bottles. That couldn't be right. I was buzzed, but not as drunk as I should have been off of a whole six-pack on a woefully empty stomach. I chucked the bottles in the trash on my next trip to the kitchen and continued my assault on the rest of the beer in our fridge.

Around ten or so my phone shrieked on my desk, and I paused in my breakneck typing pace long enough to pick it up.

I'd completely forgotten about Catrina.

I was pleased to hear her voice, and I asked about what had happened in my absence. We chatted comfortably for a few minutes as we always did, and then she asked how vacation had gone.

"Well, that's a tough one to sum up." I walked outside with the cordless handset. "It was amazing, and I . . . "

The words stopped flowing in my mind. I had no idea what to say.

"What?" she asked curiously.

"Something happened," I blurted out, and a touch of desperation that I didn't like crept into my tone. "Something amazing and wonderful, and I feel like I've just been to another place where the rules do not apply, and I felt free for a while, but now that I'm back here, I can't seem to get my goddamned head to work right. I'm writing it all down, but all it does is help me remember. My brain, body, and soul have been burned to ash. I don't feel very alive right now."

The earpiece in my phone was silent, and I suspected she'd hung up during my run-on rant. "Hello?"

"I'm still here," she said, a hint of a smile in her voice. "You want to talk about it?"

"Um. I don't know. I don't know how much of this you'll believe. It's insane."

"Insane as in 'totally off the hook' or insane as in 'I killed someone'?"

"Insane as in 'weird shit abounding, no dead bodies'."

"Aha! Now, see, I can handle that," she chuckled. "As long as you're not on the run from the law or anything. Do you think you could stand some company tomorrow after work?"

"Yeah, I'll be at home." I lit a cigarette and leaned against the back door. The smoke tasted bland, and the cold concrete porch chilled my bare feet. "Frankly, I can't imagine going anywhere else like this."

"Are you all right?" she asked, sounding worried.

"Yes. No. Maybe, I don't know. Physically I'm just recuperating from a four day party binge, but mentally . . . "

"Well, I'll be over after work tomorrow," she said. "Let's see if I can make you feel better."

Her words did nothing to elevate my mood as they once might have, before. I felt nothing at all.

I did not sleep much Monday night. Every time I shut my eyes, images of the Quarter flashed through my head like elusive foxfire, evaporating if I concentrated on them too much. When I did doze, a familiar and magical melody saturated my dreams, visions of bizarre cement walkways at odd angles flitted through my head, and I knew I was walking, wandering, following forever something that stayed out of sight . . .

Every time my eyes snapped open again, I could taste beer, cigarette residue, and white pepper for just an instant. By the time the sun rose, I was deep in a hole of depression and wistful longing.

The next day at work was horrible. I answered the phone like an automaton, fired out instructions and questions reflexively, not caring that my inflection on each call was as flat as a warm beer left on the kitchen counter overnight. On my lunch break, I spent the entire time sitting in the smoking area, nursing one cigarette after another and staring at my feet in silence. By quitting time I had lost any and all momentum. The trip home was spent in the slow lane, piloting my car carefully with the radio turned off and thinking one thought over and over as hard as I could:

Can you hear me?

There was no reply.

The doorbell rang at 7:45 in the evening, an annoying *bleep bloop* sound that I hated with every fiber of my being. Any landlord who would install a device that made the noise of a dying robot when you pressed a button was surely high on a mixture of crack cocaine and paint fumes. This time I didn't mind the sound. Cat was the only person I knew who regularly rang the doorbell, and I needed some company to get my mind out of its funk trough.

I threw the door open and found her smiling, dressed in black jeans and a sleeveless brown sweater. She cut a striking figure with her long tresses in a loose ponytail and a black leather backpack slung over one shoulder (which was her usual substitute for a purse). She dropped it immediately inside the doorway and gave me a wonderfully warm hug. I crushed her to me, burying my nose in her neck and inhaling hard. Catrina always had a strange natural perfume to her skin, a pervading animal scent that hinted at burning candles and jasmine. Doing so revived me a little, a shocking occurrence of real feeling after so much void. She hugged me back intensely.

"Hey," she whispered in my ear, "I missed you."

"And I you," I murmured into her shoulder. It was strange to suddenly smell her skin, after two days of tasteless living. The fabric of her sweater smelled like the sun, and beneath that her skin was wonderful. I held her close, wordlessly, drowned in the smells of her hair, her body, and her clothes.

"Are you okay?"

I shook my head after a moment's hesitation.

"No. No, I'm not. I've had the strangest goddamned thing happen, and I don't know what to do."

She pulled away softly, and her eyes held burning curiosity.

"Let's sit down," she said, and led me by the hand to my couch. "I want to hear about this. You look like someone just told you you're dying."

Four beers and three hours later, Cat leaned back and lit a clove cigarette.

"Wow."

"Yeah," I breathed, and emptied the last swig of my drink. "That's about the size of it."

She blew a smoke ring at the ceiling, and fixed me with a brilliant gaze. Her countenance was serious, with a touch of something I'd not seen before in her eyes. It was a strange, feral fire, one of pure hunger, and I felt those strange urges spark up inside me again.

"You're not lying," she said flatly. "I can tell. This really happened to you."

I nodded.

She stood up, and I thought she might grab her stuff and go. Instead, she crossed the few feet of carpet between us and sat next to me.

Her arms on my shoulders. Eyes that I could sink into. The light touch of her hair as she pushed me back against the couch and leaned forward to press her lips to mine. It was a sensational kiss, and it felt like I was drinking life from her, taking back what four days of redlined living had sandblasted from my soul.

With one hand cupped to my face, she pulled away by a few inches and breathed heavily.

"I've never seen you like this," she said softly, and her voice was laced with a hint of pity. "When you were talking just now, it was like... I dunno. Like you're frayed and empty."

I had no words to reply, so I grabbed her by the back of the neck and kissed her again. Waves of erotic heat flooded through me so strongly that

I found it hard to take another breath. We kissed hard, lingering, devouring. Her mouth moved against mine with the same fury, sending bolts of white-hot exhilaration down my spine. Growling, I slammed her against the sofa cushions and buried myself in her warm tongue, felt her body move against mine. Her hands arched into wicked hooks and she pulled me tight up against her, kissing, tasting, and wanting.

"I need you," I murmured, my voice near breaking from the sudden influx of stimulus on all levels. For the first time since I'd returned, I felt alive.

"Good," she said, and gazed at me the same way that a hungry leopard would eye a crippled duck. "I've been thinking about you the whole time." Her hands found mine, and with a deft movement she ducked off of the couch, spinning me around. "Come with me," she said, and if the way she'd wrapped her grin around those words hadn't been enticing enough for me to follow her orders, then the scorching look in her eyes would have surely overwhelmed any resistance on my part.

Walking backwards with her fingers tangled in mine, she led me to my room.

Breathing hard, feeling incredible, I shut the door and turned the dimmer on my lights down low. Before I could turn around, she pressed up against me from behind, her sharp teeth slicing shivers into the skin on the back of my neck while her hands busied themselves with my clothes. I moaned and clenched my teeth, almost shaking from the desire that was flaring through me like slow, dazzling pyrotechnics.

"So, lover," she intoned with the hot breath of a succubus, "still interested in making love to me?"

"Woman, you have got to be joking." I spun on my heel and wrapped one arm around her waist. My free hand clapped to her wrist like a manacle, and I guided her hand down. She grabbed me through my pants while smiling.

"I guess I'll take that as a yes," she said, and I kissed her again. Our hands ran rampant over one another, and I peeled her sweater away to expose her perfect, petite breasts, like a kid stripping the wrapper off of the world's most incredible candy bar. She gasped when my mouth found one of her nipples, lingered, and then traced down the curve of her ribs to her stomach, nicking her skin with tiny bites and reveling in her hands on my shoulders, squeezing, wanting. I stopped at the waist of her jeans, and looked up to meet her eyes.

"You're sure you're ready?" I asked, carefully running my fingertips along the inside of her waistband. She nodded and bit her lip, a strong and steady fire in her gaze.

Stifling the urge to take her as roughly as a wild boar would, I used my hands to carefully push her back to my bed, laying her down with boots and naked chest, loving both the feel of her flesh on my hands and the hunger it inspired.

Most men fumble with combat boots. I tore them off of her deftly, having had plenty of practice with my own, then moved to the button of her jeans. As it came undone, I planted my lips on the small triangle of soft, supple flesh that appeared between the panels of denim. The zipper came undone slowly, and she gasped as my mouth followed the movement, stopping when the metal teeth did. She was heart-thumpingly bare beneath the denim, and by grasping a handful of fabric in each hand I was able to slide the jeans off of her in a hard, smooth pull.

She was scrumptiously unclothed now; completely bare on my sheets and every breath I took was filled with that strange, musky animal fragrance flowing from her skin. I tore my shirt up over my head and dropped it on the floor, then undid my belt as fast as my frantic fingers could manage. As soon as my slacks started to drop her hand reached up and traced a couple of fingernails down the painfully sensitive edge of my cock, with enough pressure to slice white-hot points of fire into me. I sucked in my breath sharply, and she smiled while wrapping her thumb and forefinger around me.

"It seems you're ready, too," she said through her teeth, and gave me a squeeze that made a couple of my blood vessels want to burst. The nerves in my body seemed to be sizzling with heat as I placed one hand between her breasts and pushed her back onto the covers of the bed. First things first, no matter how much I wanted to drive into her as hard as I could. My tongue found the velvety surface of skin where her thigh and pelvis joined, and I worked my way downward with the patience of a saint. She arched her back and cried out like a wild animal as I danced my teeth lightly around her clit, my chest over her stomach and holding the backs of her thighs in my hands as I kneeled next to her on the bed. She made a wordless keening sound and curved her fingers around the back of my head, barely thrusting toward my touch. I applied tight, tiny circles of pressure with an even rhythm as her cries slowly escalated. She tasted divine, sweet and as clean as fresh rain. After some minutes of my teasing and exploring I concentrated harder on her clit, and she began thrusting faster, moving her hips in time with my touch. When her orgasm hit she came like she was dying, shoulders and the heels of her feet lifting the rest of her body off of the mattress while her hands held my head in place in a grip I couldn't have broken if I'd wanted to. After almost a full minute with her voice caught in her chest, she exhaled in a half-sigh and collapsed back to the sheets.

Some women like to pause after coming, and I knelt next to her to stroke the skin of her forehead.

"Was that alright?" I asked, intoxicated by her reaction. I love making a woman hit that physical high note of pleasure. In answer, she opened her eyes and smiled at me with a look that bordered on greedy.

"More," she said, and dragged me toward her.

I paused just long enough to slip a condom on. She grabbed my wrists and pulled me on top of her, then guided me in with one hand. A circle of tight, hard pressure engulfed me, and I moved in and out of her a couple of times in shallow strokes. She moaned as her eyes slammed shut, and then gave me a half-lidded, wild look.

"Please," she said, and thrust against me hard, her heat swallowing me in an instant, tight and smooth. I gasped hard as she did, and then pulled back to plunge in again. We seemed to be a perfect match in shape, and she was able to take all of me in each slick, piston-like movement. Shoving hard now, I felt like my own peak was not far away, and yet . . . I was still in control. My mind was in a familiar, hedonistic state of containment, both reveling in the animal ferocity of our motions together and keeping a rein on my body's reaction to make the pleasure sustain longer. She buried her teeth in my shoulder and growled, locked her legs into mine and used the extra leverage to fuck me back at a furious pace.

"Please, please, *please*," she began to chant, and a minute or so later the word dissolved into another wild cry as her internal muscles collapsed, crushing, violent spasms. I held back, enjoying the feel of her heartbeat through the constrictions inside her, basking in that wonderful heat. She shivered, then after a few minutes gave me a languid kiss.

"Not finished yet?" she asked, wiping her brow with the back of a hand. Our flesh was slippery with sweat, and the feel of her breasts sliding across my body was exquisite. I shook my head, and she laughed as a woman only can when she's had good sex—an honest chuckle, with no subtle undertones.

"No worries," I murmured, moving a little bit inside her. "I'll get there, and I'm enjoying the way you fuck."

"Mmm, and I you." She stretched her arms over her head, and I propped myself up without pulling out of her. "Care to change positions any?"

And then I did disengage, using my hands to roll her over on her stomach. She followed my guidance immediately, on all fours in front of me and offering the rounded, muscular curve of her ass. I positioned myself hungrily between her legs and slipped myself back into her, my hands on her hips and pulling her hard against my stomach. Cat was almost painfully hot inside, and she rocked back and forth with slow, deliberate strokes. Our bodies began moving faster, and I felt her begin to flex, to pulse again. This time I was more than willing to join her, with a knot of pressure building hard and hot inside me.

She came an instant before I did. We froze together; locked in place by that wonderful shared sensation that lovers receive when they fuck in a way that hits all the right spots for both people. A blazing nova of ecstasy flared through my head, scattered all coherent thoughts like a pile of kicked autumn leaves. My voice was trapped in my throat by the sheer intensity, compounded with the fact that I hadn't taken pleasure in *anything* for forty-eight hours. It felt like I was exploding, gushing, dying, and burning.

We slumped sideways on the bed, and enjoyed oblivion for a while. She nestled against me perfectly. After a time, I was able to begin thinking again. The feeling of not quite being alive had evaporated. I flexed my fingers around her breast, relishing the curve and softness of it, and she made a very pleased noise.

"Was that all right?" she asked quietly with a smile wrapped around the words. I chuckled.

"Oh, it was acceptable," I said as sarcastically as I could.

"Yeah," she said with a giggle. "You were tolerable, too."

"I mean, it'll do for now," I said, wrapping my arm around her waist and holding her close.

"Yeah, I guess."

"After all," I said, nuzzling her neck as my cock began to stir again, "We can try again and get it *right* this time."

"Mmm," she said, and reached down to fondle me. "Yes, it looks like we can."

My lips lingered on hers for a moment, and then gave her a great big grin.

"Thank you, woman."

"For what?" she chuckled.

"For bringing me back to life."

"Huh?" She drew back with one quizzical eyebrow raised.

"I'll tell you later," I growled, and dived back into her.

We spent the hours late into the night rampaging across the bed, mercilessly exploiting each other's erogenous zones and pausing only to change the condoms and get something to drink. Catrina was, without a doubt, both a lover worth waiting for and the most talented partner I'd ever encountered. Predatory, hungry, aggressive and sensual, she made love with no compunctions or hesitation. As strange as it seemed, her touch woke me that night and restored my ability to *feel*. The damage done to me in New Orleans was healed in her arms, and I felt strangely energetic when we finally collapsed at four in the morning, sticky from each other and fully sated. She was soon asleep. I put on my bathrobe and walked outside with a beer, relaxing in the chilly autumn air. My lighter snicked a flame onto my cigarette, and I took a deliciously deep breath in the dark, listening to the silence of the Dallas suburbs. No melody entered my head. The town was voiceless, and as empty of consciousness as an old eggshell lying in the garbage.

I looked to the southeast, in the general direction of Louisiana, and smiled. The soul sickness had left me. It was good to be back home, and She'd told me I that I could always return. Life was once again wondrous and strange. I had been blessed with an encounter that would leave me forever curious, no matter where I went. Every city I visited from here out would find me more observant, straining to hear if some new town had a song to sing or words for me. And perhaps in my later travels I'd find someone else who could hear what I heard in that city.

I butted the cigarette, and made up my mind to do several things. The first was to take Catrina to New Orleans. Either she believed me or thought I was a nut. Either way, I would get it out of my system, and be a goddamned, religious asshole just this once. Secondly, I would go back to that city every Halloween. That kind of magic had to happen at least once a year for me, or I'd go insane out of desire for it. We all needed a little bit of magic, whether it was in a movie theater and suspending disbelief, or talking one-on-one with a goddess. I'd finally found something that had truly slapped a taste of the miraculous into me, and it was possibly enough to carry me through the rest of my life.

The beer was cold, and the night breeze traced the stubble on my head. Somewhere else in the world, I was sure that other Predators were relaxing, taking in the night for all of its beauty, and remembering places where they'd felt wonderfully alive.

NOTE

Written on that final morning, in a filthy public restroom, right after the city made me cry from beauty:

I want to:

Fight in Los Angeles.
Eat in Chicago.
Find love in Rome.
Feel the melancholy rain of Paris.
Dance in Tokyo.
Sleep in my sweet bed in Dallas.

But when I have to die, oh whatever great powers that be, when my death comes to rip my last fucking breath away, let me die in the sexy cruel arms of New Orleans.

And I mean that. If I die elsewhere, I shall think of her with my final thoughts. Cremate me, take my ashes to the French Quarter, where the music is never-ending, the laughter is a constant background melody, and the alcohol flows like a river. Take me to Decatur Street, and fling wanton handfuls of my cremains into the streets, at the sidewalk, at the earth of every tree, until I am spread across that place, never to leave again. Then drink one for me, toss beads at a woman whose breasts are pendulous, and laugh for me, friends. I will have finally come to the place I love best, forever.

EPILOGUE

The plane landed at 9:09 pm local time one night in April. We bustled from it quickly, hailed a cab, and told the driver where our hotel was.

On the long stretch of highway, Cat noted that even by night the cemeteries were astonishing, stretching away as true Necropolises. I murmured something nervously and turned my focus back to staring at the skyline.
　Her hand found mine, clasping it in the gloom of the taxi.
　"Well?"
　I shook my head.
　"I can't really hear anything yet . . . it's like it's there, but ever since I got off the plane, it's been . . . . Distant."
　She nodded and left me to my listening.
　At the hotel we paid the cab driver and checked in hurriedly. I dragged her out the door at the first moment I could, frantic now, still unable to hear a melody. It was like the city was a person far off in the distance, the presence there again but terribly faint.

Our feet hit the cement, and an idea occurred to me. Catrina in tow, I walked at furious pace, stomping wonderfully familiar chunks of concrete with each stride, wild now, listening, listening desperately. In minutes, we were thrashing our way through the cacophonous whirl of tourists on Bourbon St., recklessly diving between clusters of Friday Night Revelers. I found the bar I was looking for, and yanked Cat inside. Money changed hands, as did two giant green tumblers.

Back outside, I found a quiet side street with Cat and handed one to her.

"This better work," I said, disturbed to hear a tremor of fear in my voice. "Ready for your first Grenade?"

"Absolutely," she said, and we clocked the tumblers together in a toast.

I sucked on the straw, and the familiar tropical, shallow flavor gushed across my tongue, a rushing cascade of melon juice, hard alcohol, and food dye. As it washed down, it seemed to melt a frozen chunk of my brain. I swallowed, and by doing so flushed away whatever it was that was blocking my skin, ears, eyes, and mind.

The song of countless walking feet filled my heart with a melody that could not be transcribed. A million strands of beads in every color flashed through my brain.

Welcome back, Traveler.

Hello, lovely, I replied, continuing the long pull at my drink. *Did you miss me?*

I paid no heed to your absence, but it is good to have you back, the city said, and Her smile made of a thousand flaming butterflies coursed through my body.

"Wow," Catrina said next to me, "This drink *is* pretty good."

"You have no idea," I said through a familiar grin.

-Fini-

ACKNOWLEDGMENTS

I would like to thank the following people for making this book possible, since that's the thing to do nowadays and there are some folks who need acknowledgment. This was mostly written while listening to the music of Johnette Napolitano (in the bands Pretty and Twisted and Concrete Blonde) and Danny Elfman, two incredible musicians that have improved the world with their talents. They cannot be thanked enough. Thanks to Poppy, Cam Rogers, Paul Tremblay, and everyone else who helped me market this beast or gave me pointers as a n00b. I owe you all many libations and parties.

Big props and thanks to Sean of Prime Books for giving this novel a home. He's put up with far too much from this ridiculous cartoonist. May his beard ever flourish like a patch of mighty ivy.

Huge thanks to the readers of FLEM Comics for supporting me in this endeavor. Once again, couldn't have done it without you. Especially those who preordered a book that was, essentially, vaporware.

Thanks to Melissa (above all else) for putting up with my crap and not throttling me in my sleep in June of 2003, and to my mother as well for not doing the same thing when I was a teen.

And, of course, thanks be to YOU for reading this. I hope you liked it.

—J. L. Grant
www.jameslgrant.com